The Complete Book of

FRESHWATER
FISHING

The Complete Book of

FRESHWATER FISHING

Text and Photographs by

KEN SCHULTZ
DAN D. GAPEN

THE STEPHEN GREENE PRESS
PELHAM BOOKS

THE STEPHEN GREENE PRESS/PELHAM BOOKS

Published by Penguin Books USA, Inc.
Viking Penguin Inc., 40 West 23rd Street, New York, New York 10010, U.S.A.
Penguin Books Ltd, 27 Wrights Lane, London W8 5TZ, England
Penguin Books Australia Ltd, Ringwood, Victoria, Australia
Penguin Books Canada Ltd, 2801 John Street, Markham, Ontario, Canada
L3R 1B4
Penguin Books (N.Z.) Ltd, 182–190 Wairau Road, Auckland 10, New Zealand

Penguin Books Ltd, Registered Offices: Harmondsworth, Middlesex, England

First published in 1989 by The Stephen Greene Press
Published simultaneously in Canada
Distributed by Viking Penguin Inc.

10 9 8 7 6 5 4 3 2 1

Library of Congress Cataloging-in-Publication Data
Schultz, Ken.
    The complete book of freshwater fishing / by Ken Schultz and Dan Gapen.
        p.   cm.
    ISBN 0–8289–0678–5
    1. Fishing. 2. Fishes, Fresh-water.   I. Gapen, Dan. II. Title.
SH441.S384 1989
799.1′1 — dc19   88–39429
                                                                         CIP

Printed in the United States of America
Set in Janson and Cheltenham by AccuComp Typographers
Designed by Deborah Schneider
Produced by Unicorn Production Services, Inc.

CONTENTS

INTRODUCTION

A few years ago, after a day of river walleye fishing in Manitoba, we were discussing our past book-authoring activities. Somehow we got on the topic of writing a book about all major species of freshwater fish, a proposition that we both thought had merit, but that neither felt comfortable doing alone in its entirety. This feeling is due, in part, to the fact that angling in the modern era has become so popular and that there are so many species, techniques, aspects, and variables to be acquainted with, no one knows enough about all these matters to give you, the reader, your fair due. Together, however, we thought we could measure up to the task. And that's how we started on the first collaborative writing effort for either of us.

Like a fish swimming against the current, this book runs counter to the present trend in fishing-book publishing: books devoted to a single species of fish or to one aspect of fishing for one or several species. While there are enough people who have a singular interest in such specialized information to make that approach appealing, there are also many anglers who fish, not for one species, but for many; who fish for whatever they can catch at the time that they are free to go fishing; who may, at a later date, develop a fanaticism for one species or method of angling, but presently are content to dabble in many disciplines; or who want distilled, basic information on how to catch certain species without sorting through reams of technical and sophisticated detail.

We have, therefore, out of practicality and enormity of task, had to scope things down. Given the book-size constraints imposed by the publisher—who, quite rightly, didn't want this to become an epic encyclopedia—the biggest problem we had to deal with was what *wasn't* going to be in this book. For example, how were we going to write one single chapter on everything there is to know about angling for a particular species when we've previously written an entire book on that subject alone?

So we had to leave some things out and hope that you will understand why we have skipped a few matters. We have not, for example, described in detail how to slow-roll a spinnerbait over a log, how to tie good fishing knots, how to cast a fly, or how to use sonar. But we have provided what we think is the critical, basic, and broad information you need on where to find various freshwater species, what to use and when to use it, and how to go out and catch fish.

In the chapter on largemouth bass, for example, which kicks off this book because of the enormous popularity of this species and its widespread distribution, we've devoted a lot of attention to lure usage and angling technique. More has been discussed on this subject in all forms of media in recent years than on any other aspect of fishing.

Indeed, bass anglers have more terminal tackle choices to make than nearly any angler other than stream trout fly fishermen (and even in that case, the choice is more type than category). However, like the restaurant diner confronted with a six-page menu, such an array of lure choices often stymies the fisherman looking for a clear-cut solution or a quick and obvious fix. We've tried to cut through the complexities to get you out of the maze. We've also simplified this broad subject by addressing the seasonal aspects of bass fishing. Since spring and summer are the foremost bass angling times, we've provided correspondingly detailed information on fish activities and angling tactics during those two seasons.

We've devoted separate treatment to smallmouth bass, unlike other books or many magazine articles (which tend to lump largemouths and smallmouths together). Treating them the same is a mistake because their habitats are significantly different, and angling techniques therefore vary considerably. Smallmouths are much more of a river fish — especially in cool, quick-flowing waters — than largemouths, so the chapter on bronzebacks was designed to address the pertinent aspects of lake and river fishing for this species alone. Again, we've put a lot of emphasis on the appropriate lures to use and places to fish, and we've even discussed the oft-overlooked (in print) subject of trolling, which accounts for more success with smallmouth bass than is generally realized.

Panfish enthusiasts should like the fact that we've treated these most popular, mainstream fish in the same exalted manner as the more glamorous game fish. Crappies get full-chapter treatment, and we segmented Chapter Five to cover rock bass, bluegills (bream), and yellow perch individually. From habitat to lures to bait to seasonal locations, there's plenty here to get you catching fish.

Where catching is concerned, no species outdoes striped bass in the variety of ways in which they can be caught. The chapter on stripers discusses each of these in detail, hopefully simplifying the business of searching for these fish; locating stripers — unlike some species, such as bass — is at least half of the fishing chore. Hybrid stripers, which at last count were found in over thirty states, are addressed in detail at the close of the chapter.

Thanks to tremendous stocking efforts on the Great Lakes, chinook salmon have become dear to millions of anglers, most of whom are stirred by the line-peeling actions of 15- to 40-pound fish; salmon that size aren't uncommon. The salmon fishing scene through the year is primarily a trolling one and is as different from most other freshwater fisheries as you can get; he whose favorite sport is tossing buzz baits to shallow largemouth bass can't readily adapt to running cut plugs tight to 12-pound cannonballs 90 feet deep over 300 feet of water. Nevertheless, we switch strides to provide the pertinent details on this explosive fishery. Although the chapter starts with a seasonal approach, which should be of use to those whose Great Lakes angling is clustered into a certain time of the year, there is information in each section that applies to other times of the year, as well as to salmon fishing in general. Landlocked Atlantic salmon, now something of a stepchild in the lake fishing scene, are discussed in detail also.

The chapter on trout in lakes is much like that for salmon, touching on all the bases and major species, but with a lot of attention to understanding the behavior and activity of these fish, which is distinctly different from that of their river-dwelling brethren. Temperature is a critical point, especially after spring, and anglers who don't take temperature into account are missing a major link in this activity, so we have focused closely on this aspect. Places to locate fish, tackle to use, and lure presentation techniques are thoroughly discussed, and seasonal matters are given special consideration. Whether your trout-in-lakes quarry is brown trout, rainbow trout, lake trout, or steelhead, you'll find this chapter fruitful.

Brook, brown, and rainbow trout get the attention in the chapter on fishing for trout in rivers. We separated river and lake fishing for the trout species because they are as different as night and day. The habits of these fish are reviewed, and detailed, illustrated sections of this chapter deal with specific, prominent river trout locations. Don't be fooled by the use of the word *river*, as we're talking about all flowing water here. A prominent large-water boating technique is prominently detailed, and seasonal considerations, plus bait and lure presentation methods, are thoroughly reviewed.

As we did with trout, we give walleyes separate lake and river chapters. While there is some overlap in lure and bait usage from these environs, fishing techniques and lure presentations differ greatly, both in locale and depth. A lot of attention is paid to behavioral patterns, as anglers need to know what walleyes do and where they go. In both environments we've focused heavily on prominent places to find and catch walleyes, adding specific information on techniques to use and the appropriate manner of fishing in those locales. With the help of detailed illustrations, a reader should feel he has a good enough grasp of basic walleye fishing matters to go right out and do it. We haven't neglected the burgeoning trolling scene in lakes, and the latter part of Chapter Nine reviews the salient points of lake trolling. There is additional focus on presentation methods in rivers.

In times past, pike and muskellunge were often joined under the same heading, but we haven't done that. For one thing, there is much more trolling done for muskies than for pike, particularly on big waters like the St. Lawrence River, Lake St. Clair, and mid-South reservoirs. The musky chapter contains a lot of specific information on trolling, not only on lures to use but also depths and presentation techniques and patterns. Even more attention is paid, of course, to casting, particularly the lures used, the places worked, and the techniques applied. There is, because of tradition and species availability, a good deal more bait fishing done for pike than for muskies, so the pike chapter contains specific information on that aspect of angling. We think you'll find the up-to-date information in these chapters very beneficial, either in getting started after these species or in refining your present angling methods.

One popular category of fish that gets short shrift in much of the media is catfish, but we've devoted an entire chapter to specific details on where to find and how to catch these whiskered creatures. Emphasis is directed individually at channel, blue, and flathead catfish, with specific attention paid to baits used and the manner of presentation, which is very refined in some instances.

This book wouldn't be truly broadly based if it didn't touch on the fact there are some species that have regional distribution but high angling merit and some species that are generally disregarded or even disdained but not completely worthy of being ignored. Included in the latter group are carp, whitefish, gar, sturgeon, and suckers, which are the subject of attention in the chapter on rough fish. Included in the former group are white bass, American shad, and chain pickerel, which are the focal species of the closing chapter. Both chapters contain specific information on lures or bait to use, in addition to general how, when, and where information.

We hope that you will find the chapters to be straightforward and comprehensive, with plenty of fundamental information about where to find, what to use to fish for, and how to catch the most popular and available freshwater game fish in North America. This information will enable anyone to go out and catch fish in freshwater environs.

On a closing note, when we opted to undertake this project, we decided to stress in this Introduction what our professional standing is as authors regarding products and manufacturers. We feel a need to do this because we've noticed that a good number of fishing books being published today are written by (in many cases, written for) individuals who are closely affiliated with (sponsored or even subsidized by) particular fishing tackle industry interests. We want you to know that the both of us are completely free of any such entanglements. When we mention a product by name, it is not because we are *tied* in any way to the manufacturer of that product (we are not sponsored by any firm) and are trying to help sell it, but because we know that it works well and believe it is really worth telling you about it. We have actually kept specific product references down to a minimum, including those about items that Dan, once a small lure manufacturer himself, produced in the past. And we selected photographs strictly on the basis of their relevance, not because they featured a certain type of motor, sonar, or other item, as is being done too often in some books and magazines.

Perhaps it seems strange to mention this, but we think that we're different from the many personalities who write fishing books. There is, unfortunately, so much promotion of goods and services by some writers, professional anglers, and television celebrity-anglers, that we want you to know that the only thing we're promoting is fishing how-to. We're not even telling you what great anglers we are by detailing various exploits through anecdotes. That's because we want to boil out the frills and beef up the facts. That may not be the most entertaining way to go, but it is the most straightforward. As good chefs know, the best sauce in the world won't make up for a poor main dish.

We don't pretend that this is the be-all and end-all of fishing books, but we do think that this book contains solid information that is valid in the modern era and will be valid for a long time to come. We hope that *The Complete Book of Freshwater Fishing* is a book you'll refer to often in the future. — KEN SCHULTZ and DAN D. GAPEN

CHAPTER ONE

LARGEMOUTH BASS

Largemouth bass are so adaptable that they thrive in all states but Alaska, as well as north and south of our borders, and in Europe, Japan, and Africa. A warmwater species of fish and opportunists, largemouth thrive in relatively fertile lakes, where water temperatures are warm enough for most of the year to be conducive to their growth and normal feeding activity. They adapt to the circumstances in any given body of water, within reason, but where they have the choice, they will generally seek the temperature of water that is most comfortable for them, provided that they can find forage there. Largemouth bass are most active when the water temperature is in the 60- to 78-degree bracket. The 65 to 72 range is likely their optimum temperature, but they function well above and below this range.

Largemouths are found in creeks, ditches, sloughs, canals, and many little potholes that have the right cover and forage, but they principally live in reservoirs, lakes, ponds, and large rivers. They orient toward cover, usually toward bottom. Most of their preferred food is found in or near cover of some form, so this, plus the need for security and protection from sunlight, is a factor in their specific habitat preferences.

These habitats can roughly be separated into visible cover (that which can be seen in relatively shallow water) and nonvisible cover (existing entirely below the surface and usually in moderate depth or very deep water). Visible cover includes logs, stumps, lily pads, brush, weed and grass beds, bushes, docks, fence rows, standing timber, bridge pilings, rocky shores, boulders, and points. Submerged—nonvisible—cover includes weed line edges, stone walls, timber and stumps, creek beds, house foundations, road beds, points, ledge-like drop-offs, humps, shoals, and islands. Submerged cover is found generally in deeper water than visible cover.

The turbidity of bass water varies markedly from one lake to another all across the country and even varies in a particular lake through the course of the fishing season. Many of the larger lakes and reservoirs in northern areas are reasonably clear. Light penetrates deeply there, and bass are either well secured in what thick cover might exist, or more likely, are deep enough to avoid the discomfort of light. In such waters you can see a brightly colored lure 6 or more feet below the surface. Here, bass tend to be spooky, and a refined fishing presentation, utilizing small- to moderate-size lures and light line, is very beneficial. Other waters may be blue/green in color and allow visibility for 3 to 6 feet below the water's surface. Such a condition is considered very clear by many Southern anglers, who never see the ultraclear waters of mountain-region lakes.

Largemouth bass inhabit a wide range of environments and can be caught on many different types of lures, making them a challenging quarry.

Many largemouth waters are off-colored, allowing limited visibility. This is the only type of condition some anglers see, and it does not require such a stealthy approach or light line use as clearer waters do. Muddy, milky, slate-gray, and tea-colored water is common in many reservoirs after heavy rains, due to farmland runoff and sediment brought into the water via the tributaries and as the result of bank erosion. You may only be able to see a light-colored lure a few inches below the surface. In some large lakes, the upper ends are only affected like this, while the lower ends remain relatively unchanged or at least unaffected for several days. In still other bass waters, particularly in Florida, the high tannic acid content gives the lake a blackish brown tint. In all these highly turbid waters, where visibility is limited, bass are likely to be relatively shallow and holding tight to cover, especially in the early part of the season and when water temperatures are not excessively high. Turbid water can be good for fishing success, and certain types of lures, such as big spinnerbaits, crankbaits with good vibration qualities, and noisy surface baits, are well-suited to angling under these conditions.

One of the characteristics of largemouth bass fishing is that lures which catch these fish don't necessarily have to resemble closely actual forage, although at times this is helpful. That forage is primarily such fish as shiners, bluegills, shad, alewives, and minnows, as well as crayfish. Fingerling-size fish of forage and game fish species are the main food for largemouths, though larger specimens may be preyed upon.

SEASONS

Spring

Every body of largemouth water goes through a cyclical transformation through the course of a season. In early spring, the surface layers and shallows warm up first. As the surface water surpasses 50 degrees, bass become a little active. When the shallows are warm enough, the bass spawn. Depending on locale, this occurs from mid-spring to early summer. Eventually the upper layers warm past the preferred temperature range, and the fish begin to go deeper, where water temperatures are cooler. In the fall, the upper layers and the shallows cool off. Bass react to these changes in accordance with the type of water they live in, the amount and location of food supplies, and the availability of cover.

The most popular time to fish for bass is in the spring, when largemouths are shallow, close to shore, and fairly vulnerable. Paying attention to water temperature is one of the best things that a spring bass angler can do.

Small lakes and ponds that are generally shallow throughout are the first to warm up and are often best for early spring fishing. A shallow pond will warm up weeks ahead of a deep lake even if they are side by side. In the beginning of the spring, if you have the option to fish two such lakes, focus on the small one first.

The surface temperature of large lakes, reservoirs, and small deep lakes doesn't rise as dramatically in a given day, but temperature can vary at different areas of the

Early spring is opportune for good, shallow-water angling, particularly late in the day, when water temperatures have warmed.

lake. Shallow flats, coves, feeder creeks, and tributaries are generally much warmer than the main body of the lake and are prime locales to induce significant fish activity when the rest of the lake is still too cold. Northern and northwestern sectors of a lake, particularly the coves and bays, warm up slightly ahead of other areas, as they are exposed more to the sun.

Regardless of lake type, afternoon fishing is often best in early spring. Water temperature in shallow lakes and in shallow areas of larger lakes can rise several degrees during a sunny day. Fish that have been subdued by cool nights and cool, shallow-water temperatures respond to the afternoon warmth, becoming more acclimated to the conditions and thus chase bait more aggressively.

Nearly all lures have merit at some time during the spring season, yet crankbaits and spinnerbaits are the most functional throughout this period and throughout the different stages of lake development and bass behavior.

The type of crankbait to use—shallow-, intermediate-, or deep-diving—depends upon various factors. If the water is very cold, you'll likely have to use a lure that gets down 5 to 10 feet and is worked on points, steeply sloping banks, and shores with a breakline (distinct drop-off to deeper water) at the 5- to 10-foot level. In shallow lakes that have a lot of stumps, flats with cover (though cover is barely starting to emerge when the water is still cold), and the like, a shallow- or intermediate-running crankbait is likely to be best. As the water warms and the cover—which may be grass, milfoil, or cabbage weeds—begins to grow up, the same crankbaits can be used to skim the edges and tops, and only speed of retrieval may vary.

Crankbaits are particularly productive in large lakes with a lot of deep water. Worked parallel to the shore, they can be the hot ticket for early fishing success. Crankbaits can also be hot in lakes with stump fields, timber flats, timbered coves, etc. Bass get into these areas in the spring before and after spawning. Another choice crankbait locale is where the outside bends of submerged creek or river channels meet the shore, often by a bluff.

Silver and white crankbaits are especially effective. Most of the time, these colors are referred to by manufacturers and anglers alike as *shad*. Other colors that may have merit, especially where largemouth bass are concerned, are bone, chartreuse, gold, and chrome. Color choice in lures has a lot to do with the clarity of the water. In northern lakes, where perch and walleye are abundant and where small members of these species are available and eager to prey on bass fry in early to mid-spring, shallow-running crankbaits with perch or walleye finishes are good largemouth baits. The same can be true with bluegill and catfish imitators.

Spinnerbaits can be fished deep, but they are most effectively employed in the shallows, preferably within sight. Spinnerbaits don't become principal spring bass lures until the water warms enough to stabilize fish behavior and keep bass in the shallows.

A trailer hook is an indispensable spinnerbait addition in the spring. One of the most prominent attributes of spinnerbaits is that they are relatively snag- and weed-free and can be fished in nearly all types of cover. In the spring, vegetation, such as moss, pads, weeds, grass, and the like, is almost nonexistent early in the season but thick by the end of it. Spinnerbaits will be effective here until such cover becomes impenetrable.

Other forms of largemouth cover—particularly stumps, timbered flats or fields,

A spinnerbait, which caught this fish, is excellent to use around most of the different forms of cover that harbor largemouths.

fallen trees, and brush — are ideal places to work a spinnerbait. The trick is to cast beyond the target and bring the lure past it, sometimes nicking or bumping the object. An especially productive tactic is to retrieve the lure up to a stump or log from behind, then let it fall over the object and flutter down in front of it before continuing the retrieve. This technique, called slow-rolling, works best with a large, single-bladed spinnerbait.

Shallow-running, floating-diving, minnow imitations — in single and jointed models — are very effective for both largemouth and smallmouth bass. These lures can be worked as swimming plugs or crankbaits in shallow water on a steady retrieve or in a stop-and-go manner. They are very productive surface lures, worked in a pull-pause twitching action and are the primary spring, surface, bass bait. The colder the water, the less likely bass are to strike any surface lure. In early to mid-spring, a slowly worked, fairly noiseless plug such as this is more likely to garner results than other surface plugs.

During the spring, of course, largemouth bass will spawn. This occurs earlier in the south, and as late as the end of spring in most northerly locales. The nest site of bass is generally in shallow water. The depth is usually 1 to 4 feet deep, but may be up to 6 or 8 feet if light (and warmth) can penetrate. Nests are dish-shaped and fairly large, usually being at least 2 feet in diameter. Some anglers confuse bluegill or sunfish nests with those of bass, but the nests of the former are smaller, close to one another, and sometimes in the open. Moreover, bass spawn before bluegills and sunfish, which have not constructed their nests at the spawning time of bass. Bass will not make nests too close to other bass nests, and they like to have some type of fairly substantial object, such as a stump, log, rock, etc., nearby, generally to the back side of the nest.

Nest sites are usually found on particular shorelines and in coves where the water is likely to be, and stay, warmer than other areas and which are fairly well protected from strong winds that could damage the nest. This can be a clue to finding them. The north, northwest, and west banks of creeks, bays, coves, and the like are often favored by spawning bass because they warm up first.

Spawning time is the period when big bass are most likely to be caught. Aggressive females loaded with eggs can be enticed into striking a lure before spawning. A male bass guarding the nest can be aggravated, and both sexes can be caught (male first, though) during spawning. Bass don't eat at this time, but they will strike objects that come into—or close to—or that threaten their nest site. A live baitfish, a plastic worm, a spinnerbait, and a few other lures can catch spawning bass, as long as they appear to be a threat to the nest and the eggs and provided they are placed in the midst of the activity.

Bass will be eager to eat after spawning is completed, though don't look for them to be super-aggressive immediately afterward. They go into something of a withdrawal stage, and it may take up to two weeks of the immediate, post-spawn period for bass to get in sync and get back to striking terror in the hearts of their prey.

The issue of fishing for spawning bass is a complex and controversial one. In areas of extreme fishing pressure and particularly in small bodies of water or where growing seasons are short, the removal of spawning bass can be a detrimental influence on the fish population. We urge you to use discretion.

Summer

Summer is an entirely different story than spring. The bass in summer are shallow, deep, or somewhere in-between, in or near cover, on or near the bottom in open water, or suspended. If that sounds confusing, it is; bass fishing in summer is a bit perplexing.

It is generally understood that bass are harder to catch in the summer than in spring or fall. That may be more a state of mind than an actual fact. Some anglers have excellent success—and catch their largest bass—at this time of year. Most successful summer bass fishermen simply work harder at what they're doing than those who are resigned to poor results and sluggish activity. Good summer fishing, however, means putting in time, finding bass, and making good presentations, which is simple to say but harder to accomplish.

Your first summer bass prospecting inclination should be to run for cover—the thickest cover that bass could hide in. If you fail to find any, go to deep-water structure. These are two tactics, however, at which most people are not very adept. Some fishermen don't ever come to grips with matted wads of vegetation or the flooded timber that hides fish. And some are just overwhelmed at the prospect of searching and probing for deep bass. Deep, of course, is a relative term, but for most anglers, deep water is that which is over 15 feet.

Those who probe certain deep-water environs meticulously can find the best fishing of the season, if not in numbers of fish caught, then in size. The key is identifying deep-water places that hold largemouths, fishing the edges of those spots, and presenting lures in a particular way. Look for humps, long points, old roads, and dams well away from shore, with approximately 12 to 15 feet of water at the shallowest spot dropping off to 25 on the edges. It is the edges that you should concentrate on.

In the summer, you often have to fish deep water structure meticulously. This August-caught bass came from 25 feet of water and fell to a Carolina-rigged plastic worm.

Locate these structures with sonar and put marker buoys in the water as references. Then, using an electric motor, circle the edges of these locales v-e-r-y s-l-o-w-l-y, precisely, and several times, being sure that your lure, preferably a Carolina- or Texas-rigged plastic worm, inches through the 17- to 22-foot range. It's a technique that takes much patience.

It's ironic, perhaps, that the thing most bass fishermen are best at — fishing shallow water — can be both their crutch and their downfall in the summer. Certainly there are bass in shallow water all season long, even when that water is tub-warm. Most fishermen are tuned into casting to and around visible cover and shallow or near-shore cover. If they catch a fish or two, they keep at it. They take a fling at deep water and, failing to have some relatively quick success, go back to the bank. In some waters, particularly man-made impoundments, there isn't a profusion of cover on the banks, and the fish there have been hammered by anglers throughout the season. They are making a mistake by not taking deeper water angling more seriously.

We prefer to fish shallow water (10 feet or less), too, but that's usually most profitable if there is heavy cover, such as various types of vegetation, or timber, or clusters of debris (piles of flotsam) to work with jigs and worms (probably by flipping). In the backs of creeks, where there may be cooler water, and if there is abundant cover in the form of brush, logs, standing timber, or vegetation, spinnerbaits and plastic worms, worked in and close to the cover, can be effective.

Otherwise, shallow-water fishing in the summer is best confined to the use of surface lures early and late in the day, or to fishing thick vegetation with plastic worms or weedless spoons during the day. Many anglers pass thick vegetation up as being impossible to fish. That's also a mistake. It may be *hard* to fish, but it's not impossible.

Bass can and will live in the densest salad (moss, hydrilla, milfoil, lily pads, etc.); there is food and comfort here.

While probing the edges and pockets of such cover is a tactic that may work early and late in the day and at night, you often have to get into the midst of this cover to be effective. That may necessitate frequently cleaning the propeller of your electric motor or poling your boat. It may mean using fairly heavy slip sinkers to drop a plastic worm through matted vegetation or creating a hole in the salad to drop a lure in. There's no speed-fishing through this cover, making quick retrieves to entice eager fish. You have to plod along, working all spots deliberately, probing carefully. As with deep-water fishing, you have to spend the time at it.

While most forms of vegetation are quite obvious, locating them is not always a sure thing, a fact that may come as a surprise to anglers from some parts of the country. Submerged grass and weed beds are common in many places. Pinpointing the location of weed lines is often a crucial element in determining boat position, lure presentation, and fishing technique. A depthfinder can be a big asset in this situation. The point is to be aware that there is both submerged and emergent vegetation.

The most obvious, most often used, and most easily managed way to locate bass in vegetation is to work the edges. In large, fairly thick concentrations of grass, for example, bass stick close to the outside line, most likely because they can see and ambush prey there. This is especially true if the grass is so congested that you can't work any type of lure across the surface without it getting fouled up.

Milfoil beds are a prime example of this type of cover. Here, you may have to work the edges with a plastic worm, dropping the worm on top of the milfoil just inside the edge, then slithering it off and letting it drop vertically along the edge.

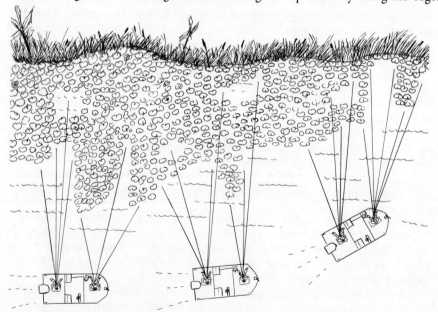

Fishing lily pads. As illustrated, isolated patches, deep holes, points, and irregular features are the types of location to fish when working thick vegetation, including lily pads.

Most strikes will occur within a foot or two of the edge. Any irregularity in the weed line, such as a protrusion, pocket, etc., may be an especially significant place to fish.

Frequently the key to unlocking the bass-catching secret in sparse grass is to fish isolated clumps—patches that are small but thick and that stand off from the main mass of vegetation (they may be inside the main body as well as outside). When the vegetation is thin and sparsely submerged, you won't be able to identify isolated patches. However, if you are using a depthfinder, you may be able to identify the thin and thick sections, as well as drop-offs or holes, by traveling across the area first.

If the vegetation—either emergent or submerged—is thick and has visible pockets or holes in it, start casting. Clearings in the grass are prime fishing locations, and they are easier to fish than congested spots.

The plastic worm can be one of the most tangle-free lures and is the most acclaimed and successful vegetation-fishing lure. It's a good idea to peg the slip sinker of a Texas-rigged plastic worm in this cover rather than let the sinker slide freely. In grass or pad stems or other types of vegetation, a free-sliding slip sinker often pulls off the object, leaving the worm behind. The two should work close together to effect a proper, natural presentation. A slip sinker that has been pegged with a toothpick to keep it from sliding does the job. An alternative is to use a weedless jig head or a plain jig with the hook imbedded in the worm.

While the plastic worm is the prime lure for vegetation fishing, bass do not always go for a worm. Often you need to give them something moving more enticingly, with a flash of metal, to get a strike. This is where combinations of spoon and pork chunk, or spoon and plastic skirt, come in.

After you've tackled vegetation fishing for a while, you'll find that it seems to be more productive in low-light situations than in bright daylight. Bright days drive bass deeper and further into the vegetation, where they are harder to reach effectively. Dawn, dusk, and overcast days offer the best vegetation fishing conditions. Night is a good time as well.

Flooded timber is another form of thick cover that summer anglers may face. It presents a different problem; in above-water timber, everything looks like it could hold a bass and in submerged timber there is nothing visual to go by. One of the keys is edges, another is channels and roadbeds; these are readily observed where timber is above the waterline and found through sonar use where timber is submerged.

In timber, sites that are a little different from the surroundings are often the places that will attract bass. The outside bends of channels and the junction of two channels, for example, are good places to concentrate fishing efforts. In the summer, bass will hold in timber adjacent to boat lanes if there is a good change in depth there. Plastic worms and jigs have the most merit in these situations in the summer, though a carefully worked, deep-diving crankbait may also produce.

Bass will also suspend in the midsection limbs of submerged trees (maybe 15 to 25 feet deep, although overall depth may be much greater), sometimes being schooled there and susceptible to vertical jigging with a jigging spoon by dropping the spoon to the bottom and then slowly jigging it up through the branches. You may be able to catch a number of fish in the same spot. Bass in this situation are likely to be active, whereas bass suspended in deep, open-water locales are a more finicky proposition.

In summer, don't overlook the possibility of having better fishing success at night, particularly with surface lures. Surface lures that are successful at night should create

Submerged timber is a good place to find bass, especially when using plastic worms and jigs.

a commotion. Noise is often a paramount factor for good, night, bass fishing. Wobbling surface plugs are tops. Crazy Crawlers (Heddon) and Jitterbugs (Arbogast) are equally successful, particularly in large sizes. Maintaining a steady, slow, retrieval cadence is the key to effectiveness.

Buzz baits are perhaps as equally effective on the surface as wobbling plugs. They are best in 3/8-ounce — and larger — sizes for night use. Another surface lure with after-dark value is a propellored stick bait. Instead of retrieving this in the normal, pull-pause tantalizing action, speed up the retrieve to a quicker, more direct pace.

Surface lures don't work all the time, of course, so don't stick with them if results aren't encouraging. Shallow-running crankbaits, spinnerbaits, jigs, and worms all have merit for night bass fishing. Try spinnerbaits in and around grass and pad coverings, along shore, and in shallow water. The spinner blades impart vibrations in the water and enhance the lure's detectability. Worms, though not good for covering a lot of territory in the dark, are great for fishing specific locations, and, since they are rigged to be fished weedless, don't invite many hang-ups.

Fall

Fishermen often think of fall bass as being more accessible and easier to catch than deep summer fish, but that isn't necessarily the case. In many bodies of water, bass in early fall still follow the deep-water behavior that they exhibited in the heat of the summer. If you aren't catching bass shallow at this time, then you need to move into deeper water and begin making appropriate presentations. In early fall on deep lakes, that may even mean deep vertical jigging.

Bass can be accessible, too, of course, in shallow or near-shore environs, and in or around cover. That's why water temperature can be something of a guide. If the water is warm early in the day, say in the upper 60s (which it will be in some places in October), you may try the shallows, but know to move quickly to deeper water if they don't produce. If the water temperature is cold to start with, such as in the upper 40s or low 50s, there's a good chance of finding fish near warmer, close-to-shore shallows, especially late in the day when the sun has had a chance to work on it. This isn't a foolproof system, but it can be helpful to use water temperature this way, according to the habitat available in the body of water you're fishing.

Temperature and habitat conditions vary markedly in the fall by geographic areas, and one bonus in far southern climes is that they experience favorable fall fishing conditions for a longer period of time than northern areas. In fact, their early fall angling can be much like summer fishing.

We're partial to ponds and small lakes in early fall—especially if they have a lot of grass and stump cover. Searching for bass in a limited amount of time isn't as difficult as it is on large lakes and reservoirs, especially if you're unfamiliar with those bodies of water.

The drawback to small waters, however, is that they are quick to cool. A succession of cold nights will draw the temperature down, and it takes Indian summer conditions to warm them back up. Larger bodies of water, which are usually deeper, take longer to cool off and thus can be relatively warm when the ponds or small lakes are already cool. That makes the latter good to fish in early fall and the former good to fish later in this season.

Spinnerbaits and crankbaits come into their own in the fall as prime bass lures. Jigs still continue to catch fish, particularly as the water gets really cold (which is when spinnerbaits become less effective). Plastic worms diminish in success as fall wears on, but surface lures, or minnow-imitating plugs worked either on or just below the surface, can provide action. It pays to be versatile and adaptable, therefore, when fall fishing, and not to be locked into only using one or two types of lures.

TECHNIQUE/TACKLE/SAVVY

How you fish for bass throughout the seasons is as important as when, where, and with what you fish. One of the elements of successful bass fishing is boat positioning: keeping your boat in the proper position for the time required to thoroughly fish an area. The most regularly fished area of a lake for all bass fishermen is the shoreline. When there are a lot of objects such as fallen trees, stumps, rock piles, etc., it is advantageous to position your boat 30 to 40 feet from shore and cast perpendicular to them. However, sharply sloping shorelines are better fished by casting forward over the bow of the boat, when the boat is positioned close to and parallel to the shore.

Another time when you should get close to shore is when there is thick brush and grass at the edge, and an immediate drop-off of 3 or more feet is present. Jigs can be worked vertically in this brush as you move along, or floating/diving plugs can be *jiggered*—zigzag fashion—in, out, and around the shoreline with a long rod. This is very effective and something that cannot be accomplished adequately by perpendicular positioning.

There is also something to be said for keeping your boat close to shore and fishing outward. Stump beds or rock piles or other objects that are far enough away from shore that they might be under the boat can usually be worked if you are positioned between them and the shore, especially if the water beyond them—away from shore—increases in depth. Deep-diving lures would probably be best here. Even if you do not see or locate underwater objects away from shore, it pays to cast deep-diving plugs out the other side of the boat occasionally.

Working a visible straight line of grass beds is another example of how it is worthwhile to fish close and parallel to the shore. However, when the grass is punctuated by cuts, channels, pockets, and the like, it is advisable to keep the boat out a bit and cast in, concentrating on the irregular features and the holes in the interior of the grass patches.

Points are always a good bass fishing location and are places that should be fished more thoroughly than many others. Three basic boat positions—on either side of the point and straight out from it—should be taken, and a range of casts should be made from each location. If you have a depthfinder, you should watch it as you work around the point; concentrate on the break area where the point tapers off to deep water.

A depthfinder is a substantial aid to all bass fishermen anywhere on a lake, regardless of the type of boat they use. In most cases, proper boat positioning over areas likely to hold bass but not visible to fishermen can only be accomplished through the use

The shoreline gets most attention, but there are many times when bass are located well away from shore, and fishermen should not overlook this.

Some of the better bass fishing may be found in not so readily identifiable places, such as points that extend well into a lake, the edge of deep submerged weeds, and shoals. Deep-diving crankbaits are often used in such locales.

of a depthfinder. By watching this instrument and following the contours of a promising spot (such as a mound, rock pile, deep grass bed, etc.), you can keep your boat on the fringe of the likely area and your lures in the fish-catching zone.

Working not-so-readily identifiable bass habitat is where many fishermen fail to operate to maximum potential. Take, for example, a situation where a deep weed line exists off a bar or point adjacent to deep water. Some anglers, intent on the immediate shoreline, may not discover the grass at all or not work far enough out from shore. Others will only give this spot a few quick casts en route to other places. Since bass will hang in the deep weed line and at the end of points where they break to deep water, a prime location combining both of these attributes should be thoroughly worked, approached from all angles, and covered with a range of lures. It pays to keep watching the depthfinder while manuevering the boat back and forth and in and out of such an area.

There are many fish-holding locales that should be fished thoroughly and for which various boat positions are advantageous. These include pilings, docks, fallen trees, bushes, and so forth. The important point always to consider is how to present a lure most effectively and how to position yourself for thorough fishing.

Effective presentation is the hallmark of one close-to-cover angling technique of substantial popularity: flipping. Flipping is a controlled, short-casting technique used in close quarters for presenting a moderately heavy jig or plastic worm in a short, quiet, accurate manner to cover that cannot be properly worked by a lure cast from a long distance away.

At a time when bass are probably more attuned to the ways of man and likely more skittish and aware of outside influences, flipping is a good technique to be used when bass may be holding very tightly to such cover as brush, standing timber and stumps, logjams or debris-filled flotsam, heavy lily pad and vegetation clusters, steep craggy ledges, docks, and boathouses.

The tackle required is a long rod, heavy line, and a jig or worm. The rod should be between 7 and 8 feet long, with a long straight handle. It must be stout, because bass are often violently jerked out of heavy cover on a short length of line, and the bigger the bass, the greater the stress and the degree of difficulty. Most flipping rods are one-piece bait-casters with an upper section that telescopes down into the handle for easy transportation and storage. Most flipping is done with bait-casting rods, but some anglers prefer spinning gear. The same rod features, however, are applicable. Flipping takes a toll on your arm muscles if you do it for a long period of time or for hours and days on end; because of this, a graphite rod, weighing considerably less than fiberglass, is very beneficial.

Most flippers use 25- to 30-pound-test line, and some even use 40. They go to such strengths because of the lack of stretch, less effect of abrasion (you often fish in abrasive areas), and need to horse big fish out of thick cover.

Black or brown jigs, primarily in 1/2-ounce sizes, but also a little lighter and a little heavier, are the most popular flipping baits. These should have fiber weed guards when fishing in all but rocky ledge areas, and they should sport a "living rubber" type of skirt and a large hook. They are adorned with all manner of enticements, including worms, curl-tail grubs, pork strips, and the like, but pork chunks (No. 11 Uncle Josh in black or brown) are the most popular.

Some prefer to flip a plastic worm, however, using a 7- to 9-inch worm on a 5/0 hook for this, and a heavy (1/4- to 1/2-ounce) slip sinker that is pegged to prevent it from sliding up the line. This seems to get hung up less frequently than a jig, and, when you have a strike, you can hesitate for the slightest moment to get a firm hook-set.

To flip properly, you must remember that your goal is to make a pinpoint bait presentation to a particular object within 10 to 20 feet of your boat and to do so in a quiet, splash-free manner.

Pinpoint presentations are more important in largemouth bass fishing than in most other forms of freshwater fishing. When casting to potential largemouth-holding objects, accuracy is a must. The first cast to a likely bass hole is often the most important one, so it pays to be able to make each cast count. This requires practice, but it also helps to use fish sense while casting. Every cast should have a purpose. It should be directed at a particular spot because it is a likely looking bass hideout, and that spot should be fished in a deliberate manner.

If, for example, you are fishing crankbaits along a rocky shoreline that drops off dramatically, it does no good if your lure constantly lands 6 feet out from shore. The fish could be hugging the bank or be on bottom 12 feet down, but no matter how deep your lure dives, it will have missed a prime area right from the start.

Make every cast count by knowing what types of visible cover are preferred by bass, then place your casts in the position likely to do the most good. Make casts to all sides of likely places. And learn how to feather your casts so that a lure doesn't come crashing down on the water's surface like a bomb.

Among the keys to successful largemouth fishing are being able to identify places that attract bass, being able to cast well and make good presentations, and being able to use your lures most effectively. When you put all these skills together, you have a good chance of catching a nice bass like this.

In addition to inadequate casting skills, another reason why bass fishermen are unsuccessful is that they fail to get their lures or bait down to the depth at which their quarry is located. Exactly what is deep? This varies among lakes and among fishermen. Anything over 10 feet is relatively deep. Yet in some areas, like Florida, few lakes have water over 15 feet deep. In others, most of the lake is over 20 feet deep; bass have been caught as deep as 80 to 100 feet in some places. Getting your offering down to these fish is often more of a problem than getting them to strike.

Very few of the standard variety of crankbaits will go deeper than 10 feet on a cast-and-retrieve. Often, bass fishermen working a bank will find that the fish are 10 to 20 feet deep along the shore, but their plugs will not get there, or will only reach the right level if they stick their rod tip deep in the water. The most recent trend in bass plugs, however, has been large-lipped crankbaits that do, in fact, dive to 15-, 20-, and even 30-foot ranges, so there is an opportunity to use plugs that will get pretty deep, unweighted and on a cast-and-retrieve. Remember that line diameter affects the depth attainment of any lure and the way in which it works.

Jigs, of course, are a prime bottom scrounger. The bigger and heavier the jig, the faster it will fall. In really deep water, most jigging is done straight below the boat. In less deep shoreline areas, jigs can be retrieved to cover a lot of bottom terrain. Worms, too, will go as deep as you like, but they are best fished on the cast-and-retrieve, rather than vertically, and are of limited value beyond 20 feet.

Any lure that sinks, of course, will achieve the depth you desire. The drawback here is that it takes time to get them to the desired depth. You can determine the sinking depth by counting until your lure reaches the bottom (as signified by slack line), trying to maintain a drop of one foot per count.

There are other ways to get lures deep, of course, the primary ones involving the use of weights. Sometimes small weights, such as split-shot or rubber-core sinkers, will be enough of an aid in that regard, though they may affect lure action. One of the better types of weights, especially for river trollers, is the bead-chain sinker. This is available in weights ranging from 1/4 ounce through 2 ounces, and it features a long, barrel-like weight on a snap-swivel assembly. The device prevents line twist from occurring, does not get hung up too readily, and works with all types of lures. A leader is utilized to connect the weight to the lure. Another device is the Bait-Walker, mentioned in detail in later chapters.

Obviously there is a host of lure types available to largemouth bass fishermen. Many of these overlap in application and technique, while others are suitable only to particular conditions and require specialized usage. In generalized terms, here is how the lure situation shapes up for bass fishing:

For shallow-water fishing, which is where everybody likes most to chase bass, floating/diving plugs and spinnerbaits get the call. In the plug category, minnow-imitating balsa or plastic lures that float at rest and dive only a foot or two on retrieve are traditional, proven baits. Spinnerbaits are excellent lures, particularly in the spring when fish are shallow, and also when fishing vegetation. They can also be used quite effectively in deeper water, crawled slowly across the bottom, or jigged.

A floating/diving minnow imitation plug, like the one that caught this largemouth, is one of the premier surface and shallow-water bass fishing lures.

For medium-depth angling (4 to 12 feet) you'll generally want to fish with a straight-running, dive-to-the-bottom-on-retrieve lure. Bottom-hugging crankbaits are manufactured in shallow, medium, and deep-diving versions, all of which are determined by the size and shape of the lip protruding from each one. Medium- and deep-divers are usually the most useful to bass fishermen, and these come into play in spring, parts of summer, and fall in many locales. Worms and jigs are also highly effective bass baits in this depth range.

For deeper fishing, the bass angler without a plastic worm or who doesn't know how to use it is in for a rough time. It is a fact that bass seek the comfort of cooler, deep water temperatures in late spring, summer, and early fall, and plastic worms are probably the most effective lure at these times. Jigs, of course, particularly jig and pork combos, can be fished extremely effectively in very deep water (and, in reality, at any depth), as well as along rocky, sharp-sloping bluffs and shorelines, and on underwater mounds. And, as noted previously, the new breed of super, deep-diving plugs is also a candidate for deep-water work.

Surface fishing is a favorite technique of bass anglers and one that is generally less productive than below-surface methods at most times. This is due to the habits and habitat of the quarry and the fact that there are generally fewer times when surface techniques have merit. Surface lures run the gamut from soft-plastic floating baits to wood or plastic plugs that twitch, wobble, chug, sputter, etc.

Live bait, of course, has some largemouth fishing devotees. Worms, minnows, crayfish, large shiners (and occasionally shad or alewives), frogs, salamanders, leeches, waterdogs, and a few other creatures are fished.

The tackle preference for live bait fishing usually runs to spinning and spin-casting equipment with the small- to medium-sized bait offerings, since it is easier to cast

Shown, from left, are some of the main types of largemouth bass lures: tandem-blade spinnerbait, walking surface plug, medium-diving crankbait, minnow-imitating plug, and rubber-legged jig.

and position them with this gear. Bait-casting tackle can be used with larger, heavier presentations. A lot of bank fishermen and some boat anglers still use cane poles. Live bait is fished with a variety of hooks from No. 6 for smaller bait to 5/0 for the largest; usually single hooks are used, but sometimes you may prefer treble hooks, particularly in open water. Split-shot is needed with small bait to keep it at the proper level and, unless you are live-lining the bait, some type of float, or bobber, will be necessary. Largemouth bass are not too shy about snatching bait, so line size usually isn't too critical, as long as it isn't too heavy in relatively clear water.

It's an old axiom that big bait catches big bass but one that has a lot of validity for largemouths. In Florida, it's common to fish with 9- to 12-inch shiners for trophy-size (over 10 pounds) bass. Remember that a largemouth has a prodigious mouth and is capable of consuming fairly large prey. If you are using small minnows for panfish, you may catch small bass, but you'll probably have to move up in size to appeal to the heartier appetite of bigger bass.

Live bait must act naturally and be lively to get the attention of bass. Change baits whenever the current offering seems to be losing its vitality. If you can keep your bait cool and well-aerated, it will stay in good condition. Live bait anglers should realize that bass with hooks in them may survive. If you've hooked a bass that you can't keep (perhaps because the season isn't open or the fish is under the minimum size limit) or that you don't want to keep and you leave the hook in the fish, there is a good chance that the bass will survive. Clip the line off above the hook. The hook will deteriorate within a few weeks if it is not stainless steel or cadmium-tin. If it is not bleeding profusely, and if you have been careful to handle it as little as possible, the fish should survive.

As for bass tackle, there really isn't one outfit that will adequately handle all aspects of largemouth fishing. Serious bass angling involves a range of fishing conditions, lure styles and sizes, and fishing methods. Adaptability, versatility, and preparedness are keys to success, and your fishing tackle must be able to meet the respective tasks.

At one end of the bait-casting and spinning tackle spectrum, there is heavy and medium-heavy equipment. This tackle borders on the unsporting side at times, considering that the majority of bass caught by all anglers weigh less than 2 pounds. In locales where brush, timber, and grass are exceedingly thick, and big bass are reasonably numerous, strong equipment has merit—but within reason. Super-heavy tackle does help anglers free lures from impenetrable tangles, and it does help manipulate lunker bass in tight quarters. But when you evaluate the situation honestly, how fair is it to catch bass, even fish up to 8 pounds, with a broomstick-type of rod and 25- or 30-pound-test line? There is good, medium-action equipment available that will handle big bass and bad conditions and still be sporting. With it, reasonable strength line can be used, switching to heavy line when the worst conditions are prevalent.

Keep in mind that a largemouth bass is a close-quarters, object-oriented scrapper. Largemouths found in or near weeds, stumps, bushes, fallen trees, rocky ledges, boulders, lily pads, and such—in effect, most of the areas where they live—have to be forced away from these objects after being hooked or they may be lost. Since this covers most of the places where largemouths are found, the importance of this element is significant. With light and ultralight tackle it is difficult, if not impossible at times, to work weeds and lily pads properly, and to finesse a weedless spoon, plastic worm, surface lure, or even a spinnerbait through them.

Bait-casting tackle, being used by this angler, is preferred for most largemouth bass fishing because of the types of lures used and the places in which largemouths are caught.

By practical elimination, medium-duty tackle, packed with 6- to 14-pound-test line, can be assigned to handle the majority of bass fishing circumstances (with a few notable exceptions, such as flipping and vegetation fishing) and still retain an element of fun and good sport in the bass-catching process. Use equipment that best does the job under existing circumstances without sacrificing the element of sport.

Bass fishing with artificial baits principally involves these different angling devices: spinnerbaits, crankbaits, worms and jigs, floating/diving plugs, and surface lures. With a good rod — one that has guts and sensitivity — you can fish the first three categories effectively. For the others, you still need a rod with guts but with a softer tip action to impart effective lure motion.

We're partial to bait-casting rods for most bass fishing, particularly crankbait and worm fishing and working in heavy cover. A bait-casting rod offers slightly better casting control and is much more conducive to the use of big lures, and baits weighing over 1/4 ounce.

Our preference runs to 6-foot bait-casting rods, which are distinctly advantageous for casting (as opposed to short, 5-foot models) — though admittedly a little harder to use in close quarters — and to straight, rather than pistol-grip, handles. The long rod helps you achieve distance, if that is necessary, and makes fish playing and control better.

CHAPTER TWO
SMALLMOUTH BASS

If a smallmouth bass grew as large as a striper or a salmon, there'd be no arguments about what was the gamest fish to catch. Think about it! A smallmouth that weighs 20 pounds! How *hard* it would pull! What a relentless consumer of prey it would be! The kind of jumps it would be capable of making, the spectacular photos we'd have! Imagine what an awesome fish that would be!

We're dreaming, of course. There's nothing wrong with the smallmouth the way it is right now. In fact, on an equal-size basis, there is no freshwater fish that pulls harder, jumps more, or fights as tenaciously as a smallmouth bass. It is an ideal fish to play on light tackle; it has discriminating habitat and food preferences; and it is challenging to pursue. The smallmouth is an impressive quarry.

Smallmouth bass are a cool-water, bottom-oriented fish that provide excellent light-tackle angling.

LAKES

Let's talk separately about river smallmouths and lake smallmouths, dealing first with the latter. There are three especially influential elements in the life of smallmouth bass in lakes, ponds, and reservoirs: cool water, a rocky bottom, and crayfish. The applicability and importance of these natural factors vary from region to region and from one bass environment to the next, but generally the home of the smallmouth has all of these features. And they influence growth as well. A typical smallmouth bass reaches sexual maturity when it is three to four years old. At this time, it will be between 9 and 11 inches long. A 16-inch fish, which might weigh about 3 pounds, would probably be 8 years old. In the most northerly reaches of its range, it would be even older. A 5- or 6-pound smallmouth, which is recognized as a trophy everywhere, is obviously one of the elders of the bass world.

In their northernmost range, where water temperatures are unlikely to exceed the low 70s throughout the summer, smallmouths may be found in shallow to mid-depth environs throughout the fishing season. But where water temperatures in the shallow and near-shore areas exceed the low 70s for a long time, bass move deeper. Smallmouths are regularly found in lakes with at least modest depth, generally of 15 to 25 feet or more. Shallow lakes usually only support these fish if they are spring-fed or are located in northern environs where cool summer evenings temper the effect of daily warmth.

Smallmouths typically inhabit rocky terrain. Their native range is typified by somewhat infertile, natural, rocky-shored, northern lakes. Their expanded range now includes southern impoundments with shoreline and deep-water rock structure. Smallmouths don't inhabit lily pad beds or grass fields, though they may be caught along the edges of such vegetation. They aren't found around stumps and timber with sandy bottoms, though they may use such objects as cover in rockier locales. They make their beds on a hard gravel bottom, as deep as 10 or 12 feet in some places, but they prefer 2- to 6-foot depths.

Smallmouths are located around rocky points; craggy, cliff-like shores; rocky islands and reefs; and rip rap shores. They prefer golf-ball- to brick-sized rocks if they have a choice, but larger rocks, including boulders, are also suitable. In the spring, prior to spawning, smallmouths in lakes that are completely rock-laden prefer to be near large rocks, and you may be able to work a shoreline quickly by keying on every big boulder in shallow water.

Perhaps the primary reason for the smallmouth's fondness for rocks is that they harbor crayfish. Where crayfish are abundant, they are the principal food for smallmouths. Certainly smallmouths eat whatever is most abundant in their environment, and they'll readily consume small fish when they are plentiful or when the proper opportunity presents itself. But crayfish are their staple.

There's no doubt that live crayfish make excellent smallmouth bait. Soft-shells (called crabs in some places) are preferred by most bait anglers but are usually hard to obtain, and in most areas, fishermen use hard-shells of varying sizes. When still-fishing, leave your bail open, hold the line in your free hand, and periodically give a light tug to the line to keep the crayfish from burrowing under rocks. In drift-fishing, close the bail and keep the rod tip high to detect a strike.

Typical lake smallmouth habitat includes rocky points, islands, shoals, and reefs.

We prefer to fish for smallmouths with lures, for the fun and challenge, and because we release most of our bass, few of which are deeply hooked or injured when using artificials. Many bass are gut-hooked on live bait, and, if you want or have to release such fish, you must cut the line and leave the hook in it.

Crankbaits are excellent smallmouth plugs. Not surprisingly, they look somewhat like a crayfish in their diving/swimming action, size, and, when used in brown and white, in color. Crankbaits can be productive for cast-and-retrieve use all season long if smallmouths aren't too deep and are especially valuable in the spring. Medium to deep runners are generally best and should be fished fairly slowly and in contact with the bottom.

Bottom scratching is critical in most bass fishing situations with crankbaits. Try to keep your plug rooting along the bottom, over objects, and along impediments. This is no problem with the right floating/diving crankbait. For the sinking version, let it settle to the bottom (or count it down to a particular level) and make your retrieve at a rate slow enough to keep the plug on or as close to the bottom as possible.

Floating/diving crankbaits are exceedingly buoyant, a feature that adds a different dimension to their "fishability." If you stop your retrieve, these plugs will bob toward the surface like a cork. You can take advantage of this feature in your fishing techniques. A pull-pause action is easily accomplished by retrieving in the standard fashion and stopping momentarily, then repeating the procedure. In its most exaggerated form, this can be extended to stopping the retrieve long enough for the lure to float to the surface and then resuming the retrieve.

The best way to fish smallmouth-holding structure with a crankbait is to cast beyond it so that when you retrieve, the lure will be able to get down to its running depth before it reaches the object. Similarly, be sure that your crankbait actually gets down to the depth that you need to reach. When fishing along riprap or sharply sloping shorelines, this is particularly important.

Another key pointer for successful crankbait usage is how to present your lure and position your boat when working the shoreline or a deep breakline (the spot where the bottom slopes off sharply). The best way to cast a crankbait to such areas is by working parallel, rather than perpendicular, to it. When two anglers are in the boat, it is a good tactic for both of them to fish from the front (as when casting from a bass boat), with each one's cast overlapping the other as the boat is manuevered close, and parallel, to the area.

Another highly effective plug for smallmouth bass is a floating/diving minnow. This is more of an early- and late-season bait, except in the most northerly waters, where some smallmouth can be found shallow even in the summer.

These lures are most effectively worked in a deliberately erratic fashion to imitate a crippled bait fish. If you have ever seen a dying shad, alewife, sunfish, perch, shiner, or other small fish, you may have noticed how it lies on its side, wiggles its tail fin occasionally, goes around in circles, and sometimes gets up enough energy to swim a few inches underwater before bobbing to the surface. This is essentially the type of activity you want to mimic in the retrieval of a floating/diving lure.

Thus, your objective with a floater/diver is to make it gyrate as enticingly as possible in a stationary position. Keep the rod tip pointed low toward the water and use your

When smallmouths are shallow, try a minnow-imitating plug on or just below the surface.

wrist to move the rod. Jiggle the rod tip in a controlled, not frantic, fashion. Then jerk the lure back toward you a few inches. Then gyrate it some more, all the time reeling in an appropriate amount of line to keep the slack down to a minimum. This is really not very difficult to accomplish, particularly if you have a rod with a fairly limber tip. The 4-inch-size lures, being light, are easiest to cast with spinning tackle and 4- to 8-pound-test line anyway, especially under windy conditions.

Another way to use this lure type is on a straight retrieve, allowing it to run a foot or two beneath the surface. This is more like using it in the style of a crankbait, and sometimes bass will strike it this way. For colors, the silver version probably out-catches all the others combined. Gold is good when the water is certain colors, and sometimes, in clear lakes, perch, smelt, and bass patterns may be productive.

Another excellent smallmouth lure with application in all bass environments is the grub. Three-sixteenths- and 1/4-ounce lead heads are used, with avocado-, black-, or smoke-colored soft-plastic bodies. Let them sink to the bottom, then nudge the rod to make them hop slightly along. It helps to have a light line (4- to 8-pound-test) and a fast-action rod with a sensitive tip to detect soft pickups and to keep your rod tip angled upward for better feel.

To work grubs, first let them settle to the bottom wherever you've cast. When fishing a moderately sloping shoreline or point, you should pull the lure slowly a little bit off the bottom; let it settle down while keeping in contact with the lure; take up the slack; and repeat this. When working a ledge, or a sharply sloping shoreline, slowly pull the lure over the structure until it begins to fall; let it settle, and then repeat. Don't hop the jig up quickly here, as it will fall out and away from the bottom and likely miss a good deal of the important terrain. With grubs, it is sometimes a good technique to make them jump quickly off the bottom rather than make short hops. You can also swim a grub on the edges of cover by reeling it slowly across the bottom and giving it occasional darting movements with manipulation of your rod tip. The majority of your strikes while jigging will come as the bait falls back down, so be alert for a strike then and keep both a good feel, and an eye, on your line to detect this.

Perhaps these jigs look like small crayfish to bass, which find their slow crawling movement appealing. The same can be said of larger jigs sporting a rubber-tentacled skirt and pork chunk. These are best fished on slightly heavier line and a stiffer rod than grubs, and, while they won't catch as many smallmouths as a grub, they do have a strong appeal to large fish.

Rocky banks can be a strong jig and pork locale, particularly if they have a very steep drop-off and possess a lot of craggy, ledge-like formations. Bass will seek refuge in the crags and under the ledges but are often not susceptible to diving plugs or other lures. Here these jigs can be flipped or cast. In both cases, present the jig close to the edge of the rock and allow it to fall vertically close to the bank. Crawl it off each ledge, over each rock, swimming it along as unobtrusively as possible, and working it under the boat or as deep as your cast will permit. Always work the lure slowly, keeping light tension on the line, and be prepared to set the hook the instant a strike is detected.

The weight of the jig to use depends primarily on the depth of the water but is also dependent upon wind and current conditions. For deep-bank work, a 1/4-ounce jig on light line might do the trick, but you may need to go heavier. The color is

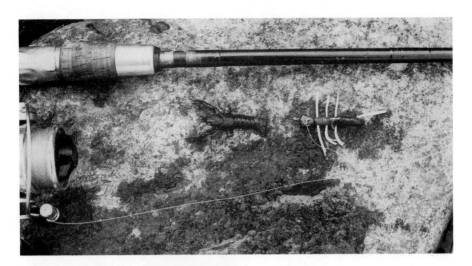

Crayfish are the primary food for smallmouth bass in nearly all places where these bass are found. Jigs, including the soft-plastic-bodied rubber-legged version placed next to the live crayfish, and the jig-and-pork chunk combo dangling from the rod of this bass angler, are premier smallmouth lures.

usually dark, with black, brown, or purple the best bets. For pork chunks, try a No. 11 Uncle Josh pork rind in black, brown, or brown and orange. The chunk, incidentally, can be trimmed with a knife to make it fall faster, if that seems desirable.

Smaller jigs, those with soft plastic, curl-tail bodies, don't look like a crayfish but are also highly effective smallmouth baits, as are hair-bodied jigs. We like the latter in brown or black colors, and the former in purple, black, or dark green (though white and yellow appeal to other fishermen). Give these a try if the bass won't hit the grubs and seem to want a more diminutive meal.

With all jigs, the lighter the line and the heavier the lure, the easier it is to reach the bottom. The stronger the line, the greater its diameter and the more resistance it offers in the water. A 1/4-ounce jig will fall quicker on 8-pound line than it will on 14-pound line, for example. The advantage here (the magnitude of which depends on fishing conditions) will be that it is easier to get your lure to the bottom, and keep it on the bottom, with 8-pound line than it is with 14.

Once you are on the bottom, of course, you need to maintain contact with it. Assuming that you have cast your jig out, let it settle to the bottom, and are now retrieving it toward you, you should keep it working in short hops along the bottom as long as the sloping bottom and length of line out enable you to do so. If you are in a boat and drifting, the jig will eventually start sweeping upward and away from you and the bottom as you drift, unless it is very heavy; so you need to pay out more line occasionally until the angle of your line has changed significantly, then reel in and drop the jig back down again. When drifting, incidentally, face the wind or current and drop your jig out on the windward side of the boat. If you drop it on the lee side, the boat will soon drift over your line, and you'll be in an awkward position for fishing.

Choosing the right weight lure to use is critical to most types of jigging. The ideal is to have a lure that gets to the bottom and stays there under normal conditions, but which is not too large to be imposing to bass. Most anglers who fail to reach bottom not only don't use the right retrieval technique or compensate for wind or current, but also use too light a jig for getting down to the bottom.

While jigs and crankbaits account for most lure-caught smallmouth bass, there are times when other lures may be successful. Spinnerbaits can produce nice smallmouth action, though they are not universally appealing. When bass are shallow and aggressive, as they are in the beginning of the season, spinnerbaits may be especially successful; but later, as the fish move deeper and become warier, spinnerbaits don't produce unless you want to spend time fluttering single-blade models off deep ledges. Small lures, no more than a 1/4-ounce, are usually best, and in some waters you may find spinnerbaits appealing more to pickerel or pike than bass.

Smallmouths may be taken with spinnerbaits when they are in shallow rocky environments close to shore, when they are on shoals to feed, and when they are on beds in sparsely covered terrain. While we have caught some big-lake smallmouths on spinnerbaits fished along rock- and boulder-studded shores, we have also found them reticent to hit these lures under similar conditions on other lakes. We know one excellent spring lake where small, in-line spinners will take bronzebacks that refuse spinnerbaits, and another where shallow bass occasionally strike a plug and quickly take a jig but repeatedly pass up the spinnerbait. So it pays to be adaptable.

Spinners, in 1/8- to 1/4-ounce sizes, and in black, gold, silver, and combined colors, have been traditional smallmouth catchers, particularly in northern locales and in streams. They may imitate small fish or emerging aquatic insects, and though they can't be fished as slowly as a jig, they should be retrieved at a pace that keeps them near the bottom and with the blade turning freely.

Surface lures are mainly applicable for smallmouths when the fish are shallow, but there's a variety of these lures that are worth trying. As previously noted, a floating, minnow-imitation plug provides exciting fishing in the spring when smallmouths are nesting in shallow water. At the same time and in the summer in areas where bass are shallow during the day, a stick bait such as a Zara Spook has merit.

Stick baits with propellers, either fore and aft or just aft, take many shallow smallmouths in various regions of the country. These lures are basically shaped like small cigars or torpedoes; they may feature propeller-like blades both fore and aft or they may only possess one blade at the rear. They are manufactured in roughly 2- to 6-inch sizes; the 3 1/2-inch-size model is the most productive one. The basic retrieval technique is similar to that of floating/diving minnow plugs, which is a jiggling-jerking-pausing motion that is erratic and representative of a struggling or crippled baitfish. Keep the rod down, utilize the rod tip to effectively impart action, and make your wrists do the work.

Propellered surface plugs can be fished in the spring, summer, and fall, though summer appears to be the most productive period. At that time, it is best to fish them for the first few hours of daylight and occasionally in the evening.

We've had more limited success with other types of surface lures, but some lakes have their own oddities. We have taken big smallmouths on a Jitterbug fished explicitly for largemouths, for example. There are places where the night-time use of surface wobblers and poppers is most effective, even though these lures usually don't attract smallmouths in other lakes.

Peculiarities pop up everywhere, of course. For instance, live leeches are a popular smallmouth (and walleye) bait in the spring in the upper Midwest, but you don't find fishermen using them extensively in other regions. We regularly hear about fishermen who have tremendous success in Canadian lakes with live frogs, and some anglers drag weights over rock bottoms to stir up bait and then catch smallmouths by livelining crayfish just off the bottom.

Great Lakes practitioners of the latter technique call it "center-line drifting." They fish areas near shore that have a softball-size cobblestone bottom, in depths that range from 20 to 30 feet. They bait No. 4 hooks with soft-shell crayfish (locally called crabs), which ring a smallmouth's dinner bell like no other form of food, and put a No. 1 or 2 split shot about 18 inches above the hook. The key to this technique, besides using soft-shells and knowing the prime locales, is drifting a 40- to 50-pound weight along the bottom, using an iron or steel block that doesn't snag up, and securing it via heavy rope to the gunwale amidships so the boat drifts sideways with the wind. The anchor drags bottom fairly close to the boat, stirring up rocks and leaving disturbed crayfish in its wake. A chum line of sorts is created, and smallmouths are not only attracted to the free chow but even follow the dragging anchor.

There are some environments (Lake George in New York, for example) where anglers catch smallmouths 100 feet deep while using downriggers, and, while that it is a little extreme depth-wise, the use of downriggers for trolling, in fact, has a lot of merit where smallmouths are concerned and has only recently become a little more widely practiced.

By using downriggers you are able to get lures down to the bottom, to be in constant control of the depth that is being fished, and to cover effectively wide expanses of desirable territory in a fairly short period of time. In large, clear lakes where bass are found very deep, fishermen equipped with a downrigger may have better action using this gear because they can cover a lot of ground and can employ light line in

Trolling is an overlooked smallmouth bass angling tactic, but one with a lot of merit, especially when these fish are deep. This angler is using a downrigger to troll in an impoundment with smallmouth bass.

the process. If a concentration of bass is found, stopping to jig or fish bait may have merit.

With or without downriggers, there are times and places in which trolling is a good way to get your lures in front of bass. Lakes without vegetation or submerged timber and lakes with plenty of deep water are very likely to yield bass to trollers. This is especially so in the summer. Then, the water is warm, fish are deep and not readily located, and it is difficult to make effective deep casting presentations. In appropriate places, trolling can be a good way to find and catch smallmouth bass (sometimes largemouths, too).

The most successful and functional lure for bass trolling is a small- or medium-sized crankbait. All else being equal, crankbaits achieve much greater depths when trolled than when cast, making them especially useful for light-line (6- to 8-pound) fishing and scouring 12- to 25-foot depths without the use of sinkers or weighted lines.

It isn't always necessary to get deep, however. In the spring, on large lakes, bass come out of their winter haunts and orient from deep to shallow waters. You can catch a lot of bass then, especially smallmouths, by trolling small-lipped, shallow-running 4- to 6-inch–long, floating/diving minnow plugs. These lures don't dive appreciably, but, if you troll them on a light line 150 to 225 feet behind the boat, they'll get down to 5- to 8-foot depths without being weighted.

Another primary lure type for bass trolling is a spoon, such as 1/8- to 1/4–ounce, thick-bodied spoons up to 3 inches long, and lighter, thin metal spoons of a similar length. The former can be cast or trolled while the latter are strictly for trolling. These are the same types of spoons used for trout trolling.

Spinners are not usually thought of as a bass lure by many anglers these days, but spinners are one of the most popular lures in the world. A favorite single-blade spinner for trolling is the so-called June bug spinner, which features a long-shank hook and a single rotating blade with beads along the shaft. Variations of this are a highly popular lure for bass and walleye fishing in many locales, most notably Lake Erie. There, they are garnished with a live worm and drifted or trolled across reefs. Drifting with the wind is akin to slow-trolling, and, as in motor-trolling for bass, getting the lure down to the bottom and keeping it there is critically important.

Using split-shot, rubber-core, or bead-chain sinkers is a technique often used for trolling minnow plugs, spoons, and sometimes diving plugs, in addition to spinners. Another device that is extremely useful for getting lures deep (including depths they would not reach on their own, such as 20 to 40 feet of water) for bass is the Gapen Bait Walker. This is a rig shaped like an open safety pin or a spinnerbait, with a lead body on the bottom and a swivel at the end of the top arm. Fishing line is tied to the midsection, and a drop-back leader 18 to 30 inches long is attached to the swivel.

This bottom-walking rig comes in a wide range of weights and can be used to cast or troll lures. It is also remarkably (though not completely) snag-free, due to the shape of the lead weight and the angle of pull. A good use for this device is in trolling minnow-imitation plugs or tiny crankbaits (try shad or crankbait patterns), to bring them down to a depth that they couldn't reach unaided. The biggest trick is selecting the right size weight, without going too heavy, in order to reach the bottom. Besides being trolled, this rig can be cast (carefully) or drifted, but it should always be run slowly along the bottom.

When you are trolling for bass, always be cognizant of the bottom depth where

Light and ultralight spinning equipment brings out the best in the zesty fight of smallmouths.

you are fishing, the level at which you believe bass are located, and the level that your trolled lure is working realistically.

Regarding tackle for smallmouth bass in lakes, light- and medium-duty gear, packed with 4- to 8-pound-test line, can be assigned to handle the majority of smallmouth bass fishing circumstances. This will allow you to enjoy the spunk of a smallmouth without overpowering it and hauling it in the boat.

Light (6- and 8-pound) and ultralight (2- and 4-pound) lines are practical, even desirable, for smallmouths. This is because smallmouths are residents of open water, and, when hooked, do not have to be powered away from obstacles other than the bottom. Also, in many regions, they inhabit relatively clear, deep lakes and are an especially wary fish, so delicate presentations involving light, thin-diameter line, small lures, and corresponding rod and reel combinations, make light and ultralight tackle a fundamental part of smallmouth fishing success.

RIVERS

As noted earlier, smallmouths are inhabitants of both lakes and rivers, and, while it may be in the former that they grow largest, it is in the latter that they are most feisty. We could argue this point forever, but smallmouths in flowing water may be the most sporting freshwater fish (and certainly warm-water species), pound for pound, that exists.

Those who have fished for both know that the river smallmouth is far superior in fight to its lake-dwelling brethren, which is saying a lot because the lake dweller is no slouch. True to the character of its flashing, fire-red eye, a river smallmouth possesses demon-like determination. Once hooked, this fish will explode high above the surface in a continuous series of leaps. Then it heads deep, sluggishly holding back. Moments later, it again breaks the surface in a final attempt to dislodge the hook. The fight usually ends with the bass completely spent.

River smallmouth bass get their added strength from the environment in which they live. Surviving in fast-flowing currents tends to slim and condition this fish, and, unlike largemouth bass, or lake smallmouths, river bass are more streamlined and lack a drooping potbelly.

Body coloring will vary with the environment. Clear-water streams hold fish that range in color from a pale amber to a light green along the back and upper sides. In dark waters, muddied by stream corridor conditions or rusted by swampy discharge, the smallie's back and sides vary from ebony-black to darkened brown. Stomach colors will likewise vary according to natural surroundings but are still primarily shades of white. Gray and yellow stomach coloring is evident when river structure contains a great deal of clay or discolored sand and gravel. Darkened water must be present as well to produce these two belly colors. Only when dark rock and black loam blanket river bottoms will the smallmouth's lower sides darken to a near black.

Finding river smallmouths in good numbers is usually the main concern of all bass anglers. First-time river anglers are often reduced to countless hours of catching only a few of the 1/4- and 1/2-pound buck bass and not determining where to look for bigger fish.

The best thing to do is probe a river for a structure called *hardpan*. Hardpan is that section of a river's bottom where it hardens, lifts, and forces current toward the surface. In most cases, you'll discover hardpan by looking for a distortion of current pattern on the river's surface. A small boil, large swirl, slight rippling, or visible drop indicate that the river bottom below has hardened. Boulders, rocks, gravel, stone, shale, and hardened clay or sand are all considered hardpan. It is a natural part of any river bottom created when moving water can no longer cut a channel through softer elements such as silt, loam, soft clay, or fine sand. Unable to cut the bottom away, water is forced up and around the hardened structure. In so doing, a highly desirable holding and feeding station is created.

Similar conditions are created by various obstructions, such as fallen trees and up-rooted stumps, rocks, large blasted stones, current-diverting structures, and bridge pillars and pilings. These can all be holding areas, though they are not nearly as produc-tive for river smallmouth as natural structures.

River smallmouth hold in these places because of the availability of food. Minnows, crayfish, hellgrammites, nymph larva, and leeches gather here for protection, reproduc-tion, and feeding. By simply placing its nose in behind a small, protruding rock or ledge and allowing downstream backwash to hold it in place while gently finning, a bass can easily hold in the fastest waters without extreme effort. Once stationed like this, smallmouths are able to easily gobble up critters who pass this place of ambush. Remember that in a river, much of the system's food comes via the current. Forage—be it minnows, crayfish, or hellgrammites—will seek out protruding rocks while they are being whisked downstream. The very spot they seek as shelter is a holding area for a predator bass.

Rivers provide a lot of good smallmouth habitat, as well as vigorous fish.

Look for hardpan structure in rivers where banks pinch in toward one another, at off-river points where rocks are visible at the point's end, when surface waters quicken and become disturbed, where single rocks protrude above the surface, where waterfalls or small dams drop away, beneath exposed tree limbs that indicate that a main tree trunk lies below, and where riprap is exposed above the surface on the river bank. Most of all, such structure exists beneath any visibly noticeable surface disturbance.

Because river smallmouth bass spend a major portion of their existence on and above hard river bottoms, crayfish are a major source of food. Crayfish, which are also known as crawdads or crawfish, are found in many environments across North America, include a variety of species, and thrive wherever running water travels over a hardened bed of rock.

Once their protective cold-weather shell is shed—which is when water nears 64 degrees—crayfish are readily sought by river bass. In many places, the crayfish at bait dealers are distinguished as either *hard shells* or *soft shells*, and it is usually the soft shells that are preferred.

With hard-shelled crayfish, you can crack off the tail, peel a bit of shell back for scenting benefit, and use it as is or tip it on the hook of a jig. Always run the hook from the under-tail side of the crayfish to come out the top-tail side. With whole crayfish, put the hook in the tail section so he runs backward naturally. Crayfish, like their lobster cousins, are backward travelers. Try snaring them from the front with a catch-net sometime and watch them scurry off in reverse.

Another good natural bait for smallmouth bass is a night crawler, hooked in the head, which becomes very effective as the water temperature reaches the mid-60s. Crawlers work well for other fish, too, of course, especially once the water warms up in mid to late spring. However, night crawlers become less effective with the arrival of cold fall winds.

Live crayfish and crawlers can be worked behind weighted, bottom-bouncing rigs, employing egg sinkers, walking sinkers, pencil leads, Bait-Walkers, or three-way rigs. Most of these must be worked downstream and brought up against the current.

Crayfish-imitating crankbaits are a popular river fishing lure and are made by a host of plug manufacturers, particularly Rebel, Norman, Bagley, Mann's, Bomber, and Rapala. They are representative of crayfish in color, certainly, and to some extent even in shape. When worked across hardpan shallows, these lures effectively entice smallmouth. Pick crankbaits 1 1/2 to 3 inches in length for river crayfish imitation.

Plastic worms and spinnerbaits work on smallmouth but generally are fished in slower, deeper river systems like the Mississippi, Tennessee, and Columbia/Snake rivers. Use dark worms; purple and grape are particularly good choices. Use spinnerbaits in small, colorful models. Brush piles, sunken logs, and uprooted stumps along big-river riprap make excellent targets for the angler using spinnerbaits or plastic worms. Fish both lures slowly, allowing them to fall deep as they drop down along the structure. Do this also wherever there are small eddying pockets of water by riprap.

Fly fishing has merit at times in flowing water, too. Some fly rodders use nymphs, small jigs (1/64- and 1/32-ounce), and semi-submerging flies like a Muddler Minnow during summer months. These best represent the natural food that bass feed on, of course. In spring and fall, use streamer flies, which represent minnows. Preferred patterns are those with black or brown backs, yellow or gray sides, and white bellies. Streamer

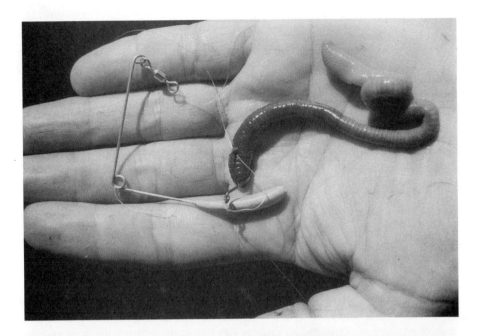

Nightcrawlers are a popular natural bait for smallmouths, and this one is attached to a bottom-walking sinker rig. Crankbaits, particularly those with a crayfish-imitating pattern, are a prime river artificial where there is enough depth or flow to use them.

fly size varies from No. 8 to 1/0, with long shanks. Popping bugs are used in late fall also, which we'll discuss momentarily.

Jigs are an excellent, and perhaps the best, river smallmouth lure. Jigs can be tipped with a small crawler tail or short pieces of night crawlers. Cut the crawler in four or five pieces and use each piece individually for tipping, running the jig hook through either end. Don't double up on crawler pieces. This causes the jig to ride unnaturally and may attract too many small fish to your offering.

Any jig that looks like it might represent a crayfish or hellgrammite (another important river smallmouth forage), acts erratically, and is darkly colored is considered excellent river smallmouth bait. Jigs sprouting rubber legs are such a lure and have become favorites in many rivers. The Ugly Bug jig, a lure with brown body, orange head, and four sets of rubber-tentacled legs, may be the king of unsightliness, but it has been a lure used effectively by ardent river smallmouth anglers for many years. This and other jigs are preferred in brown color and should be worked with the current to be most effective.

Working with current is one of the most important points for river smallmouth fishermen to understand. The faster a river system flows, the more food it forces downstream. Therefore, logic dictates that you work your offering with the current to represent the natural movement pattern of food in a river. Working a lure with the current doesn't always mean retrieving directly downstream, however. When working a boulder-strewn shoreline, for example, cast upriver at a 45-degree angle and retrieve in a similar manner. This enables you to use any lure and dig deep enough to be effective. Smallmouths, like all river fish, are most often found holding close to the bottom.

There is, however, an opportunity to catch river smallmouths on the surface, particularly late in the season. Many river systems host frog migrations in the fall (in the north in late August and in the south in early October), and you can often see frogs migrating upstream along the banks. There is good reason for this. Frogs that are in tadpole stage get swept away by river currents and are forced hundreds of yards, even miles at times, downstream. To get back to their place of birth, which is a natural instinct, they travel upstream. Unable to swim against the current, they must use the river bank. But frogs often get in the water. Where there is an eddy, for example, they swim to the head of the eddy and then leave the water. In the water, of course, they are victimized by smallmouths. A likely place to find frogs is riverbank areas which house weeds and gently circulating eddies. If these eddies rest between a series of short, low, stony points, so much the better.

Fly rodders will find this a great time to use Popping bugs. Use 8 1/2- to 9-foot rods capable of handling 8- and 9-weight bug taper lines. Use one line size over the rod rating if you will cast only Popping bugs, but stick with the rated line if you will also be casting streamers and wet flies.

Spinning tackle users will find selection of surface lures quite easy. Any floating frog imitation, blunt-nosed popper, or stick bait with rear-end propeller will do the trick. For some, color makes a difference, but we've found that white, yellow, or green belly colors work equally well, remembering that the belly is what a bass sees when he's looking up (as opposed to the color on the top of the lure). What does make a difference is the action given to such a bait. Work surface lures slowly, allowing time between each hard twitch. Even when the lure floats with current flow, allow time between twitches.

One of the things to realize about river smallmouth is that they will not only lie below obstructions, but also above them. Anglers casting to the eddy directly downstream from a structure will encounter bass, of course. During the day, small fish will be directly behind the rock, and larger fish will be holding along the current cuts some 10 to 15 feet downstream. That's the norm, however. What many fishermen fail to realize is that one or more very large bass will often hold just upstream from the structure. Naturally, these spots should be approached first.

On a bridge abutment, a slightly different situation occurs. Anglers will find small bass directly downstream from this structure, with some large fish 10 to 20 feet farther down along abutment-created, current cuts. A current cut is that area where swirling eddy water, created directly downstream from structure, and fast, downstream-descending current meet. All river structures have current cuts downstream from them.

Like the rock mentioned before, there will be a large fish or two directly upstream from the bridge piling. They are able to hold here because of the backwash created as current forces in on the top side of structure. Anchoring above and fishing down may be the only way to get at them.

In fast-water areas, waterfalls, small drop dams, or shallow gravel rippling, anglers tend to fish below the structure. In the spring, when spawning occurs, that's fine. But during the balance of the season, fishing above these structures will produce more and larger smallmouth bass than will fishing below them. Here, such forage as minnows,

Current cuts below dams and bridge abutments are a good place to look for river smallies.

crayfish, hellgrammites, and nymphs take advantage of the upstream bottom conditions. Smallmouth bass find staging easy here, and there is well-oxygenated water and food always available.

The lure and live bait approach to such areas can be accomplished by upstream casting and downstream retrieving, by wading or anchored-boat anglers, or by trolling. The deeper such an area is, the more apt the angler is to use a sinker rig. Jigs and crankbaits work best when such upstream areas are shallow.

When the river you fish is less than 20 feet wide and has an average depth of 2 feet or less, anglers must change their approach. Wading is best here. Small johnboats and canoes will work but often have to be run with the current. Such a maneuver will set up a series of disturbances that in turn telegraph the angler's presence to the waiting prey. Wading, in contrast, should begin from a downstream point and continue upstream as the angler casts up ahead. This automatically forces the lure to be retrieved with the current, which is a proper and natural presentation.

Small streams generally receive little fishing pressure and therefore are some of the hottest smallmouth hiding places. On these small streams, work the undercut banks, sunken logs, stump roots, and short rock walls. The water around these types of structure may only appear 4 to 6 feet deep but generally hold bass.

By using a dabbling technique, you can drop a small, live, bait-tipped jig (1/16- or 1/8-ounce) in a small creek hole, work it ever so slightly, and draw a strike. Dabbling is a simple method of vertically jigging a lure, and it especially works in creeks. There, gamefish recover quickly from an angler's intrusion, especially if it comes from downstream. That's because the vibration from your approach returns downstream away from fish. The same is true for any disturbed materials you might have dislodged from the creek bottom by walking.

Once summer heat sets in there is no better place to catch smallmouth bass than under the shade trees along a farmland creek, wading in shorts and tennis shoes. If

Don't overlook small creek fishing and wading for smallmouths. Not all the best action is in the larger rivers.

the creek is wide enough you might try "body" fishing, which is wading deep and using your body as structure to attract fish. Creeks or small rivers having a scattering of rocks that stick out of the water slightly work best. If there are no rocks, stumps or pilings will do. These structures should be waist-deep.

On very hot days when river water warms, there is often a smallmouth movement pattern that gets established, with schools of smallmouth moving from one structure to another. Six to ten bass may be involved, although the larger the fish the fewer the number. Each stop behind each rock will last from 15 to 30 minutes. (Incidentally, walleye, pike, suckers, white bass, and carp all work this same pattern.)

The idea here is to use your body as structure. Face downstream in waist-deep water, allow the current to rotate around your body, and form a series of eddies below you. Place your body midway between two structures. Stay at least 20 minutes before changing position. In that time, a school of fish may pull into the eddy created by your body. If not, move to another spot and set up position. The key is to place yourself on a direct line between visible natural structure to which schooled fish might travel. Most of the time, there is little need to change spots. Schools of fish will come and go continuously throughout the fishing hours if you stay in a good spot.

The key here is being in waist-deep water. If it is any deeper than that, it becomes difficult to work your fishing equipment, and if shallower, you may not create enough of an eddy structure in front of your body to attract fish. Use natural baits, 10 to 12 inches behind split shot, or use small jigs. Just drop your offering straight in front of you and under the nose of the fish. This is an unusual wrinkle to fishing for smallmouths in flowing water, but don't count it out until you give it a try.

CHAPTER THREE
CRAPPIE

The crappie is every fisherman's "fall-back-on" favorite fish. Crappies have saved the day for numerous anglers by being available when the primary quarry (usually bass) was not. But that doesn't mean they are a simple fish to catch or that they can always be found. Crappies can be as elusive and mysterious as other prime game fish species.

Perhaps the most basic mystery is the subject of what fish we are actually talking about. The black crappie and its cousin the white crappie have more aliases than any other freshwater species. More than fifty-five nicknames have been attributed to them. Some of the more popular ones include: slabbies, barfish, calico, lamplighter, sac-a-lait, sand perch, sand bass, sandies, old silversides, strawberry bass, speckled perch, and tin mouth. In each area of America, local customs have taken root in naming crappies, but whatever they may be called, these fish are among the most favorite freshwater species.

Known by many names in different areas of the country, crappies are highly sought for their spunky fight and tasty flesh.

Beautiful in design, the crappie's silver body and mottled black markings easily identify it and distinguish it from other panfish. Crappies are relatively slow-growing and short-lived. They live from 4 to 8 years, attaining an average length of 2 to 3 inches after their first year, 5 to 8 inches at two years, 7 to 11 inches by three years, and 10 to 14 inches at four years.

The rate at which crappies grow is related to conditions in their particular aquatic environment, especially food availability and competition with other fish. In lakes with poor growth conditions, it's not unusual to find old-age crappies weighing a mere 4 ounces. Conversely, lakes with good growth conditions can harbor plenty of 1- to 2-pound crappies, with some fish getting even larger. Good fishing isn't usually produced in crappie waters unless the crappie can attain a length of 10 inches in four years. Nationally, the average crappie caught by anglers is about 3 years old, weighs about a pound or slightly less, and is 10 to 12 inches long.

The two crappie species are similar in some ways, different in others. The black crappie prefers cool, clear lakes and slow-moving rivers. It is a little more particular about its environment than the white crappie, which flourishes in warm and more silted water.

The black crappie generally has a silvery-olive side coloration which shades to olive-green on the back. Black spots or blotches are scattered irregularly over much of the fish. During spawning season the splotches seem to grow in size to turn the entire fish a deep purple-black. On white crappies, the spots are not as dark and are arranged into seven-to-nine vertical bars extending down the sides of the fish from its dark olive back.

The easiest method of identifying the species is to count dorsal spines. Usually the black crappie has seven or eight dorsal spines, while the white crappie has six. This identification technique, however, is not foolproof, because some white crappie have been found with seven spines.

The surest means of identification is to apply the following formula: for the black crappie, the distance from the eye to the start of the dorsal fin is equal to the length of the entire base of the dorsal fin; for the white crappie, the distance from the eye to the start of the dorsal fin is greater than the length of the base of the dorsal fin.

The original range of the black crappie is from lower Manitoba east to the upper St. Lawrence River and completely southward. They are found in the Mississippi River drainage as far south as Texas and on east throughout Florida, and they have been widely introduced into waters of the northeastern states and many of the western states. White crappies are found from Nebraska eastward to Lake Ontario and southward through the Ohio and Mississippi River watersheds to Texas and Alabama. It, too, has been introduced in lakes and reservoirs in many other states; some white crappies, for example, still survive in San Diego, California, where they were stocked in 1891. Although the range of these cousins overlaps greatly, white crappies are more abundant. Location, then, is not a guide to identification, and fishing regulations pertaining to creel limits do not distinguish between crappie species.

Crappies feed primarily on insects, mollusks, crustaceans, and small fish. Insects and minnows are most important. In southern reservoirs, gizzard or threadfin shad make up more than 50 percent of the crappie's diet while in most other areas, particularly in northern states, insects play the greatest part in their dining habits. Crappies, perch, and white bass, surprisingly, all may prey on young walleye, northern pike, largemouth bass, and other gamefish fry. For this reason alone, stocking of very young walleye and pike in panfish-dominated waters is often unsuccessful.

In the spring, when water temperatures climb into the 60-degree range, crappies move into the shallows to build nests and spawn. In some environments, spawning activity begins as soon as the water temperature reaches 55 degrees, but, in most, 65 to 68 degrees is preferred. As with other sunfish, the male crappie prepares the nest by fanning out a circular spot on the lake bottom in water that is 3 to 8 feet deep. In some northern habitats, crappie may nest in water so shallow that their backs protrude above the surface while they're in the spawning process.

Nests are usually built on sand, gravel, shell, or loosely packed clay and limestone bottoms. Scattered brush, stickups, reeds, and the previous year's aquatic growth helps entice spring spawners. The female leaves the nest after depositing her eggs, and the male remains to guard them. Eggs hatch in seven to fifteen days, and the young fry suffer severe predation from parents and from other fish.

Spawning-time crappies are reasonably predictable and easy for anglers to catch. But with warmer temperatures and the onset of summer weather, they become less predictable and more elusive. After spawning, crappies move to deeper water, gather in schools, and begin to wander. They may range far, seeking food as well as cool, well-oxygenated water.

Finding places that provide comfortable temperature conditions is the key to summer-time crappie fishing. Though many crappies can be found from 3 to 40-plus feet deep during summer, most crappies stay deep when shade isn't available. They congregate tightly in sunken weed beds, drop-offs, offshore brush piles, flooded timber, and sunken cribbing. During the hottest part of the day, crappies are situated on the cool,

In the spring, before the water gets very warm, crappies are found in shallow, brushy environs.

shaded side of such structures. Peak feeding periods are early morning and late evening.

Massive schools of crappies form at different levels of the lake wherever these fish locate ideal water temperature. The large schools are spread out laterally rather than vertically. This phenomenon is especially notable in crappies that inhabit large reservoirs; there, temperature varies considerably from surface to lake bottom compared to smaller bodies of water, where temperature is more uniform.

As the days grow hotter and the water temperature continues to rise, crappies may head even deeper to find cooler water or they may seek out stream channels or any depressions in the lake bottom. Springs and small streams which bring cool water are other popular resting areas. Other shaded areas may attract some crappies as well, though not necessarily large schools. These include bridges, piers, boat docks, and the bases of old tree stumps. Additionally, many crappies are caught in 10 to 15 feet of water amongst tree limbs in standing timber.

In the fall, crappies may move into even deeper water to gather around underwater structures such as old channels, rocky ledges, or weed beds. Though they will move from top to bottom to find food and occasionally into shallower water, crappies will generally remain in deeper water until spring.

Crappie fishing equipment isn't at all complicated and consists of light line, a balanced rod and reel, live bait, and small (1/16- to 1/32-ounce) lures. Fly rods, open-face spinning rods, spin-casting rods, telescoping fiberglass rods, and cane poles are all popularly used.

Crappies will concentrate together, and it's possible to have a lot of fun on light spinning tackle when you find a cluster of these fish.

For the most part, modern crappie anglers use ultralight, open-faced spinning reels equipped with 4-pound-test line and 5- to 5 1/2-foot rods. Using such gear, light terminal tackle such as split-shot sinkers, pencil-style bobbers, baited hooks, and tiny lures can be cast with pinpoint accuracy in and about brush piles and submerged stumps; crappies battle like champions on this equipment.

Cane poles or telescoping glass rods play a large, traditional role in crappie fishing. Eight- to 12-foot poles work well for boat anglers, but bank fishermen prefer 16- to 20-foot rods. The line is seldom longer than the length of the pole. Live bait is used, and dabbled in place after place.

Regardless of rod (or pole) length, for live bait fishing you should use a fine, wire hook (often the Aberdeen style) in sizes 4, 6, or 8. These hooks straighten out when snagged in brush and wood and are easily rebent to be used again. This is important, since so much fishing is done around cover that is easily snagged.

One of the best ways to fish for crappies is with small jigs. Marabou hair, plastic, or tinsel-covered jigs all work. The preferred size is 1/16-ounce, closely followed by 1/8- and 1/32-ounce sizes. Effective crappie jig colors include white, yellow, chartreuse, blue, green, and silver. Again, hooks should be fine wire.

Crappie jigs must be worked slowly. In the spring, near and over the spawning grounds, jigs are suspended below bobbers and fished without action. By tying the jig to the line with a knot that keeps the jig horizontal (put extra loops around the

A small jig is the foremost lure for crappies; a yellow marabou version caught this large, nicely colored fish.

line tie with a clinch knot), the crappie angler is able to present his offering horizontally to the bottom in a manner representing a minnow. Crappies will inhale the jig and hold onto it, sinking the bobber above.

Minnows are the key bait for crappies. As a general rule, small minnows (no longer than 2 inches) will catch more fish, but when crappies are on a feeding binge, larger minnows will catch larger crappies. And when crappies are biting sluggishly, smaller minnows will catch more big crappies.

Proper hooking is important. Minnows must be hooked securely but in such a way that they remain alive and lively. When still-fishing with a plain hook, the minnow should be impaled high in the back, just below the dorsal fin, or through the mouth by inserting the hook into the lower lip and on through the top of the nose. For casting with a jig, the minnow can be hooked through the head and out its lower jaw.

The jig-and-minnow combination is deadly for crappies, but many anglers believe it can be even more devastating with the addition of a spinner. The spinner creates the illusion of a minnow, or at least something edible, through vibration, flash, and motion. When a plain minnow or jig fails to attract crappies, the bright, glittering flashes of a spinner will often be the tidbit that prompts a strike.

Spinner blades come in various colors, including black, white, and yellow, and while these are sometimes effective, the polished brass and nickel-silver finishes are more popular. Brightly colored spinners seem to take more fish, especially in the muddy, turbid waters populated by white crappie. A yellow jig with a silver spinner has proven deadly for black crappie in clear northern lakes, and in southern and western reservoirs.

While minnows are the most popular live bait, there is a devoted corps of panfish anglers who swear by using meat, employing either a small strip of pork rind attached to a plain hook, or a 1/4-inch-wide strip of flesh (about 1 1/2 inches long) taken from a crappie and attached to a No. 6 hook with a silver spinner. When crappies aren't falling to other tactics, and especially in midsummer, this may be worth a try.

The summer crappie angler is more of a hunter than a fisherman. That's because a lot of scouting has to be done to find fish, and this can be a lesson in frustration. Because schooled crappies string out in a horizontal manner, which is a reaction to being in their temperature-controlled comfort zone, they may not provide much of a target on sonar units. Even when crappies hold on bottom-anchored brush piles, they seldom group in a vertical fashion. In fact, in some lakes, crappies suspend away from the bottom in a narrow band of water no thicker than 18 inches. Such staging is most difficult for anglers to work. Fishing a foot above or below these schools may not produce fish, so the angler must be "right on." It's worth the effort, though, as some of these narrow-banded schools of open-water crappies cover several acres.

Fishermen without sonar can locate such schools by lowering a lively minnow, hooked through the lips or back, to the bottom. Allow the minnow to work for a few minutes about 1 to 2 feet from the bottom. If nothing happens, raise the bait 2 or 3 feet, and again allow the bait to work while occasionally twitching the rod tip. Continue this procedure until the bait reaches the surface. After three or four unsuccessful attempts, move somewhere else and try again. You might try drifting while you are doing this.

Drifting is probably the best technique for catching lunker crappies. Wind speeds measuring from 5 to 10 mph, which are quite common in summer and fall, will

Among natural baits, a minnow is the favorite crappie attraction. With a livewell to keep crappie fresh and a bucket for the minnows, you're in good shape.

push the average boat along at a speed that is perfect for deep-running crappie lures.

When wind conditions are not right, either in velocity or direction, trolling can be productive. To achieve a proper trolling speed, many anglers prefer using an electric motor. This is best accomplished with a small outboard motor, and, in some instances, with electric motors. You may have to troll with the boat headed in reverse in order to maintain a slower speed. Remember that crappies strike slow-moving baits best.

Trolling is more productive in the morning or evening. Work slowly along the shore, particularly around rocky points, weed beds, trees hanging over the water, the ends of boat docks, and the edges of drop-offs. When you find a school of crappies, mark the spot so you can either anchor just outside the school and cast into it, or continue to troll or drift around the concentration. Any commercially made, small buoys will work for marking. Some crappie anglers use a plastic bottle or small piece of styrofoam to act as a marker. Make sure the line from marker buoy to anchoring weight is long enough to reach the deepest part of the water you fish.

Many who troll for crappie in summer use deep-probing devices such as a Bait-Walker; a weighted, three-way swivel rig; or a Wolf River rig to walk the bottom. Rig weight will vary with the depth of water. Sinkers in 1/4-, 3/8-, 5/8-, 1-, and 1 1/2-ounce sizes are used. Even the best crappie rig won't produce, however, unless it is pulling the right bait or lure. During summer, the successful crappie fishermen rely heavily on live bait (such as minnows or worms) on small, long-shanked hooks.

Many deeply worked artificials can be deadly, including spinner-fly combos, small stick plugs, beetle-type spinnerbaits, 2- or 3-inch plastic worms, hairy marabou jigs, and sinking lead swimmers. Floating/diving-style crankbaits can also do the job at times, if you can get them to run at the appropriate level. Large crappies will strike 3- and 4-inch-long crankbaits, although you might be better off to use a crankbait as a locator and then switch to jigs (clean or baited) or small spinnerbaits to work an area thoroughly.

Summer fishing for crappies should be predicated on two major factors: wind and light. Fish do not have eyelids or irises to shut out or reduce the amount of light that strikes their eyes. Light penetration is not a problem in spring when the sun's rays strike the water at an oblique angle. But in summer, as the sun moves higher in the sky, light penetration increases. Thus, crappies are forced to find shade around structure or by moving deeper. Keep this in mind and plan accordingly.

The preeminent structure in many crappie locales is some form of wood. In southern waters especially this means drowned or flooded timber. Many huge impoundments that have been created in the last fifty years provide an abundance of timber, so this is where crappie anglers in such places should head first. Besides flooded timber, the reservoir angler might look for crappies along old river channel drops, shoreline riprap, old flooded roadways, inundated hedgerows, and sunken islands. In each case, your chances will improve if these structures hold a flooded dead tree or two. In many bodies of water without timber, especially large impoundments, anglers plant brush piles in order to attract and hold crappies (and other fish, too). They may plant many of these, in places known only to them, and they will visit them often, primarily using jigs or small minnows to work the structure. If you're contemplating doing such a thing, first check the legality of this in the state where you'll fish and also check with the agency, if any, that controls the body of water. Pre-planted brush piles are often the savior of otherwise "crappie-less" anglers in the summer.

Drowned and fallen timber create good places to find crappies; many anglers plant brush piles to attract these fish as well.

On warm sunny days, crappies will pack tightly in deep water or in areas providing optimum shade; this includes under docks, in weed beds or brush piles, or even inside hollow stumps. On cloudy, cooler days, crappies usually will not school as deep and probably will be scattered over many different areas.

Whether it is a sunny or cloudy day, wind can be important to summer fishing. With the right wind speed and direction, you can drift slowly over old underwater channels, along sheer drop-offs, or a flooded forest, and other structures. When the wind is either too gusty or nonexistent, you should move into sheltered bays and fish weed patches. A little ripple of wind on the surface will not adversely affect success. But as wind and waves increase, crappie fishing productivity diminishes. As a general rule, as winds increase, start fishing deeper.

Summer, incidentally, poses an opportunity for the fly rodder, though you wouldn't ordinarily think so. To the fly fisherman, crappies can be an exciting bonus or a bore. Due to their deep-water posture 80 percent of the year, crappies seldom afford much chance to the fly rodder. There is the obvious opportunity when the fish are in shallow water in the spring, yet there is also another time when crappies are available to fly fishermen. That is on hot summer evenings, just as the sun sets. Then, crappies are drawn to the surface of lakes, rivers, and reservoirs by hatching insects, feeding ravenously on nymphs and adult flies. If the hatch is heavy, surfacing crappies may cover several surface acres, and a feeding binge may go on long after the sun has disappeared.

Watch carefully as the sun goes down for a dimpling of surface water in bays and inlets. A variety of fish may be active at this time, but crappies, unlike other fish that feed on the surface, seldom splash when sucking in an insect. The upper mouth, head top, and shoulder portions of crappies roll slowly above the surface. Don't rush through an area where crappies are feeding on the surface; drift to it or slowly use an electric motor to quietly get on the periphery, then use a dry fly or nymph to cast to rising fish. This can be great sport.

Fall is something of a forgotten season for crappie fishing. Yet, as water begins to cool, crappies again become mobile, moving longer distances to find suitable cover and feeding more voraciously than before. Crappies will continue this behavior through the fall and winter.

Fall crappie fishing has its challenges, of course. Fish that are found in 8 feet of water one day may move to a 20-foot depth the next. They may hover over a brush pile in the morning and move into a deep weed bed by early evening. Generally, the most successful fall anglers fish mornings and late afternoons. Beginning in September, crappies feed primarily during these two periods, a habit they will maintain through the winter.

With cooler temperatures, crappies resume their finicky eating habits. They'll consume more than they did during the summer but take their sweet time at it. Accordingly, the angler should turn to smaller minnows or worms and night crawlers. Crappies are also fond of white grubs and will rise more readily to surface flies. To overcome nibbling tactics, switch to small bobbers or quill corks. The quill cork reacts to the slightest disturbance, providing that sinker weight is kept to a minimum.

Crappies also offer a prime opportunity for winter fishing, and many northern ice anglers make these fish their number one pursuit. The biggest attraction of ice fishing for crappies is its simplicity; this is just a matter of cutting a hole in the ice, baiting a small hook or ice fly with a 2-inch minnow, and you're ready for action.

Though little investment is needed in winter fishing equipment, diehard winter anglers enjoy the comforts of an ice shanty and its small stove. These shelters are generally handmade and constructed of wood. There are some commercially made portable houses, however, and many crappie anglers opt for the lightweight, collapsible version that can be moved to a new location in a few minutes. This is beneficial because when action slows in one spot, it can often be resumed by cutting another hole in the ice a short distance away. The ice fisherman who moves around, cuts new holes, and periodically changes the depth of his bait will usually be the first to discover action.

Most anglers use small bobbers and small bait for ice fishing. Crappies are finicky feeders in the winter and often will nip at bait. If you're using a large bobber, there will be no clue to what is happening in the depths below. This problem can be overcome by thinking small, using bobbers that are no larger than a bottlecap in diameter. Your bait should also be diminutive; a 2-inch minnow is good, as are any number of grubs, including waxworms, golden grubs, mousies, and others.

Crappies show a distinct preference for feeding at certain times of the day in the winter and apparently don't like snacking between meals. The best time is probably the first few hours after sunrise. Another common feeding time is late in the day, extending until midnight. Many a winter crappie angler swears by night fishing only.

When searching for crappie in the winter, keep in mind that they are usually found in relatively deep water now, from 20 to as much as 50 feet deep. First try the middle

Crappies may be deep in the winter, but the reward for finding them is considerable.

of large sheltered bays, out from rocky points, or about 50 to 100 yards straight off weed beds. The water depth, of course, will determine the distance you fish from shore. Oxygen is often at a premium in some lakes during winter, particularly shallow bodies of water. There, crappies may congregate in areas where oxygen enters, such as the inlets of creeks and streams.

Although winter crappies are usually caught near the bottom, you can never be sure at what level they have schooled. We've caught them just 2 feet below the surface of the ice in 30 feet of water, so it pays to keep working various levels.

There are a few other pointers, not directly related to catching crappies but still helpful to know for angling for these fish throughout the year. One of these is that boat fishermen will improve their chances on new or unfamiliar waters by using sonar and a contour map to search for appropriate habitat as well as fish. They should also employ two anchors, one at either end of the boat, to keep the wind from forcing the boat's stern off the school. It also helps to have rope tie-off tethers in each corner, with or without brush clamps.

Crappies have extremely tender mouths. Not only will these fish tear off a rope-style stringer, but they often tear off the hook while being lifted into the boat. Instead of placing crappies on a stringer, use a boat livewell, ice cooler, or wire mesh basket for storage. To avoid having fish get off your line, do not reset the hook a second time or pump in the fish. Pumping, as is done with other, usually larger, species, is not needed when playing crappies because pumping repeatedly increases pressure on the hook, which tears the fragile cartilage of the mouth. What starts as a tiny puncture soon becomes a gaping hole from which the hook can easily slip out if the crappie turns quickly or if any slack line results. Keep your line taut. Even without pumping the rod, the hole in the mouth will grow larger as the fish is reeled in. And if the line is slackened, the lure may fall out.

Using a net is a sure way to land crappies, but many anglers don't want to mess with a net when they're on a school and the action is fast and furious. A technique used commonly by cane pole fishermen and spin-casters is simply to hoist crappies into the boat or on shore. More fish are lost this way, but it remains popular because it is fast and easy. To increase your chances of landing crappies this way, gently raise the rod and swing the fish into the boat. Don't jerk the fish from the water. By maintaining an even, continuous motion, and being careful to lift the fish smoothly from the water, a crappie is momentarily calmed (like putting a chicken's head under its wing). Seldom, if ever, will it flap during the procedure.

We won't devote any space here to ways to clean and cook crappies, but it should be noted in closing that crappies are delicious fish and that their edibleness is one of the things that motivates fishermen to pursue them so avidly. In many places, crappies are quite plentiful, and creel limits are liberal, so it does no harm to keep a batch of these fish for deep-frying enjoyment. This, coupled with the fun of catching, makes for double-barreled pleasure.

CHAPTER FOUR
PANFISH

There are many panfish that provide great sport and table fare for young and old, novice and veteran anglers. In fact, panfish as a whole are actually the most popularly sought fish in the U.S., according to surveys by the Department of the Interior. There is more time spent fishing for panfish, in fact, than bass, though bass are much more glamorized and publicized. Much of the attention paid to panfish, of course, is through very casual fishing; yet there are many panfish species that are pursued fervently by some anglers, using very sporting tackle and prizing their catch for food value. Crappies, to which we've devoted a separate chapter, are foremost among these panfish. Other popularly sought panfish include yellow perch, bluegill (referred to as bream in most southerly locales), and rock bass.

ROCK BASS

Rock bass are the least avidly pursued of these three species, usually caught incidentally to other fish. There is really only one state — Indiana — in which rock bass are regarded as a prized game fish. In Indiana, the rock bass, which is also known here and elsewhere as a goggle-eye, is eagerly sought. In waterways such as the Tippecanoe River, for example, which bisects northern Indiana, rock bass and smallmouth bass are taken in similar numbers and dedicated anglers prize them equally. Actually, Indiana is roughly in the middle of the range of these fish, which tends to be mostly northerly.

Rock bass inhabit both lakes and rivers, spending much time around rock and wood structures. Any sunken log or tree stump would be an excellent place to search for these fish in areas where they are known to be found. (In some locales, one lake has rock bass and another nearby lake doesn't.) These fish spawn in late spring or early summer when shallow waters exceed 65 degrees. They fan out a bed where there is either sand or gravel, usually near their home base. If a school of rock bass lies beneath a sunken cottonwood tree, they will generally nest there as well. They know no migration except to go deep or shallow, movements which are determined by water temperature and atmospheric pressure.

Rock bass may remind the first-time angler of some kind of part-crappie, part-bass, part-bluegill type of fish that eagerly attacks garden worms wiggled before its nose. Like his bluegill cousin, the rock bass is easily enticed by insect and wiggly type baits. Unlike a bluegill, however, the rock bass prefers to feed deep below the

Rock bass eagerly take live and artificial baits and are often found in concentrations.

surface. He is a fish who strikes out from a deep, dark hiding place, a place which provides protection from predator and sun rays alike.

The main foods preferred by rock bass are crayfish, insects, and a variety of small minnows, with crayfish being foremost among these. In fishing with bait, night crawlers or garden worms are most productive. The most common angling method involves nothing more than placing a small worm or 1 1/2-inch piece of crawler on a No. 4 short-shanked hook, adding a couple of small split-shot and dropping this down along a sunken rock or log. Once it hits bottom (if the fish allow this; they may not when plentiful and hungry), raise the bait up 6 to 10 inches and wiggle gently.

Anglers who fish for smallmouth bass at the same time that they pursue rock bass (or vice versa) might use small jigs tipped with a piece of crawler. Both fish love the scenting created by a worm. Rock bass can also be taken on live, or dead, minnows, artificial flies, very small crankbaits, small spinners or flashy spoons. The latter usually only produces rock bass during the spawning season. Surface poppers, at times, work on rock bass, but only when this fish is situated in very shallow water beneath the protection of such structures as fallen trees or overhanging rock ledges. These same fish may be easier to catch on below-surface lures, but it can be fun to use a small spinning popper or fly rod bug or popper on them.

No matter what lure or bait is used for rock bass, there is little need to retrieve or work it rapidly to be successful. Rather, a slow, steady action is preferred. At times, no action is best. Like their bluegill cousins, rock bass will move in on a stationary bait, watch it, then flare their gills and suck it into their mouths.

As noted, sunken logs, flooded stumps, and large submerged rocks are prime places to hold rock bass. Besides these, look to deep-water rocky ledges, quiet still pools along river banks where large rocks are present, deep-water gravel beds where a large weed structure begins, and beneath overhanging willows along a river or lake shoreline.

Rock bass can be found around much of the dead and dying timber in river back waters.

Once rock bass are found, vertical jigging may be the single best way to catch them. Rock bass aren't easily frightened off their holding structure. The angler can move his boat directly on top of a submerged brush pile or log, and jig a bait directly below.

No matter what time of the season, wherever a single rock bass is found, there surely will be others nearby. During spawning there may be as many as twenty-five to fifty rock bass beneath a single object and most, if not all of them, can be caught by an astute fisherman, particularly with live worms or a jig/worm combination.

The tackle for rock bass is relatively simple. Many veteran rock bass anglers prefer to use a long limber rod (sometimes a fly rod) with a spin-casting reel loaded with 6-pound-test line. This setup easily works the smaller live and artificial baits used on this species. Others use a fly rod and reel, with fly line and tapered leader, to fish nymphs as well as live minnows. Though fly fishing equipment is preferred by the ardent rock bass angler, most fishermen use conventional ultralight spin-casting or spinning tackle. Five- to 5 1/2-foot rods are quite adequate, as is 4- or 6-pound line. Balanced light or ultralight outfits bring out the best in the spunky rock bass.

We should note, incidentally, that rock bass make excellent table fare. Their meat is pure white and flakey. In some instances, however, usually where there is an overpopulation and excessively warm water temperature, this fish can be infested with grub worms and therefore unsuitable for eating, so be aware.

BLUEGILLS (BREAM)

Bluegills are plate-styled members of the sunfish family. They are the most available sunfish and are found with, or similarly to, such companion species as the redbreasted sunfish, green sunfish, pumpkinseed, shell-cracker, and the long-eared sunfish, all of which are similar in configuration but different in appearance when viewed closely. On each the opercular flap, which overlaps the gill plate, is different in shape; body markings and colors are equally different. When viewed from the side, the opercular flap resembles an eye, albeit one that is much larger than its natural companion. Perhaps this is nature's way of camouflaging sunfish against predators; a predator descending on a sunfish is apt to take the enlarged flap as a very large eye on a much bigger fish and not attack.

Bluegills and their relatives are well distributed in the United States. They are vigorous little scrappers whose fighting ability, ounce for ounce, may be the toughest in freshwater. It's nice to imagine what these sunfish would be like on a fishing rod if they weighed about 10 pounds each. Having caught some 2-pound bluegills, a size that is quite large for this species and fairly rare, we can say that they are indeed a "game" quarry.

Bluegills spawn when the water temperature reaches the mid-70s, and this is when they are most easily caught. With nest-building in full gear, this fish becomes extremely aggressive and extremely protective of its nesting grounds. Lures or bait dropped in the center of their nest are instantly eaten, roughed up, or forced away. Even lures retrieved near nesting areas are eagerly struck or slapped (the fish often swipe at an intruding creature or object in an effort to ward it away).

Bluegills can be very aggressive, even taking plugs at times; they are more commonly caught on smaller offerings.

While the propriety of fishing for spawning bass, which are a taxonomic relative of bluegills, is a hotly debated issue in many places, the same is not true for bluegills and other panfish. These panfish are prolific creatures that readily overpopulate many places in which they are found, especially small lakes and ponds. Fisheries biologists encourage people to spend more time catching these fish and also keeping as many of them as feasible for consumption.

Bluegills and their panfish cousins are found in shallow areas close to shore as the water temperature rises. Their spawning beds, which are circular depressions, are readily discerned in coves and bays. Though they are aggressive, that doesn't mean you can blunder right into a bedding area and catch fish. Whether you fish from shore, wade, or cast from a boat, you still have to use some stealth. Often, bluegill beds will be clustered closely together, and a lot of fish can be taken in the same locale by the careful quiet angler. But being noisy and causing a lot of commotion will stir the fish up in an alarmed way, and they may move off the bedding area for a while.

This may happen in any event, once you've caught several fish in the same locale; in this case, fish elsewhere for an hour or so, and, when you return, you should find the fish more accommodating once again. It's a good idea as well to try to steer hooked fish quickly away from beds and the general bedding locale to minimize the possibility of spooking other fish.

Beds may be located in water that is only a foot deep, or up to several feet deep, so a variety of angling methods have merit. Certainly the chief method, and a great one for youngsters, is fishing with live worms and bobbers. This is particularly effective where the water is 2 to 5 feet deep, provided a small- to medium-sized bobber is used, and the right size hook is employed. A No. 8 or 10 hook is about right, as

A light fishing outfit, a bobber, a worm, and a bluegill add up to a happy youngster.

bluegills don't have very large mouths. Fish it unweighted or with just a small split shot. Use a long-shanked version to facilitate unhooking, and keep a degorging tool or hemostat handy to help with deeply hooked fish. You might also try crickets, the tiniest minnows, and meal worms. Cane pole anglers have a lot of success at this time of year by using just a baited hook and bobber and deftly moving their offering from spot to spot via their 10- to 12-foot–long pole.

Small jigs are another fine bluegill catcher. Jigs weighing from 1/8- to 1/32-ounce, fished on ultralight line, take many a bedded bluegill, and there is generally no reason to be selective as to color. Small spinners and spinnerbaits (or jig-and-spinner combinations) are also effective, as are fly rod poppers and nymphs, the latter being allowed to sink and be retrieved in a series of short stripping actions.

The key to success with nearly all offerings is being right on the bed itself. While bluegills will rise to the surface and move laterally to strike a lure or bait, they will almost surely do so if the offering is in, or moving directly through, the bed. Being able to see beds, therefore, is advantageous. Fishing from an elevated position in a boat and wearing polarized sunglasses are very helpful.

Light lines and light tackle are best for bluegill fishing at any time of the year. Two- to 6-pound lines; whippy 7- to 8-foot fly rods; ultralight spinning or spin-casting outfits; and 1/8- to 1/64-ounce lures are standard. Light tackle not only is good for effective fishing, but it brings out the best in these fish. A 3/4-pound bluegill can provide plenty of rod-bending activity. His battle is always deep, stubborn, and circling. If there are weeds near the place where a bluegill is caught, the fish will surely entangle itself in their midst. Many a trophy bluegill has been lost when 4-pound line was wrapped around the stems of tough lily pads, so you have to take this into consideration when fishing and try to promptly steer a fish away from such habitat.

Fishing for bluegills isn't always done from boats. Much angling, in fact, is done from the bank or by wading. But fishing techniques vary widely, as do the places where bluegills are found.

Thick, lily pad clusters are a foremost bluegill habitat. Often you hear the fish snapping and sucking insects from about the pads before you see them. Fly rod poppers in No. 8 to 12 sizes work especially well for these fish. Also, a long (12 feet or more) cane pole with a short line, small bobber, and a cricket on a No. 10 hook will be the ticket in this cover. Look for openings in the pads, drop your cricket and bobber into it, and await a strike. Once the fish is hooked, the pole is lifted high and thrust past the angler, which swings the bluegill to your feet. Getting a large fish out of the opening without tangling in the pad stems can be exciting. Fifty percent of the time you fail, but the use of cane poles is very popular with bluegill anglers, who are able to drop their offering from place to place with relative ease and quiet.

Weeds are consistently a good holding area for bluegills. Vegetation provides plenty of food, such as water mites, shrimp, larva, nymphs, leeches, and small minnows. These same weeds provide protection for bluegills against predators. With this combination of food and cover, vegetation is often a prime place to seek bluegills. In lakes, ponds, and river backwaters, stumps, logs, and fallen trees provide a similar protection for this fish. In many cases, this structure is found where there is a loam bottom, which produces a high volume of insect life. A slow retrieve, whether using lures or live bait, is best. If you fish a small popper on the surface, for example, do so very slowly, popping it only when the rings disappear from the previous movement.

Surface fishing for bluegills may be at its best late on summer days, as the sun is fading. Bluegills are often drawn in great numbers to the surface by the hatching and presence of insects. The daytime temperatures have been extremely hot, and as cooler air meets the water's surface, insects become available. Bluegills seem to come to the surface not only for food but also because of the cooler water. Any angler who is able to cast a soft fly, one which lands upon the surface without disturbing the fish, can have a ball using No. 10 and 12 dry flies, nymphs, or wet flies. These late-evening fish are often spotted when a school of them erupts on the surface after being startled. A careful angler can spot these schools before disturbing them if he keeps the sun at his back and wears polarized glasses.

In the Midwest, where black leeches are popular bait for walleye and smallmouth bass, small sizes (1 to 1 1/2 inches) of these creatures work well on bluegills when fished with split shot and suspended beneath a bobber. Some anglers prefer to use a slip bobber rig so they can set their bait deep while still being able to reel it up and cast it.

A less common technique, though one that produces larger fish, is drifting or trolling along a deep, underwater weed line just off a submerged reef or point. Here the water can vary from 14 to perhaps 35 feet deep. Most big bluegills seem to come from 25 feet of water. The rig employs a 1/4-ounce walking sinker or pencil lead, using a 24-inch drop-back line, and a No. 6 short-shanked hook for the leech (which is hooked through its suction cup). You can use leeches up to 2 inches long. Remember to concentrate your presentation along the outer edge of the sunken weed line. Drifting is the preferred method.

One of the toughest things about bluegill fishing is finding large fish. Usually you catch small to intermediate-size bluegills and rarely the largest ones. To have a better

Adults get pretty enthusiastic over large bluegills, such as this 2-pounder, which are not often caught.

chance of catching large (what constitutes large obviously varies, though 3/4- to 1-pounders are fairly big in general) bluegills, you should focus your attention on deeper water. For example, work 12 feet deep if you have been catching lots of small fish in 3 to 6 feet of water. Big bluegills often come from the same waters that produce big largemouth bass, so you might keep this in mind if you would like to try specifically for them. This is probably because the small fish numbers are kept in check by the larger predators.

In impoundments it's a good tactic to seek bluegills at submerged hedgerows. Bluegills seem to love such structure. One of the most successful tactics here is to cast directly into the hedges, reel a few quick turns, then allow your lure to settle gently toward bottom. Just before it reaches bottom, again reel rapidly while lifting your rod tip high. Repeat this several times until you are certain no fish follows. If a bluegill strikes your offering, chances are that it will do so as it drifts toward the bottom between rapid reeling actions. Black jigs in 1/16- and 1/32-ounce sizes are recommended.

Bluegills, of course, are popular in winter, where small jigs, flies, and meal worms are used. Some anglers have taken to working winter ice flies during the summer for panfish. As in winter, small, white, natural grubs (not the plastic grub) are added to jigs to provide taste and smell. These ice flies are often worked directly beneath a small bobber. Good colors are fluorescent orange and red and dark natural colors. These same ice flies can be used on a fly rod, just as one might use a nymph. Ice fly styles include ants, teardrops, mousies, crappie slims, and dew drops.

YELLOW PERCH

Yellow perch are highly popular primarily because of their tasty, white, flakey meat. They are not a member of the sunfish family, like bluegills and rock bass, but they are considered panfish.

Though many fish bear the name 'perch,' both in colloquial as well as specific terms (crappies, for instance, are called speckled perch in many places), only the yellow perch is truly a genuine perch. Like their walleye cousins, perch are found mainly in the cooler water regions of the northcentral and northeastern U. S., and southern Canada.

Yellow perch spawn in the spring under similar conditions as, and in areas similar to, walleye and sauger. Knowledgeable anglers find thousands of these fish ascending tributaries and in the back eddies of rivers. Perch often spawn in loam-filled backwater bays, but they do not build a nest. Their eggs are sprayed into the open water and float along in a string-like gelatinous substance above bottom, and this is usually quite readily seen in clear water once the water temperature reaches and exceeds 45 degrees.

Yellow perch are a schooling fish. Once you catch a perch, it's a good tactic to mark the spot with some type of marker buoy and systematically fish the area. Small jigs, live and dead bait, small plugs, tiny flashy spoons, and flies are good perch catchers. Garden worms and live leeches are especially attractive, too, and bobbers are frequently employed with live bait. Jigs are very popular, in 1/16- to 1/8-ounce sizes, as are night crawler rigs with a No. 2 hook and No. 2 spinner up to a No. 8 hook and No. 0 spinner. Silver seems to be the preferred color for spinners. Small fluorescent jigs tipped with bits of night crawler and crawler trolling rigs are also popular in some locales. Ultralight rods and reels with 4- to 6-pound lines are most useful when perch fishing.

Yellow perch are often taken by those who search out the wary walleye and, under such conditions, are considered a pest, a bait stealer. When too many small yellow perch station themselves on your favorite walleye reef, they can be a nuisance. However, in many places where they are found, there is no concentrated effort made to catch these fish, with bass or other species being favored, and the lures used for those fish will only occasionally catch a perch. That's too bad, as these fish can generally use more harvesting in places where they are abundant. Most of the perch that anglers see are about 8 inches long, and a large perch is one 10 to 12 inches long and weighs about a pound or so.

Along Great Lakes shores, dock and pier fishermen do a lot of perch fishing. Some employ a trolley rig to bring their bait out to offshore perch schools. They make a long cast with a surf rod and send a sinker out to station the rig, which operates like a clothesline. This is one of the more inventive ways of perch fishing. Many perch are caught accidently by anglers seeking other species. If interested in a good meal, they then stop and work the area well, usually with a small jig (in spring, a minnow-imitating plug is good, too). For the most part, yellow perch like cool water and will school in deep water in places where surface temperatures get warm. They are normally slightly shallower than walleye, but, like walleye, will move into warm shallow water to feed.

Perch are great bait-nibblers and schooling fish. They can be caught on small jig and spinner combos, which is what this young angler used, and on minnow-imitation plugs in the spring in shallow water.

CHAPTER FIVE
STRIPED BASS

Landlocked striped bass are one of the largest-growing and strongest-fighting, freshwater fish; they are very similar to their ocean-roaming ancestors, except that they are found in large, freshwater impoundments. They are predominantly open-water nomads; locating these fish is perhaps a more formidable task than catching them. They are vigorous and at times gluttonous eaters, and their environments are usually blessed with an abundance of forage, which is primarily threadfin or gizzard shad, plus alewives or small panfish in locales that do not have shad.

Stripers become active in the spring when they migrate (sometimes great distances) up tributaries to spawn. This usually happens when the water temperature reaches 55 degrees. Spawning takes place in stages, generally from mid-April through mid-May or slightly later, depending on spring weather and geographic location.

After spawning, stripers are somewhat scattered. They do not travel in large schools, but migrate down the tributary to the lake. The inside bend of major tributaries is often a hot spot to catch stripers at this time. Most anglers are accustomed to working the outside bend at this time for largemouth bass, but stripers like a point where water rushes by, so they hold on the inside bend of a channel and use these spots to ambush whatever comes around.

Once in the lake, they often follow the path of channels and stream beds into deep water. From then through summer into fall, stripers school in groups of similar-sized fish, staying mainly in open water. They travel many miles and move around frequently and swiftly in pursuit of bait fish. Usually stripers are found at a depth between 20 and 50 feet at this time, sometimes suspended over much deeper water. They may locate over old creek beds and channels, near sunken islands, along ridges with quick drop-offs, at the deep end of points, near bridges and adjacent causeways, and near any natural funneling point for bait fish to travel.

In the fall, stripers move into shallow, flat areas, and chase schools of bait fish near the surface. They're on the move and vigorously following forage, so this is a very exciting time to pursue them. In the winter, stripers tend to stay deep, in many of the same places as in the summer, but they roam less.

The methods of catching stripers include using live bait, jigging, casting, and trolling. In all techniques, and with the exception of the fall chase-'em-up frenzy, it is important to have some type of sonar, either to find the types of places that attract stripers, to locate catchable fish, or to determine the depth at which stripers are located so you can place your lures or bait at the right level. You should look particularly for fish that are close to, or touching, some object (submerged trees or humps, for example),

This kind of striped bass, a 30-plus-pounder, would please any lake and reservoir angler.

as these often are more active than stripers that are suspended in mid-depths well away from structure.

Of the four basic methods of striper fishing, trolling may be practiced the most, but live bait is very popular, especially in the spring. The primary bait fish used by striper anglers are gizzard and threadfin shad, herring, bluegill (where it is legal to do so), alewives, shiners, and assorted minnows. Which to use depends on the species naturally available in your area. One of the keys is presenting the bait at the right location and making it look like a vulnerable target.

Live bait is still-fished while the boat is at anchor or slowly adrift. Depending on the depth to be fished, the size of the bait, and whether there is current or wind, you'll need from 1 1/2 ounces to 4 ounces of lead in the form of a bead-chain weight, to keep the bait at the proper depth and right below the spot where you have positioned it. The weight should be about 2 feet ahead of the bait. Use a 2/0 or 3/0 hook for small baitfish like threadfin shad and 4/0 to 6/0 hooks for larger baits. Hook them through the top of the back so they can swim freely if they are large baits or through the top of the nose if they are smaller (while using smaller hooks). Sometimes it's best to keep the bait just off the bottom, but, when you already know where the stripers are, keep it slightly above the depth at which you've pinpointed them.

Cut bait, incidentally, is also effective in some bodies of water. Take a chunk of fish flesh with a hook in it, rigged like live bait, and set it just off the bottom. If you don't catch a striper this way, you just may get a catfish.

With live bait, however, one of the keys to success is keeping bait fresh and replacing lethargic bait with a lively specimen. This requires having plenty of bait to start with and treating it properly. Abundant bait is a practical matter; if you have enough, you can change bait more frequently. Often one rod catches the most fish because it routinely has a new, fresher bait put on it. Herring, shad, and alewives, which are the most popular striper baits, must be kept in a large, circular livewell that is well-aerated. In a rectangular container, these fish cluster in a corner and die. Thirty-gallon wells are standard where much bait is used. Keep ice in the bait well in the summer to reduce the temperature and put some non-iodized salt in it. Give newly hooked bait a few seconds in the water by the side of the boat to acclimate to the new water temperature before sending it on its mission.

Most of the time, stripers take live bait very well, swallowing it and hooking themselves. However, sometimes the hook turns back into the bait fish, and, when you set the hook after a strike, you come back striper-less. Sometimes you can tell when

These nice stripers were caught on live herring, still-fished from an anchored pontoon boat, a common practice in some southern lakes.

a striper is in an area because of the action of the line, a quivering rod tip, or the float. This is caused by the movement of the bait, so it pays to keep a close eye on your tackle.

Most avid bait anglers like to use a lot of rods for striper fishing, as many as is practical and the law allows, either setting them all around the boat or setting a few lines a short distance away via the use of large, colorful cork floats. Long rods, in the 8 1/2- and 9-foot category, are good for bait fishing, not only because they help keep lines separated but also because they help muscle fish away from cover (there is a lot of standing timber in many striped bass waters).

There are times and places where anglers cast lures to striped bass, and naturally this is very enjoyable, but this is seldom done in open-water areas unless stripers are schooled up and chasing large pods of bait fish near the surface. With some exceptions, such as in tailrace areas and in tributaries when fish are migrating, you seldom cast to striped bass unless you see them chasing bait and know that they are present. Even then, they are accessible for a moment and then gone. Casting is primarily a fall activity, although surface feeding frenzies do occur at times in the summer.

There is no secret to finding schooling fish activity; often you come upon it by accident, though usually as the result of deliberate searching early and late in the day. A pair of binoculars, for scanning the horizon and pinpointing distant activity, is standard equipment. The most important trick is to be observant. A lot of boats located in one area a long distance away could signal something you ought to check out. The best evidence is a flock of birds concentrated in one locale and swooping down to the surface to pick up small fish. (Some clever striper chasers have found that a bag of crackers tossed into the water will interest seagulls for a long time and draw boats from afar, while the perpetrators chase a school of stripers by themselves.)

Generally, you need to keep an eye on the horizon, looking for sudden splashes. If you see a splash in one spot, keep your eyes fixed on it. If you see another, crank the outboard motor up and scoot over, being careful not to run into the midst of the activity (which will put stripers down). Get close fast, then idle up to the edge of the action, shutting the big engine off and perhaps using an electric motor to get closer. Make long casts as soon as you get within range and hang on for what is often a jolting strike. You'll seldom be able to keep up with the striped bass/bait fish schools, which quickly scoot away, but they'll pop up someplace else, and you have to rush over there as quickly as you can.

Your best bet is to cast right to the exact spot where fish have broken water and to do so as soon as possible after they appear. Surface plugs that walk, sputter, or pop are prime fish catchers, but sometimes they are much larger than the bait the fish are eating, and stripers won't hit them. Shallow-running plugs can be effective, too, but be sure that their hooks (and split rings and snaps) will hold up. A white bucktail jig is also a good bet here, worked vertically or cast and stripped back just under the surface.

Jigging is primarily done, however, when you have located stripers holding in deep water in a defined area, such as the trees of lakes that have submerged timber (in some, trees will come up almost to the surface in 60-foot depths). You may come upon these fish by motoring around watching a depthfinder, or by locating them in the course of trolling. When you do find a concentration, drop a marker buoy nearby and keep your boat over the fish, jigging vertically for them.

Slab jigs, as shown here, are good for
vertical fishing for stripers, particularly
those that are suspended in the tops of
submerged timber. The inverted V marks
on this graph paper are stripers, some of
which are situated inside the trees.

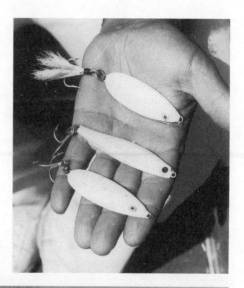

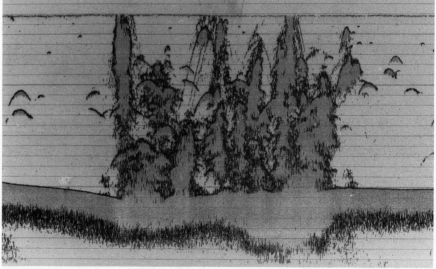

For striper jigging, use good-sized lures; 1/2 to 2 ounces is the norm. The lighter
ones can be used on light line and light tackle in conditions where such gear is appropriate. It is important, however, to use a heavy jig in order to get down fast enough
to the level of the fish, which often is 20 to 50 feet. Lead-headed bucktails work
very well and may be more productive with a curl-tailed, soft, plastic trailer. White
is the top producer, but chartreuse or yellow may at times prove worthwhile. These
jigs are also effective striper catchers when trolled behind downriggers. Other jigs
work, too. The silver or white painted, slab-sided versions, and standard jigging spoons

are specifically intended for vertical fishing, with and without a patch of hair on the treble hook.

When jigging, pay attention to your method of working the lure and to the depth it is at. If you find a school of fish at 30 feet, for example, in 50 feet of water, don't drop the jig to the bottom and work it back up. Let it out 30 feet. You can either make a long enough cast to let the lure settle down to that depth, or better yet, strip out 30 feet of line. With a level wind reel, you can determine how much line comes out with each pass of the level wind guide, or you can strip line off in 2-foot sections until you reach the right depth. Jig in short, sharp upward motions, letting the lure flutter back down each time. Remember that current and boat drift affect the line and adjust for these factors.

Another, and sometimes more effective technique is speed jigging, using 1- to 2-ounce spoons (metal slab or jigging spoons, including the Bomber Slab, Mann's Mann-O-Lure, and Luhr Jensen Nordic), 20- to 30-pound-test line, and a stiff rod. If fish are close to the lake bed, free-spool the jig until it hits the bottom, then turn the handle of your bait-casting reel five turns as fast as possible. Then push the free-spool button, drop the lure down to the bottom, and do it again, always keeping the rod tip pointed toward the water and occasionally pumping the rod. Continue doing this for several minutes. Then try making seven turns of the handle, then ten. If fish are suspended well off the bottom, count the lure down to the depth of the fish, reel the jig up for five turns of the handle, drop it back down, and reel again. Light thumb pressure is applied to the reel spool when the line is going out, since most fish hit as the lure falls.

It's critically important to bring the lure up above the fish and flutter it back past their nose, which seems to mimic the movement of dying bait fish as they zoom up toward the surface, then flounder back. While doing this method of jigging, constantly maneuver your boat around a marker buoy with an electric motor and watch your sonar for fish. Keep the lure in front of their nose. Most anglers fish below the stripers and don't keep their lure in front of them.

Because of the wandering nature of stripers and the need to locate fish and keep with them, trolling is a very popular activity through all seasons. There are several ways to troll for stripers, but the key with all of them is getting and keeping the lures at the right depth. On sonar we have watched an occasional striper swim up and come behind a trolled lure, but it is usually necessary to keep your offerings at, or slightly above, the holding level of the fish. This is primarily accomplished by using a downrigger or flat-lining (running a lure a set distance behind the boat on a generally unweighted, nylon monofilament line).

When stripers are within 25 feet of the surface, most trollers flat-line by tradition, though they needn't be restricted to this. When flat-lining for stripers, plugs, spoons, flies, and jigs can be used for shallow fishing, but only plugs have merit from 10 to 30 feet. Many striper-trollers greatly overestimate the depth at which their diving lures run or miscalculate the depth to which they are capable of diving. As a result, they often are not trolling at the proper level for success (usually they are too shallow).

Where plugs are concerned, there must be a compromise between lure size, diving ability, and strength of line to be used. Sometimes standard, black bass crankbaits (which are 2 to 2 1/2 inches long) are most representative of the size of local bait fish, but require light line to get them down (which may not be feasible). Remember that there are a lot of options available to you, and that a lure that dives 15 feet

When stripers are scattered in deep open water, you have the option of jigging for them or trolling. Using sonar is particularly important for locating the fish and determining at what depth you should work.

in a certain situation with one size of line can be made to dive deeper by using a lighter line or by trolling a greater length of the same line. So it is important to know the abilities of your striper-trolling lures when flat-lining.

Downriggers are becoming an ever greater force in striper trolling, and the use of these devices is affording deep striper trollers a greater range of lure presentation and more precise lure placement and control. There are some places, however, where striper trollers are reluctant to use downriggers. Many southern impoundments that are home to large populations of pure or hybrid striped bass have a significant amount of standing timber in them. This timber often holds bait fish and stripers and poses a problem for anyone who would troll an 8- to 12-pound downrigger weight, not to mention a lure, in their midst.

We have done this and can say that it is not impossible to use a downrigger for striper trolling in these circumstances, provided you know your underwater terrain well, constantly watch your sonar, fish with another capable angler who is always ready to raise the weight, keep the clutch setting loose, and aren't afraid to lose some tackle now and then.

Finding stripers and presenting your lures at the appropriate level is more than half the battle in striper trolling, but accomplishing both of these is no guarantee that fish will take your offering. If there are bait fish near the stripers you mark on a depthfinder, the bass may be moving on quickly in pursuit of this bait, and you'll find it extremely difficult to stay with them and continue to locate them.

Some of the stripers you find simply won't strike your lure for whatever reason, and still others may show only passing interest. Since you can never be sure when you'll have a strike, you should conduct your trolling with the thought that a fish is likely to hit at any moment; every movement should be calculated to bring about a strike. The worst thing you can do is troll aimlessly for hours on end, even if your lures are at the proper depth.

For successful trolling, you must be conscious of where your lures are in relation to the position of the boat, as well as in respect to depth. For instance, if you were to spot a school of fish and then turn the boat slightly, your lures would probably not come close to that school because their path of travel will be straighter than the boat. Keep this in mind when you are attempting to closely follow an underwater ridge line or river channel, for instance. It is often necessary to steer your boat beyond or to the side of some object or fish in order to direct the path of travel of your lures following over it.

Many of the trolling tactics and boat manipulation skills employed when trolling for any species of fish work for striper angling. These include avoiding trolling in open water areas in a straight line for continuously long periods of time, alternating between heading upwind or downwind, making turns, changing speed, etc.

Trolling with deep-diving plugs on a flat line or with various lures on downriggers is a vital part of striper fishing. This fish was caught by trolling, using a long rod with plenty of line, since large fish are powerful and can run a long way.

If you aren't running as many trolling lines as the law allows, you are not only decreasing your chances of taking fish, but you are missing an opportunity to experiment and determine what lures, lure colors, or depths should be fished. This is especially overlooked by striper fishermen, many of whom are not accustomed to trolling, or who spend a great deal of time casting for such fish as largemouth bass using only one rod at a time. Check the angling regulations in your area; most states permit the use of two rods per angler.

When trolling, you needn't travel especially slowly. Stripers are strong swimmers accustomed to chasing down prey in open water. That doesn't mean that they prefer to have to swim after a meal, only that they are capable of doing so. Nonetheless, a medium to medium-fast boat speed, as long as it is conducive to proper lure action, will get the job done.

For striper trolling, it is best to have a long rod, preferably one of 7- to 8-foot length, with moderate- to fast-action tip (the latter especially for use with downriggers). Reels may be spinning, bait-casting, or larger conventional levelwind models, but they should have a smooth, reliable drag and be able to hold a minimum of 120 yards of heavy line. A clicker is a desirable feature for bait-casting and conventional reels. Largemouth bass fishing tackle may do at times, but the rods may be too short and the line capacity too little in situations where large fish are encountered or where there is heavy current or obstructions present.

Striper fishing lures consist almost exclusively of deep-diving plugs, metal spoon-type jigs and hair jigs, and some surface lures, although trolling products for stripers may be plugs, jigs, flies, and the occasional spoon or spinner. Plugs like the Whopper Stopper Hellbender and Bomber Waterdog are favorites in many striper lakes (and some anglers take the hooks off these plugs and use heavy line to attach a 1 1/2– to 2-ounce jig behind that), though, of course, other diving plugs catch fish, too. Most striper anglers use 20- to 30-pound-test line; 20 is adequate. Twelve- to 17-pound-test line will do well in open water circumstances, provided you can fight a fish properly and use the appropriate reel drag setting. An advantage to lighter line with stripers is that it can alarm fish less (stripers are spooky fish) and draw more strikes, plus it gets lures deeper.

HYBRID STRIPERS

Whether hybrid stripers are smarter or stronger than pure stripers or any other fish is a moot point; but make no mistake—they are incredibly powerful fish, especially in the larger sizes. The fact that they are so strong and that they get fairly large pretty quickly endears them to anglers wherever they've been planted. Also, they are sometimes a more aggressive bait and lure consumer than their pure striper parent.

Hybrid stripers are the most popular and successful hybrid fish America has yet to see. They are known to many anglers simply as "hybrids," to a few as "whiterock bass," and to still others as a "wiper"—a term that seems more conducive to a throwaway product that adorns the rumps of toddlers. Now found in over thirty states and a sterile cross between the female striped bass and the male white bass (not to be confused with the so-called "sunshine bass" of Florida origin, a cross between the male striper and female white bass), this hybrid striper grows particularly fast, which means it is a good quarry for anglers.

Hybrid stripers are recognized by broken spotted lines, or stripes, on their sides. White bass and pure stripers have continuous lines. Hybrid stripers may have a few continuous lines, but some will be all or partially broken, especially near the head. You can distinguish between white bass and hybrid bass by checking the tooth patch on their tongue; the white bass has a single patch while the hybrid has a double.

Like its parents, the hybrid striper is an open water species that does not relate to near shore structure as do many other popular warm water game fish. Threadfin and gizzard shad make up the primary forage in southern locales; alewives are the mainstay in some northern waters, and bluegills, chubs or other species constitute main or secondary forage in other hybrid sites. Like pure strain stripers, hybrids follow bait fish schools, feeding heavily on them.

The most popular season for hybrid striper fishing is spring, though good success can be had in all seasons if you spend a lot of time on the water and can track the movements of these fish. In spring, hybrids attempt to spawn in tributaries when the water temperature reaches the mid to upper 50's. They usually are right on the heels of white bass, and just before pure stripers, though in many of the lakes where hybrids are stocked, one or both of the parent species do not exist.

Hybrids travel in schools. When located, it's often possible to catch more than one or two. The most exciting fishing for them is the frenzied jump fishing that occurs

The hybrid striper on the left weighs about the same as the pure strain striper on the right but is shorter and fatter, which makes for a hard-fighting fish.

early and late in the day from late summer through fall when hybrids locate a school of bait fish, pin them against the bank, a sand bar, or the surface of the water, and pounce on them. Fishing tactics then are like those described previously for pure strain stripers.

Hybrids are primarily sight feeders. Lures that work well for them are those that imitate small bait fish: hybrids favor white, silver, chrome, and clear or translucent finishes. For trolling, diving minnow-shaped plugs—like a small Rebel Spoonbill Minnow or Mann's Stretch 20+ or medium- to deep-diving crankbaits—are good.

Places to locate hybrids include gravel and sandy bars, points, tailrace runs below dams, spillways, the mouths of rivers and creeks, between submerged or visible islands, along dropoffs, and above humps or levees. They are often found on humps, ledges, and points in the summer, and, in some really warm southern waters, hybrids will be down roughly at 21 to 22 feet around the thermocline.

Many of the places that attract white bass or pure stripers also attract hybrid stripers, and in lakes where both are found, it's not uncommon to catch a hybrid in the midst of other fish. Most of the fishing techniques that apply to pure strain stripers also apply to hybrids.

CHAPTER SIX
SALMON

Salmon are quite the glamour fish these days, particularly the chinook and coho salmon of the Great Lakes. Naturally, because of their size and fight, these salmon are prized by big water anglers more than any other fish. In lakes, they are hard to find, yet some anglers consistently track them down and catch more than others do, which proves that, as in other forms of fishing, there are ways to increase angling success and make the salmon-catching endeavor more than a haphazard, luck-will-prevail proposition. Among the key elements are knowing the behavior of these nomadic fish, what lures to present, and when and how (especially how fast) to present them. We'll focus on these and other factors as they pertain to salmon fishing in lakes, recognizing that there is also a good deal of river and stream fishing for salmon but that those fish are more concentrated and the range of angling techniques narrower.

Salmon fishing, by and large, poses a big water dilemma: where are they in terms of locale and depth? The answer, through much of the season, is just about anywhere. A radiotelemetry study of Great Lakes salmon indicated that they travel an average of 7.8 miles a day in the spring and summer, and may travel as many as 20 miles in a day. While finding them is of primary importance, fishing for salmon in open water is an ongoing quest in that you seldom get to keep plying a specific spot or school but must keep on the move, experimenting with depths, lure types and colors, speed, setbacks, and other factors. To catch salmon with regularity you must work at it.

Coho and chinook salmon roam open waters and return after three to five years at large to the rivers and streams of their birth; there they spawn and die. Their movement in open water is largely governed by water temperature and food. They put on many pounds through spring and summer, their principal forage being smelt and alewives. These bait fish, which mass in large schools, come inshore to spawn when the water warms up in the 50's, and this helps draw salmon close to shore. Afterward, however, both smelt and alewives stay in the strata of water that is most comfortable, which is roughly 48 degrees for smelt and 54 degrees for alewives. These bait fish range widely, and salmon follow them. Salmon are also comfortable in that same temperature range. Water temperature, however, is influenced by weather and prevailing winds, so that conditions that may be conducive to the presence of bait and/or salmon in a particular place at one time can be markedly altered within a few days.

Chinook salmon range widely in the Great Lakes, following the bait fish inshore in the spring and then moving deeper into the thermocline as surface waters warm. Early season fish are brightly colored and strong fighters.

SEASONS

Spring

Fishing begins in earnest in early spring, gains momentum in late spring and summer, peaks in late summer and early fall, and continues through mid-fall. In pursuing spring salmon, anglers usually scour the water from top to bottom. Just as salmon range widely over a lake in the spring, so, too, are they dispersed at all water levels from the surface to 40 or 50 feet deep because of the uniformly cold water. Most spring salmon are caught within 25 to 30 feet of the surface, over a bottom depth that ranges from a few feet deep to as much as 100 feet. They may move slightly offshore over this greater depth, yet still be close to the surface, when inshore boat activity and/or bright light forces them to relocate.

Though there are days when success comes consistently at a certain depth, this depth may not be the same from day to day. Assume that conditions will change daily so that you are flexible enough to try various methods and to fish at differing water levels. There are times when you catch all your fish at the same depth on the same type and color lure, but there will also be times when there is no consistent depth, lure type, or color pattern, and you will be forced to experiment.

Salmon are here-today, gone-tomorrow in the spring, especially on the Great Lakes. Unlike fall salmon, which cluster near tributaries and are preparing to run upriver to spawn, spring fish have no compulsion to linger. Passing through, they are temporarily attracted to tributaries (also power plant discharges) because of the warmer water and food to be found there, but so are other species of fish, plus boats and fishermen. When boat traffic in warm shallow water is too great, salmon leave. That's one reason why it pays to start early in the day; salmon that have come into the areas near tributaries overnight may still be available for those first-light anglers. A typical salmon outing starts before dawn in the spring (and again in the fall).

Primarily, lake warming is initiated by tributaries. When the water temperature is in the low to mid 40s, a 50-degree day with rain might send enough warm water down a tributary to warm the environs of a tributary mouth up a few notches, and this could spur fish activity. Often there will be a mud line created around tributary mouths, which results from the stained or muddy spring runoff, and it may extend a short distance to the east or west depending on lake currents; salmon may be caught on the edges of the mud line because there is usually a thermal break here as well, with the inner edge being warmer.

Elsewhere, the upper layer of water may be warmed up a bit on a mild sunny day, and this might cause fish to be caught in very shallow water. As spring progresses, pockets of warm water or vertical separations of different temperature water away from immediate tributary areas can produce fish. It's a good idea to monitor shallow-water temperatures as you fish, both to look for these things and to determine if fish that you do catch are in a particular area because of the temperature difference.

Most inshore fishing concentrates on immediate tributary environs. Good places to fish here include the heads of piers, the river alley between piers (nearest the lake proper), the harbor, break walls, troughs near shore, and nearby structure. These areas, however, are also most obvious and accessible to other boaters and to shore-based fishermen, and, while some fish can be caught when angling pressure is intense, it's good to get away from the crowd, even fishing a mile or two down the shore and away from the mouth. Try fishing tributary environs for the first hour or so of the day, and, as traffic increases, move off and look for nearby undisturbed water or places that have been left alone for a few minutes. When inshore traffic is heavy, other boaters zero in on the locale where someone is fighting a fish or was just observed to have landed a fish; this behavior often tends to cluster boats in certain places, if only for a relatively short period of time. This is when you can be trolling the vacated spots. This works for trout as well as salmon trolling; but, where salmon are sought, this is an even better tactic in fall than in spring because fall fish are in the area to stay, whereas spring salmon are going to move on.

Spring salmon trolling can be accomplished by using flat-lines, planer boards, down-riggers, or diving planers. On the Great Lakes, most salmon trolling, even in the spring, is done with downriggers (set shallow at first and then at intermediate depths), but some people have success using side-planer boards to get lines away from the boat. Running some flat-lined plugs off side-planer boards is especially worthwhile in early spring for coho or chinook salmon and is a particularly good way to catch trout at the same time. In the summer and fall, by contrast, virtually all trolling is done with the aid of downriggers, although diving planers are used at times in conjunction with downriggers. Flat-lines are rarely employed, unless there is a surface thermal bar present well offshore, and when there is one, it usually has disappeared by midsummer.

This is about the only time of the salmon season when sonar instruments are not critically important. They are needed to tell you how deep you are, and they are needed when you are downrigger fishing to make sure you don't hang the weights up and to help locate pods of bait that might hold nearby salmon. But from a fish-finding standpoint, sonar doesn't enter into the equation like it does when the water warms and you are hunting fish more than working localized areas. The fish seen on sonar in early spring are usually not the fish that are caught because you seldom see fish on sonar below the boat in shallow water.

In the spring, salmon trolling is done with flat-lines, planer boards, and downriggers, but downriggers dominate the scene afterward, with diving planers getting some use as well, as most salmon are caught deep.

Plugs are good for catching spring salmon on or near the surface, and spoons are good when fished a little deeper via downriggers. Dodger and fly or spoon combos do the job later in the spring as the water warms. Plugs can be fished on flat-lines, planer boards, and downriggers, and usually exhibit good action even when worked at the moderately slow speed that cold water spring fishing requires. That speed may range from just below 2 to 3 mph, while later in the season it will seldom be at the lower end of that range and often will be greater.

As the shallow water warms up, bait fish and salmon move offshore (depending on prevailing winds). Smelt are usually moving out of the inshore shallows by mid-May and alewives by the end of May or early June. Then, most fishing is accomplished with downriggers. Flat-lines or planer board lines may catch fish on a thermal bar, of course, and sometimes the use of diving planers, particularly the Dipsey Diver, is productive; but perhaps as much as 90 percent of the fish from here on in will be taken using downriggers fished at intermediate and deep depths.

Summer

In late spring and summer, you must *find* fish. The standard way to do this is to check water temperatures from the surface on down until you find water that is too cold for salmon to congregate in; set your lures in the 48- to 55-degree band of water, and start covering a lot of territory, always watching your sonar instrument to note the presence and depth of bait fish schools and large individual fish that may be salmon. A device that gives you constant, deep temperature readouts is very valuable for this, but an alternative is to use a thermometer attached to a downrigger weight (preferably

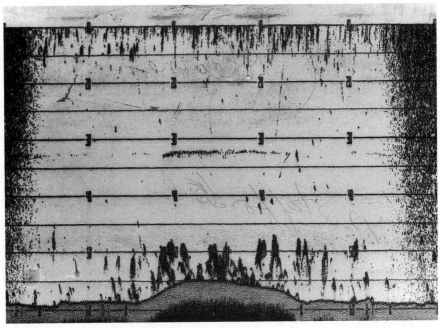

Schools of alewives show up at the 50- to 55-foot level on this graph paper readout. Below the alewives are chinook salmon. Both are clustered in the thermocline offshore.

a manual model so you can raise it as quickly as possible to check the temperature at various depths).

As the water warms up, a thermocline is established, and salmon move deeper in the lake from late spring through early September. On the Great Lakes, you are usually fishing the thermocline in June, July, and most of August. It is a mistake, however, to fish the thermocline band strictly. Look for fish and bait on your sonar and note their depths. Deliberately fish a line or two (assuming you have enough lines to do this with) on either side of the thermocline. Look for 50- to 55-degree water but don't be afraid to work a bait in 48-degree water, especially for chinooks.

When you find fish, you're likely to see them in packs — not large schools — but grouped more so than in the spring. Doubleheaders are a possibility, and when you find a school you may want to slow down a bit, change lures, shorten the leads (or setbacks which is the distance from downrigger weight or cable to the lure) behind your downrigger, and bring lures closer together and more tightly packed in the vertical space that the spotted fish occupy. Make a lot of turns, and include figure-eight boat-driving patterns as part of your presentation repertoire. You may lose the school, but you may find another one. Depths at which lures are fished range from 30 feet to 50 or 60 in late spring and early to midsummer, reaching 90 and 100 feet and even considerably deeper in late August. The bottom depth will range from 50 feet to several hundred.

Downriggers are fished in conjunction with sonar. Here, a paper graph recorder tracks the depths at which four downrigger weights and their following lures are running.

This is precision trolling, truly a controlled depth presentation, and the backbone of downrigger fishing. Really long drop-backs for salmon aren't necessary, and many times lures are run from a few feet behind the weight to 30 feet back, longer for shallow water and shorter for deeper water. With the depth of the lure assured because of short lines and downrigger weight settings, with the speed of your boat known and the depth of fish marked on sonar, you might conclude that catching is now a piece of cake. Sometimes it is; often it's not.

Remember that you do have to find the fish, then play with drop-back lengths, lure types, lure colors, speed, and so forth. The salmon you find are in the midst of an odyssey that will cause them to roam many miles on any given day. You're moving; they're moving. This is one reason why Loran—long-range navigation—is becoming a standard accessory on big, Great Lakes boats, particularly those belonging to charter captains. In the summer you may have to go many miles offshore (ten to twelve miles is common in some places, but this depends on where you are on each of the lakes and on the direction of the prevailing wind) to locate salmon.

Summer salmon may be found in areas where there is some type of bottom structure different from the rest of the underwater terrain, such as reefs, rocky spots, a trough, a sharp drop-off, and where temperature is favorable. In some areas of the Great Lakes, such locales are not very far offshore, and salmon can be located fairly regularly and caught with some consistency. The Great Lakes, obviously, are huge waters, and while there are many similarities between the five lakes, there are also differences, and these influence salmon behavior.

There is no question that salmon, especially chinook, are very sensitive to light. In spring, they are often found inshore in the wee hours of the morning and at dusk, moving offshore and getting progressively deeper as the sun rises. Getting out an hour before sunrise is usually a wise decision, not only because salmon may be closer to shore or shallower (meaning higher in the water column, especially so in summer) than later in the day but also because they are actively feeding and are more aggressive about striking lures just before daylight and at dusk. Salmon fishermen who are on the water day after day during the summer and early fall know that there is usually a one- to three-hour peak activity period in the morning and that catch rates almost invariably decline as light penetration increases. That's not to say that you can't catch fish in midday, but there are usually many slow stretches between midmorning and midafternoon. At dusk, however, the chance of renewed activity is increased.

Fall

In late summer salmon are in a so-called staging disposition, schooling up in deep offshore water and beginning to undergo the physiological changes that will ultimately cause them to stop feeding and to come into the tributary regions. When they do come inshore to prepare for spawning, there are usually plenty of fish, and the opportunities for catching trophy-sized salmon are particularly good.

The big fish and the swollen near-shore presence of salmon is what instills enthusiasm into fall anglers throughout the Great Lakes. Actually, this begins in late August and extends through September and into October. Coho and chinook salmon return to natal streams during this period, eventually entering them, not en masse, but sporadically when their biological clock nudges them to do so (they are also encouraged with each new rainfall). This explains why river mouths figure so prominently in the activities of late-season angling.

While large and small rivers attract fish, the entire tributary vicinity is likely to harbor salmon, and anglers may be more successful from a half-mile to several miles directly offshore or relatively inshore yet several miles in either direction of tributaries. It is not uncommon to find a lot of fish close to a river mouth, but on the bottom and uncooperative. These are likely to be salmon that are almost ready to run the river and which are not interested in feeding. They may strike a lure, fly, or spawn sack later when they're in the river, if it is repeatedly dangled annoyingly in front of their snouts, but an object passing by their noses in the lake doesn't antagonize them enough.

The surprise of fall fishing is that there are lake salmon that strike even though they are undergoing severe physiological changes that produce a kype (the curled lower jaw), darkening of the body color, and ultimate loss of appetite. Many such salmon are on the verge of losing their appetites completely, and probably strike more out of habit.

Coho and chinook strike plugs and spoons of varying sizes, colors, and shapes, and it is always a challenge to discover the kind, size, and color of lure that is successful. These patterns can remain constant for a season or a week, or change suddenly, and they can vary from year to year. Cut plugs, such as a J-Plug or Lucky Louie, are perennially good, fall salmon catchers, yet each year it seems the size that worked so well one autumn doesn't cut it the following year. Even smaller plugs, such as 2-inch–long wobbling crankbaits like a Hotshot, Wiggle Wart, or Tadpolly, are effective.

Running lures close to the downrigger weights is usually the rule, and 6 to 8 feet

A variety of lures are used for salmon trolling, with spoons being perhaps most widely employed. A cut-plug-style trolling lure, which caught this fish, is one of the most successful fall lures.

back is normal in deep water in the fall. Occasionally you might drop back from 12 to 20 feet. The downrigger weight piques the curiosity of salmon, or irritates them, and it apparently draws attention to the bait following it. It sometimes pays to stack lines on the same downrigger, with the upper lure a few feet above the lower one and slightly further back. This puts two lures in the same zone and near one weight.

Despite the occasional presence of salmon near the surface, late-season fishermen should concentrate their efforts at deep levels. A high line may pick up the odd steelhead or brown trout, but salmon catches occur deep. This doesn't necessarily mean on the bottom, however, or in the thermocline, or close to shore. The point is that you need to search for fish at specific levels (using some type of sonar), which are invariably relatively deep, and you still need to utilize a downrigger to make a controlled presentation at that level.

The water temperature at those depths may not be what is normally considered ideal for salmon, but temperature alone is not the guiding factor now. It's good if a thermocline is established near shore and salmon are holding in 50- to 55-degree water. The right wind (usually south or southwest) for several days can push warm water out and bring salmon closer to shore, providing an explosion in fishing action. However, a strong north or northwest wind can alter the depth of fish near the tributaries, and you need to assess the situation daily.

In late August or early September, you may see a lot of active fish on a graph recorder. These are streakers, on the move and feeding, and you may get quite a few false releases (lines pulled out of the downrigger release device) as the result of fish striking your lures but not getting hooked. These may be active fish that are more inclined to strike than stationary sulkers.

The concentration of fish near the shore at this season, whether due to the spawning influence or thermocline presence, contrasts with spring and midsummer fishing in that salmon can be anywhere and at any depth in the early part of the season and very deep and well offshore (this depends on the location of the thermocline and the prevailing wind) in the summer. While the first and last few hours of daylight remain good times to catch salmon, the fish don't necessarily disperse quite as readily as light penetration becomes greater. Some late-season salmon will disperse and others will stay in one area and be inactive.

Late-season salmon may be undergoing drastic changes that make them darker and more malevolent looking, but don't underestimate their pulling power or staying ability. Many an autumn Great Lakes angler has hooked up with a fish that fatigued his wrists. And many a salmon has gotten tougher near the boat and pulled free or made netting awfully difficult. But, of course, not all fish act the same, and some large, late-season salmon are whipped pretty handily. Part of the fun at this time is not knowing just when you'll get that tiger.

TACKLE

Irrespective of season, salmon, especially large chinooks, are among the most powerful fish in freshwater, and they have whipped many a fisherman's reel drag. We once heard a scientist say that a Great Lakes salmon was "as fast as any terrestrial animal in its ability to move in its environment." Though fall salmon may lose a fraction of their fighting vigor as they darken and get closer to running the rivers, they're no pussycats. It's not uncommon to see nearby anglers frantically pull lines and downrigger weights, then chase after a salmon heading for the next county.

The possibility of hooking a real tackle tester is one of the forces that keeps anglers after salmon, chinook especially, and late summer fish in particular. The fish will,

Big chinooks like this draw hordes of anglers to tributary areas in late summer and early fall. Note the small lure in the mouth of this over 30-pounder.

of course, be larger in the fall, but a 20-pound spring chinook, not nearly ready to succumb to the physiological changes that will occur in fall, is still one broad-tailed Goliath. Many a spring pier fisherman, using light tackle for perch, has had his rod yanked off the pier by a salmon (or steelhead), or been uncontrollably linked to a fish twenty-five times larger than what he was expecting. Trollers don't necessarily fare better, even though their tackle is stouter; more than one boat angler has been de-spooled by a powerful chinook.

Obviously it takes some skill to land the bigger chinook, though this is something that an angler with adequate tackle can master quickly. A long rod, in at least the 8- to 9-foot range, is distinctly advantageous for use with downriggers and for playing fish, and a reel should have plenty of line capacity (200 yards minimum) and a good drag. Level-wind reels are preferred for this, and line strength ranges from 14 to 25. Charter boat captains, who often have inexperienced anglers onboard, seldom fish with less than 17-pound line for salmon. Many use 20 and some go to 25. We prefer light line because it's a challenge and thrill to play these strong fish in open water with it, though light-line use can be a problem when you hook a big fish that you have to wear down and there are other boats in the immediate area. When boat traffic is not a problem, it's not hard to play a big fish in open water because there is nothing for it to snag your line on, the deck can be cleared and the boat maneuvered to your advantage, and, if the drag is set properly, the fish can take plenty of line and do its stuff. When conditions allow, we ordinarily prefer 12-pound line for salmon trolling but also fish with 6 and 8 for trout, and occasionally hook a salmon on a trout rod.

You may find it very exciting to fight these fish on ultralight tackle and super-long, so-called noodle rods. The problem with using such gear, however, is that it does take a little more time than usual to land a fish, and if the salmon runs a long way on the surface in a locale that is crowded with boats, there will be cutoffs and people who get upset because you're in their way. In the spring, when boats are clustered inshore, this is especially likely to be a problem. The solution is to fish the fringes of heavy traffic or only use the ultralight stuff when the water isn't crowded. With light and ultralight tackle, there is no doubt that you can spend a long time on a really large fish, but if you know how to play a fish properly and use wind and boat position to your advantage, you needn't spend most of the day fighting Goliath.

There is, of course, a mind-boggling array of types and colors of lures to fish. There are many brands of lures and often lure types that do the job, and you have to find what works for you under existing conditions on a day to day basis. There are no hard and fast rules where lure choice is concerned. Moreover, there are regional lure preferences, and in salmon trolling there are often hot colors and hot lure types just as there are times when people have success doing quite different things. Getting the right action out of your lures (regardless of type or color), being observant to details, and changing and experimenting are the keys.

We should note, however, that of all the colors used in late-season, Great Lakes salmon fishing, we wouldn't be without a blue-and-silver combination. This color has produced more consistently for us than any other. It may not catch the most fish in a particular year, or even the largest (though some years it will do both), but, like the baseball player who hits for average, it's always in contention. We've also had fall success with some fluorescent colors, but silver, green and silver, chartreuse with red, and green and black have been most effective at this time. This applies to both spoons and plugs, although in general we find that plugs come into their own again in fall as the more consistent chinook salmon catchers.

The premier coho salmon catcher is a fly, spoon, or rubber squid fished behind a dodger. Dodgers serve as attractors and are used in a variety of colors and sizes. Popular colors include all silver, silver with assorted prism tape colors attached to it, fluorescent red, chartreuse, blue, and green, but there are others. Sizes vary, although smaller ones tend to see more use in the early part of the season, bigger ones later in the year. Spoons, flies, and squid (mostly squid) are run 18 to 24 inches behind the dodger and are used in a wide range of colors. Coho also strike other lures fished without a dodger behind a downrigger, such as thin spoons and small casting spoons, but this combination, fished primarily off a downrigger but also behind a diving planer, is perennially a top producer.

If we had to point to one lure type to use on chinooks, it would probably be cut plugs. Typified by the single and jointed J-Plug, Silver Horde, Canadian Plug, Dandy Glo, Lucky Louie, and others, these erratic swimmers can sustain high trolling speeds and produce fish in summer and fall. Good colors include all silver, silver and blue, silver and green, green, and green and chartreuse. Other useful plugs, however, include jointed minnow imitations such as the J-11 Rapala and Sisson Minnow-Mate in fluorescent colors, and small diving plugs like Hotshots, Tadpollys, Hot 'N Tots, and Wiggle Warts in silver, blue and silver, chartreuse and red, and other colors.

As for spoons, the number of manufacturers is so great that it's hard to keep up with them. Some of the Eppinger products are well liked throughout the Great Lakes, and other very popular spoons include Evil Eyes, Northport Nailers, Southport Slammers, Flutterspoons, Suttons, Andy Reekers, Northern King, and on and on. You

A dodger (in the hand of the angler on the left), combined with a fly or squid, accounts for many salmon each season, especially coho. Coho like this are very frisky, usually jumping several times.

should realize that there are trolling spoons that cannot be cast without a weight, and casting spoons that can be trolled but often are not as useful as trolling spoons. Few of the heavy, thick-bodied spoons are used routinely for salmon trolling because they sink too fast on turns, drop an indeterminate distance below a downrigger weight when trolled, and don't have the best action at slower speeds. However, thick-bodied spoons can be useful for surface flat-lining at times without the aid of weights because they do attain some depth while trolled.

Lightweight spoons, on the other hand, attain no depth unless fished with a weight, diving planer, or weighted line, or are trolled behind a downrigger weight. The wafer-thin models are made of light gauge metal and are so pliable that they can be bent to modify their action. They also bend readily when a fish thrashes in the net with one of these spoons in its mouth, and they are predominantly worked slowly to achieve maximum action. The slightly heavier versions—still unsuitable for casting, however—are the foremost salmon spoon on the Great Lakes and they have very good swimming action over the intermediate and fast ranges of trolling speeds.

An important point to remember about spoons—and this is true whenever they are trolled—is that each type of spoon has an optimum trolling speed and an acceptable range of trolling speed, and that when you troll below that range, the lure has no action; when you troll above it, the lure spins or darts wildly and has an unnatural action. Therefore, when you are selecting a spoon to troll for salmon, make sure its speed capacity is compatible with the other spoons (and plugs) that you are already fishing, and, in general, make speed-related selections for salmon fishing based upon the design and thickness of the spoon.

It's important to get the right action out of lures that are trolled for salmon. Many trollers employ a speed indicator (like the round object on the right) to monitor boat and lure speed.

Lures with phosphorescent paint have been around for some time and have proven popular for low-light and deep-water salmon trolling. These lures must be held to a light source, such as a spotlight or lantern, to make them glow, and their illumination only lasts for 15 to 20 minutes, after which they must be recharged. Some lures have phosphorescent paint on them, but you can paint others yourself or use phosphorescent tape.

Chemiluminescent light sticks are another way to have bright lures, and this field first got started with Dandy-Glo plugs, which are plastic cutplug trolling lures that sport 4-inch-long light sticks inside them. These have proven useful for early morning, downrigger trolling for chinooks in the summer. You should activate the light stick for an hour or more before fishing, however, to let some of the brightness mellow. Using tape on translucent plugs or using darker colored plugs also helps diffuse brightness. There are similar new products which include small plugs and spoons that sport much smaller light sticks. These high-visibility lures are primarily useful in low-light situations, such as on overcast, foggy days or early in the morning or at night.

LANDLOCKED SALMON

Known for leaping, running, and pressuring light tackle, the landlocked Atlantic salmon is a fish of grace, beauty, and maximum punch per pound. It has long been a troller's favorite in the Northeast.

Fishing for landlocked Atlantic salmon is a bit different than fishing for coho or chinook. Landlocks are not quite as scattered as Great Lakes coho or chinook. Traditionally, landlocks are pursued by trollers using fly rods and weighted streamers or leadcore line and either spoons or streamer flies. Downriggers and other Great Lakes salmon paraphernalia are still relatively new to the landlocked Atlantic salmon scene, although they've made inroads and are helping to extend what has been primarily a shallow spring fishery.

While there is a more traditional attitude toward landlocked salmon trolling, the life cycle and behavioral pattern of these fish is very similar to that of coho and chinook salmon. Landlocks, for example, spawn in the fall, return to natal tributaries to do so, and live out their adult lives in the open water. Landlocks leave their natal waters as smolts and generally return to those tributaries two or three years later. Unlike coho or chinook salmon, Atlantics often survive the reproductive process and may spawn two or three times.

Landlocked Atlantic salmon inhabit large and intermediate-sized northern lakes, as well as small lakes or ponds in high-altitude areas. The predominant trolling fishery occurs in large lakes. The principal fishing is in spring, beginning right after ice-out. While some salmon may be caught when the ice is breaking up and the water temperature is in the 39- to 42-degree range, better action doesn't begin until the water hits the mid 40's. Landlocks are caught from the surface to 20 feet deep at this time (which is all uniform temperature) and can be found near shore over relatively shallow bottom or out in open water over deep water.

As the surface temperature increases, landlocks are more likely to be found near tributaries if they attract large runs of spawning smelt or inshore where schools of smelt or spawning alewives may be located. Water temperature then is in the low to mid 50's. This activity takes place in May and through June; but by mid to late June in a normal year, the surface water will be warming up, and landlocked Atlantics will move to deeper water and locate in the thermocline, roughly staying in 52- to 57-degree water and roaming as widely as the size of lake and water temperature zones will allow.

Smelt are the foremost, and preferred, landlocked salmon food. Alewives are a major forage fish in a few locales that don't have a substantial smelt population. Elsewhere, ciscos, shiners, and yellow perch make up part of their lake diet. Smelt are usually the bread-and-butter prey, and most landlocked salmon lures are meant to imitate smelt. These lures include minnow-imitating plugs in straight and jointed versions from 4 to 6 inches in length, long thin spoons, and single or tandem streamer flies.

The traditional and still widely practiced, landlocked salmon trolling method is to use a fly rod and a streamer. The fly rod is between 8 and 9 feet long and is equipped with a large-capacity fly reel loaded with 100 yards of backing, a level sinking line, and a long leader. The leader is about 20 to 30 feet long and can be of one strength (6 to 10 pounds) or split into relatively equal sections of differing strengths (such as 10 and 6). Using one continuous section is preferable because it eliminates the potentially troublesome nylon-to-nylon knot. A streamer fly is tied to the end of the leader, and a split-shot or two may be added a short distance ahead of it.

Another traditional method, used for getting to below-surface fish with either a fly or light spoon, is to use a fly rod or conventional rod with level-wind reel and lead-core line. A long leader is again employed, and the issue is one of experimenting with how many colors to let out to get down to a certain depth. In both cases, where spoons or flies are fished, most successful anglers hold their rods in their hands, with rod parallel to the water and perpendicular to the gunwale of the boat, and sweep the rod back every few seconds. This pulsates the fly or spoon and causes it to surge forward and flutter back and is an important aspect of appealing to landlocked salmon. So important, in fact, that electric devices to do this have been made locally and used for many years. These devices are essentially rod holders powered by windshield wiper motors that are timed to sweep the rod back and forth. Two or three small manufacturers make them, but they are not widely distributed. Cannon recently produced a machine that did this.

Most of the traditional landlocked salmon trollers have not employed sonar devices, although more are doing so today. It makes sense to do so, not only to know when you are nearing potentially dangerous shallow waters (many natural northern lakes have submerged reefs), but to help pinpoint schools of salmon and the depth they inhabit, so you have a reference point as to how much lead core you must let out to reach the fish-holding depth.

Downrigger fishing is growing each year on the landlocked salmon scene. Where spoons and plugs are used, downriggers are most beneficial. Spoons and plugs have an action of their own. Flies, on the other hand, when trolled, need to be jerked to look more active, and the only way to do this is with an automatically oscillating downrigger, an expensive product that few landlocked salmon trollers (other than charter boat captains) are likely to buy because they are predominantly just spring fishermen.

Flies can catch salmon when used on downriggers, however, even though they

Landlocked Atlantic salmon are less widely dispersed than chinook or coho salmon and generally run smaller, but they are no less appreciated by those who catch them.

may not be as active as you'd like. This setup may be most useful on windy days, when boat movement through waves causes some natural up-and-down weight motion, thereby adding to streamer action (if the fly is not very far behind the weight), and also for getting streamer flies down to a controlled trolling depth.

The best fishing, especially in spring, is often in the first few hours of the day, with a late afternoon or evening flurry common. Midday, particularly under bluebird conditions, is dubious. A relatively fast trolling speed is employed for landlocks, and while lines are usually set from 75 to 200 feet behind the boat on flatlines and 40 to 80 feet back on deep downrigger lines, some spring fish are literally caught in the prop wash.

Lure colors that work well include gray and black, gray and white, silver and black, silver, and copper, although streamers with a touch of red are sometimes the hot ticket. Gaudy colors, which are often so successful on Great Lakes salmon, just don't measure up. Useful lures include Grey Ghost, Red Ghost, Ninethree, and Meredith Special streamers; Rebel, Rapala, Sisson, and Bagley minnow-imitation plugs; and Mooselook Wobbler, Sutton 44, and Flutterbelly spoons.

As you probably have noticed, we've neglected salmon fishing in rivers in this chapter, frankly because we haven't done enough of it to be thorough and authoritative on the subject. One thing that we don't want to do is write poorly about a subject just to fill up space, so we beg your indulgence on this score and hope that you find the information contained here to be helpful in your lake fishing activities.

CHAPTER SEVEN
TROUT IN LAKES

Angling for trout in lakes is a completely different sport than angling for trout in flowages. Certainly creeks, streams, and rivers provide some fine one-on-one trout angling and many aesthetically pleasing moments. Yet fishing for trout in lakes is equally, if not more, challenging. And if you're interested in catching larger trout, you should be plying the lakes. Big lake trout, brown trout, and rainbows (steelhead) are more likely to be found in lakes or reservoirs because such waters often provide suitable, year-round water temperatures, have abundant forage-fish opportunities, and the trout aren't readily accessible.

It is because of the lack of accessibility—the fact that trout in lakes move a lot and aren't always confined to readily identifiable terrain—that many anglers don't want to pursue trout in lakes; after all, it's a lot easier to work a lure or fly for trout in flowing water because you can readily see the possible trout lies (if not, in fact, see the fish) and know that you are presenting your offering to a fish or working very good water. Many stream trout fishermen don't want to admit it, but few of them could find their way around and catch fish if deposited on a lake; it's often tough. For that matter, few still-water fishermen are really on top of their game when it comes to locating and catching trout in lakes.

Fishing for trout in lakes is like blind prospecting. To have regular success means covering a lot of water, hunting and pecking, eliminating places and lures and boat speeds and depths and on and on—until you unlock the secrets of those fish on that lake under those conditions and at that time of day. In some respects, it is like hunting, if you're going to be aggressive about it.

Sure, you can plop your feet back on a lounge chair, prop your rod in a forked stick, and dunk bait until a trout swims by. That is a method, but instead let's review ways you can actively pursue trout, ways in which you can find and catch them where they happen to be, which is distinctly different from waiting for them to happen by.

FACTS/PLACES/TEMPERATURE

The first thing you need to have is an appreciation of lake dynamics. Basically, that involves temperature and terrain. Where terrain is concerned, the important point is getting to know the body of water that you fish. You can do that by studying navigation, hydrographic, or underwater contour maps; by studying your sonar readings

Fishing for trout in lakes, including such large bodies of water as the Great Lakes, is an entirely different proposition than fishing in flowing water and requires a lot of hunting and experimenting.

diligently; and through observant fishing experience. It takes a combination of these. Even the best maps often fail to pinpoint certain underwater features that attract trout. That might be a trough, for instance, near shore and created by wave action. Or it might be a slight pinnacle or mound or hump that rises off the lake bottom enough to attract bait fish and thus trout, but not enough to be highlighted between charted depth sounding information.

Trout orient to objects and edges; these might be long, sloping, underwater points that drop off sharply to deeper water; reefs that attract deep-dwelling lake trout to feed; or rocky or sandy bottoms (knowing this makes a difference, especially if you have to fish right near the bottom with a downrigger weight and don't want to get it hung up). By identifying physical terrain, from depth contours to irregularities in the shore or bottom, you can get an idea what places attract bait fish, as well as trout and pinpoint possible ways to fish them.

The other important element here is a knowledge of the temperature requirements of trout and how lakes react thermally. Trout are scientifically classified as cold water fish. They are metabolically suited to cool, and cold, water environments. Lake trout have a preference for water in the mid to upper 40's. Brown and rainbow trout prefer water in the upper 50's and low 60's. This is not to say that they will not be found in water above or below this nor that they will be active only in water temperature in their preferred range. But it provides some indication of what their needs are and why they react as they do when lakes warm up.

After ice-out or in late winter and early spring, trout lakes begin to warm on the surface. Trout may be found at any level at this time, and are often within the upper strata (20 feet or less) of a lake or in shallow water close to shore. Thermal discharges, tributaries, rocky shorelines, and the like contribute to warmer water locales (warmer in this instance may be 46 degrees, as opposed to 43 or 44 through the rest of the lake). Pockets of water warmer than the rest of the lake may be found, and they can hold catchable fish.

Ultimately the upper layer of water will warm to the point where trout are uncomfortable. Then they seek deeper, cooler environs. This seems rather obvious but many anglers overlook this fact and continue to fish surface and shallow waters during the day at this time, when there is little hope of finding trout in such areas.

Eventually a lake (except those in cold northern locales) will stratify, and a thermocline will develop. The depth of the thermocline, which separates distinctly different temperatures of water, can range from 15 or 20 feet below the surface to 100 or more in very deep lakes with good oxygen levels. Once a lake has stratified, you need to start looking for the thermocline and establishing the depths of the preferred temperature of trout. In the case of brown and rainbow trout, the place where those temperatures meet with the bottom of the lake can be a very strong locale for catching fish, especially if they are prominent aspects of underwater terrain, such as a point or ledge near shore. Lake trout, which prefer temperatures below the thermocline, will orient to very deep water, often residing on or just above the bottom, where they feed. They also foray into warmer water to shoals and reefs to feed, then depart for deeper environs again. Checking the water with a thermometer at various levels is the only sure way to know where desirable water temperatures can be found.

Temperature enters the picture in a horizontal as well as vertical sense in the early part of the season, where one might be looking for pockets of warm water (near a sun-bathed rocky shore, a tributary, or a warm shallow cove), or, in larger lakes, a surface distinction between temperatures. The latter is likely to happen on huge bodies of water, such as the Great Lakes, some of which develop a vertical thermal barrier that is especially conducive to steelhead fishing and which is prominent in a typical year from mid-May through June. This so-called thermal bar is a mixing of water temperatures leading to the development of a thermocline. The important point is that the surface temperature breaks attract trout (and especially steelhead, on the Great Lakes). Remember that temperature is only a guideline for your fishing efforts; trout will inhabit warmer or cooler water if other factors, particularly forage presence, warrant it.

Another clue to solving the puzzle of fishing for trout in lakes is to know what trout feed on in a lake environment and where that forage is likely to be located. Lake trout forage includes alewives, smelt, ciscoes, chubs, sculpin, assorted species of shiners and darters, insects, and even yellow perch, crayfish, and other trout. It is usually a certainty that the prominent forage species in any environment constitutes the major part of the diet of a trout. In most large lakes and reservoirs, this is alewives or smelt. Lake trout, however, which spend a lot of midsummer time in deep environs, may feed primarily on sculpin and deviate from this relative abundance generality.

In far-northern waters that are fairly sterile, there is no great concentration of bait fish. Lake trout there eat whitefish or other trout, and we've had good success using dark-colored plugs that imitated the darkly colored lakers. In those same environments, we've caught small lakers with stomachs completely full of mosquitoes. It takes a lot of cruising to fill up the belly of a 5-pound trout with insects, so you have to suspect that there was a lack of bait fish.

Temperature is an important factor in the location of trout in lakes, both in a vertical as well as horizontal sense. Steelhead, shown here, are often found on a surface thermal bar in late spring.

On the other hand, there are many situations where trout in lakes are extraordinarily difficult to catch because there is such an abundance of bait fish available to them. When there is a plethora of bait in the active temperature band of trout, your offerings pall in comparison, and trout can be extremely selective.

It pays to know whether prominent forage is found deep or shallow at various times of the year and how bait fish temperature preferences relate to those of trout (smelt and alewives, for instance, respectively prefer 48- and 54-degree water, plus or minus a few degrees). There is often reason to suspect that trout prefer food over temperature (within reason, of course), so it makes sense to be fishing in places, and at depth levels, where both food and temperature requirements are met.

That's why reefs are attractive to lake trout; lakers can come out of deep water to stay by a reef to feed, then return to the depths. The deep water/shallow water interface near islands can be similarly productive. In addition to such deep or open water structure, a sharply sloping shoreline often provides foraging opportunities, especially for brown trout. The edges of long underwater bars or shoals are places by which bait migrate naturally, and these logically present feeding opportunities for trout.

These are the kinds of places where trout may be located, and they form another part of the puzzle of where to find and catch trout in lakes.

An ideal situation in large lakes is to find a place where all three criteria of temperature, forage, and shore structure coincide. If you are looking for schools of bait fish and monitoring preferred water temperature, you could do no better than to find both of these where the thermocline intersects the bottom. This would be a prime place to begin looking for trout in the summer on large lakes. This is particularly true of brown trout. These fish don't generally inhabit the vast expanse of open water after late spring and seem to gravitate toward places where shallow areas meet deep areas, where they can be comfortable and expect to ambush prey. If you're fishing open, mid-lake areas and not finding trout, look for fish closer to the bottom near sharply sloping shorelines. Trout may be more concentrated, incidentally, along a sharply sloped shoreline than along a moderately sloped shoreline that has a wider band of preferable temperatures; that's one advantage of the sharper bottom contour. In midsummer, deep trout may cruise over a large area in the horizontal strata of their active preferred temperature range, so in large lakes you may have a lot of scouring to do.

One of the things that you'll find true about fishing for trout in lakes is that the places that produce trout will repeatedly produce trout over time. This is one instance where trout in lakes are like their flowing-water brethren.

The more you fish a particular body of water, the more you'll discover the nuances of that lake's fish and begin to put some of the puzzle together. You may well find that bigger, older fish seem to have a stronger orientation toward temperature than smaller, younger fish; small fish seem likely to visit higher temperature zones to feed and then return to colder water more readily than canny older fish. You may find that trout in their preferred temperature range are quite likely to be active feeders; sometimes you observe this on sonar equipment. You may also discover, in nutrient-rich lakes where there is deep cold water but an absence of oxygen at deeper levels, that trout may be driven to seek relief in the tributaries during the summer. The direction and velocity of wind sometimes has a marked effect on the location of bait and/or trout.

Look for brown trout in the summer to be located where the thermocline intercepts a sharply sloped shoreline.

TECHNIQUE/TACKLE

When trout are shallow and near the surface, they can be caught by trolling, casting from shore or in a float tube, or drifting with bait. Although casting is the most fun, trolling is often more popular, because it allows you to cover a lot of ground and look for active, aggressive fish, particularly trout that perhaps have not been spooked or otherwise bothered by other fishermen and boaters. Drift-fishing with a boat usually is a live-bait proposition (many anglers are quite successful with this technique using the prominent forage, such as alewives, for bait), but it is slow and, where motors are permitted on lakes, less productive than lure trolling. If you cast from shore, you may simply be limited to one spot, such as a pier or break wall, and must cast repeatedly in hope of attracting a moving, incoming fish to strike your lure. This can pay off in tributary areas where warm river water attracts a significant number of fish. In small lakes, however, it pays to be mobile, concentrating shore-casting efforts near prominent points, inlets, steep banks, rock- and boulder-studded shores, shorelines with sharp drop-offs to deep water, and warm bay and cove areas. Try casting spoons and plugs (crankbaits or sinking, minnow-style baits) from shore for brown trout and jigs and plugs in northern lakes for lake trout.

Once the trout are deep, however, it becomes tough, if not impossible, to catch them from shore, and here the boater with the ability to get his lures down, to scout for fish with some type of sonar and with an opportunity to ply a lot of water, has a distinct advantage.

Many methods have been employed to get lures deep for trout. These include using wire line, lead core line, diving planers, heavily weighted nylon monofilament lines, and downriggers. Downriggers, which permit controlled depth fishing and allow you to fight a fish unencumbered by restricting objects, have developed into an extremely efficient and practical fishing tool, particularly where it is important to present lures at specific, deep levels. While they originated with Great Lakes fishing, downriggers are suitable for fishing in nearly any lake that has trout.

In fishing for trout in lakes, once you have established some idea of where and how deep to fish, the consideration becomes what type of lure to fish, what color, and at what speed. Spoons, plugs, and spinners all catch trout, as do jigs at times. Many flat-line trollers use fairly heavy spoons to help them get down, but light spoons (including the wafer-like so-called flutterspoons) have really come on in recent years because they can be used so well with downriggers; they don't sink as fast on a turn, they run at the same depth as the downrigger, and they have an appealing wobbling action. These same flutterspoons can be used with bead-chain sinkers or other types of weights as well.

Spoons are unquestionably the favorite lure for trout in lakes, ranging all the way from small, thin, 2-inch-long models to the 2-ounce monsters trolled for giant lakers in the Northwest Territories. Spinners take some smaller trout — and especially recently stocked trout, often near tributaries — but they don't present as much of an image of a substantial meal to a fish. Jigs are an underrated trout lure in most places because fishermen are too preoccupied with trolling other baits, or don't think they should waste their time by stopping to jig a lure in places that may not contain trout.

Plugs have a special prominence for trout in the spring and when fish are shallow. The traditional minnow-imitation-style plugs do well for brown trout, as do those

Spoons are the pre-eminent lure for trout in lakes, followed by plugs. Pictured is a lake trout from the Great Lakes.

fat-bodied plugs that may imitate alewives. Wide-wobbling plugs and erratic-swimming plugs can be productive for steelhead, as well as lakers and browns, and they help emphasize the importance of lure action and behavior. Trout are often very curious fish, and they may follow a lure for a considerable distance (lakers are especially noted for this). Floating/diving-style plugs respond well to changes in boat speed, the presence of current, a turn, or other factors that might influence or momentarily change the swimming pattern of a lure, and these are often the factors that cause a trout to strike.

One of the vastly underrated elements of lure fishing for trout in lakes is that of lure or boat speed. Many Great Lakes fishermen monitor boat speed closely because they know how speed affects lure action and which species of fish relate to slow (lake trout), medium (browns and steelhead), and fast (salmon) speeds. Boat speed and lure speed may not be the same (wind and underwater currents affect it), however, and, in addition to lure style and color, the speed at which it is fished can be an especially important element in success. Keep in mind that all lures have a top speed, after which they no longer exhibit the action they were designed to have, and that some lures are incompatible at specific speeds (in other words, the best speed for one lure may not be a desirable speed for another lure and they should not be fished together). Always be alert to how your lure is working at a given boat speed, and check this before you start fishing it.

Color, meanwhile, remains the big puzzle in lure fishing for trout in lakes. Matching the hatch, as one would by using a particular size and color of fly when stream trout fishing, can be the thing to do in smaller inland lakes but is seldom the way to go on large bodies of water. We've caught some exceptionally large brown trout in small

Minnow-imitation plugs are particularly good for brown trout trolling early in the season.

reservoirs by using lures that closely resembled (in shape, size, and color) the prominent forage fish for those trout. By contrast, on the Great Lakes we've found that you may need to use lures that are smaller than the average prey fish and nowhere near as representative in color (black, orange, and green, for instance). Color selection is becoming a more astute and closely followed aspect of fishing for trout in lakes, and usage depends not only on present forage, but on the clarity of the water, the varying intensity of light, and the depth to be fished. The better trout fishermen are constantly changing colors, using lures that mix potentially productive colors, and switching lures to find what works. And what works one day often doesn't work the next.

Notice, however, that while everyone is switching between spoons that have some blue or some green or some pink or some other attractive color to them (on one side or as a strip of prism tape), they are combining this with silver or brass colors. The question is to which color the fish are responding. It's best to keep experimenting and changing colors until you hit on something that seems to indicate a pattern. One fish on a particular color doesn't make a pattern, but two fish get us putting out more lures in that color. Some fishermen, once they get three fish on one particular color, change all their lures to that color. This so-called monochromatic fishing obviously can be a self-fulfilling prophesy. You might hedge your bets with at least one or two lures that are of a different color or shade of the hot color, especially when fishing deep enough with downriggers to allow the use of a slider rig (a second lure, usually a spoon, on a main fishing line).

In addition to finding the right color, you have to find the right distance to set your lure back. Trout in the Great Lakes are routinely caught on 30- to 100-foot drop-backs on flat-lines, downriggers, or side-planers. Where boat traffic allows, it may be advisable to get 70 to 150 feet of line back from the release to lure when flat-lining or using side-planers. On smaller lakes, however, longer lengths may be employed, including up to 250 feet behind the boat on flat-lines. When the fish are abundant and action is hot, however, you can shorten up on drop-backs and still do well.

Whatever length line you use, it's wise to spice up your presentations frequently by making turns and increasing or decreasing boat speed. Some trout appear to be followers, swimming behind lures for considerable distances before losing interest or striking. Lakers are notorious for this. Vary your trolling routine by making turns, or following S-shaped patterns; this throws a momentary change into the working of the lure and sometimes draws a strike. Periodically increase the throttle or put the motor into neutral for a few seconds, especially if you're not catching anything and/or mark fish on the graph recorder.

SEASONS

Perhaps the most popular and successful time to fish for trout in lakes is spring, when fish are relatively shallow and often fairly close to shore. Therefore, it seems appropriate to direct a few comments about that activity.

A key point to realize about trolling technique is that line placement, lure presentation, and boat control are absolutely critical for success. Shallow fish are easily spooked. You can't motor through the shallows and expect fish to stay around and/or to be exceedingly receptive to the offering you trail behind. The simplest shallow trolling

When trout, like this brown, are shallow and close to shore, they are also spooky. Good boat manipulation skills, line placement, and the use of planer boards contribute to fishing success.

of any kind is to run a flat-line straight out behind the boat. Many anglers prefer to flat-line off of side-planer boards, which bring lures further away from the boat's path of travel. Remember that the clearer the water, the shallower and spookier the fish; the more local boat activity there is, the longer the line you need.

Trout in shallow water near shore or that are close to the surface in open water move out of the boat's path of travel. That is one reason why you seldom see trout on sonar equipment in less than 15 feet of water. Proper boat manipulation can bring lures into the range of fish that may not have been in the boat's path or that have moved out of it; so be alert to this aspect of trolling and regularly alter the lure's path of travel by turning, steering in an S-shaped pattern, driving in other irregular ways, or by increasing or decreasing the speed of the boat. It is also a good tactic to sweep in and out from shore and to plan strategically advantageous approaches to such areas as points, sandbars, islands, shoals, channels, and the like.

A host of deep and shallow fishing combinations are possible in spring, too. When fishing near shore, you can run two or three strategically spaced lines off a shore-side planer board. On the open water side of the boat, you have the option of running a surface or diving lure on a long flat line, running a lure deep via the downrigger, or running one or more lures off the other side-planer. Moreover, the amount of territory that can be covered is vastly increased. If you run two side-planers boards, each 60 feet to either side of the boat, and have two fishermen in the boat, you can run four lines over a 40-yard span of water. If the bottom drops off sharply near shore, as it does in many trout lakes, you could be working over a few feet of water on the shore side of the boat and over 40 feet on the opposite side, presenting your lures to fish that would not ordinarily see them and would not be frightened by the passage of your boat. On reservoirs, which often drop off sharply near some shore areas, fish the open water side of the boat with a lure set behind a downrigger. Straight behind the boat run a shallow- or medium-running plug on a relatively long flat-line. On the shore side, run a planer board close to shore, using a shallow-running minnow plug nearest to shore on a moderate length line and then either a similar plug or a spoon on the inside planer board line. This covers the environs near shore in such a situation quite well.

Your primary quarry here will be brown trout. These fish are not extremely difficult to catch and are found close to shore, meaning that they are accessible to trollers of all levels of experience and with all types of boats and fishing equipment.

Because there is no need to venture far from shore in the spring and because there are a lot of boats trolling the same areas (especially on weekends and on the Great Lakes), fish do get spooked. Traditionally at this time, trout seek warm water, but when there are hordes of boats and hundreds of lures constantly swimming by, they move. It pays to keep an eye out for other boats to see how the brotherhood is doing, though. If everybody is catching trout, it should be obvious, and you should be catching fish, too. If you aren't, you need to make some strategic changes. Key factors in successful brown trout trolling in spring are trolling speed, lure color and type, fishing depth, and the distance the lure is from the boat. A change in one or more of these elements may be needed. If you see a lot of boats and no fish—or very few fish—are being caught, move. Get away from the pack; troll the shoreline away from the tributary; look for a shoal, small creek mouth, or pocket of warm water; and fish areas with little or no boat traffic (or the least traffic).

Similarly, if you are flexible, willing to experiment or go with hunches, you can greatly aid your own efforts. Everyone focuses on the magic lure color to fish for spring brown trout, and the fish do sometimes show preferences for certain colors. Chartreuse and green or lime green are often hot colors on the Great Lakes, as is a chartreuse and red combination. Sometimes it's all red or bright orange. This can change frequently during the season or from day to day, and you should vary the menu.

When starting for the day, put a different color lure on each rod being fished. When two fish are caught on the same color lure, put more of that color out. If more fish are caught—but all on the same rod (it happens quite often)—then it's probably the action or depth of the lure, not the color, that counts most, so concentrate similar lures at that depth. On some days, color is almost irrelevant, however, and you just have to keep making changes. Having the right speed, covering a lot of territory, and changing lures regularly then are the main factors.

Plugs are the primary lure choice in the spring, though spoons take on added stature as the season progresses and the water warms, and eventually become more effective than plugs. Jointed minnow-imitation plugs, 4 1/2 to 6 inches long, rate highest, followed by unjointed minnow plugs and shallow-running crankbaits. The jointed plugs have a strong swimming action, and the minnow style well imitate the smelt and alewives that trout forage on. Crankbaits and alewife-imitation plugs sometimes catch fish, but seldom better or more than minnow-bodied lures. Since most fishing is done in shallow water and these plugs don't dive very deep, you can effectively troll slowly (but beware of going too slow), and in a stop-and-go fashion, without getting hung up and while still getting good lure action.

By shallow water, we mean water near the shore that is several feet deep and within

Plugs like these, in assorted colors, are commonly used for trout in lakes.

the first 10 feet of the surface in water that is up to 30 feet deep. As the season advances, more trolling is done away from the immediate shore and deeper. But for much of spring, shallow and close-to-the-surface fishing, via flat-lines and side-planer boards, is the norm. Downriggers come into play when you start getting away from shore; here, set lures back about 40 feet when traffic is heavy and up to 80 feet if traffic allows.

At some point, you may employ downriggers and side-planers together and use both spoons and plugs as long as they have compatible speed capacities. Fish spoons relatively shallow on downriggers to start. Consider using spoon-rigged sliders. A slider could be fished at 15 feet while the main lure is at 20 or 30; this puts an extra lure in the water, even though it's close to the boat, and sometimes those who can run a lot of lures have the greatest success. This is an advantage that big boaters have. Therefore, sliders can be especially useful to small boaters, who also have the advantage of being able to navigate easily in close quarters and ultra shallow water and to make tight turns if trolling line length allows.

With side-planers and downriggers, pay close attention to the tension on your line release devices. This is a small item that is overlooked by many anglers and results in a lot of "dropped" fish—trout that strike a lure, snap the line out of the release, and then get free immediately or shortly after the angler plays it. The reason for much of this is insufficient release tension; fish never get hooked.

Tighten release tension as much as you think the line can stand. This will significantly increase hooking percentage. One drawback: when using heavy line, you might drag a small fish because it doesn't apply enough force to pop the line out of the release. Keep an eye on the rod tip to see if it starts bouncing a little strangely; if so, there may be a small fish on the rod.

Appropriate line size varies. It often seems that line size doesn't matter a great deal, but 8-pound line is a good choice, perhaps going even lighter, like 4 and 6, on a noodle rod for the extra challenge. However, many anglers, especially big-boat and charter-boat operators, use 14- or 16-pound line. These fishermen run many lines and often fish with inexperienced anglers. Stronger line allows them to subdue fish quickly and leave other trolling lines in the water to keep from resetting them, which increases the chance of getting additional fish.

Brown trout move a lot. Yet sometimes they are briefly clustered. Trollers should keep this in mind when they land a fish; too many trollers get a fish and then keep trolling away from the area where they've just had success. Anytime you catch a trout, make another pass or two in the same vicinity as quickly as possible afterward. If you catch two fish relatively near one another, work the area thoroughly. If nothing happens after awhile, move on. More often than not, the fish will be scattered.

Non-boaters can enjoy spring brown trout angling, too, even though they aren't as mobile as boaters. Action concentrates around warm-water locales, in bays, near creeks, along docks and piers, and by thermal discharges, often very close to shore. The most popular and accessible locations often draw a crowd. Some people fish from shore, many get in the water as far as their chest waders will allow, and a few use belly boats. Heavy casting spoons, in 1/2- to 1-ounce sizes, and weighted minnow plugs or crankbaits, are the mainstays, using long spinning rods and light (6- to 10-pound) line for achieving distance. Bait fishing with live or dead smelt, alewives, or shiners may be the ticket, too.

LAKE TROUT

Another very popular big-water activity is angling for lake trout, and since this differs a bit from fishing for the species of trout that are found in lakes, it's appropriate to direct a few comments specifically toward laker fishing. It used to be that the primary lake trout fishing technique was to troll a prodigious length of weighted line and flashy hardware using a rug-beater rod. That's still the game of some veteran laker anglers, but it needn't be only thus. Light tackle is not only a reality for lake trout fishing today, but a practicality for deep and shallow fishing; and trolling, although the most preferred method, isn't the only way to take these fish.

To enjoy fighting a lake trout, you should use the lightest line that fishing circumstances will allow. Those relatively few people who have played 40- to 60-pound lakers on 20- to 30-pound test line for 30 to 60 minutes will disagree, as will those who customarily ply north-country waters by trolling 2-ounce spoons equipped with monstrous hooks, but it's a fact that the average laker that one catches, in the states or Canada, is fairly small—3 to 6 pounds—and not much of a thrill when landed with a beefy stick and thick line. Furthermore, lake trout are a denizen of open water. They may be bottom- or reef-dwelling fish, but once you hook a laker, it's strictly an unobstructed, open-water tussle. That's prime for light-line fishing.

With light line, lake trout will give a good account of themselves, particularly those caught deep in Great Lakes waters.

Downriggers have made deep fishing for lake trout with light line particularly feasible. Four- through 10-pound-test is a good range to use, with 6 or 8 being optimum. Mitigating factors, however, include whether you are using some type of attractor, such as a dodger or cowbells, which exert a lot of pressure on the line; if your lure (and line) is scraping rocky bottom terrain, causing line abrasion; and if you are catching larger and harder-fighting fish in the same locale (such as chinook salmon, which happens in the Great Lakes).

In most places in the southern part of the lake trout's range, trolling for these fish is mainly done at relatively deep levels. This is because lake trout are attuned to very cold water (mid-40's to low 50's) that is situated below the thermocline and because they are often near bottom and some form of hard structure (primarily shoals or reefs) from late spring through early fall. The downrigger provides a means of getting to a specific depth and being able to play a fish on an unencumbered line and is easier to use than wire or lead core line. The end result is that the fish is able to be more active.

Not all trolling for lakers is done at decompression depths. Rocky islands and reefs are prime foraging grounds for lake trout, which characteristically move into such spots to feed (even in the summer and even if the water temperature is higher than they generally prefer), then retreat to deep water. Also, early and late in the year

In northern waters, lakers can be caught by shore anglers at the mouths of rivers and along rocky reefs and points, either by casting plugs, spoons, or jigs.

are good times to find lake trout in the upper 20 feet of a lake or reservoir if the water temperature is favorable. Then, light tackle is particularly advantageous, using flat lines run straight behind the boat or off side-planer boards.

Lake trout are one of the most curious freshwater fish, a fact that can make you more successful at catching them when you know how to appeal to this trait. Lakers may follow a lure for a considerable distance, sometimes nudging the lure and sometimes just staying right behind it for long distances like a bird dog. In super-clear water, we've watched lakers come seemingly from nowhere to follow a lure, which was being cast and retrieved, right to the boat. Sometimes there were several fish following. Sometimes the fish would follow the same lure a second time after it was taken out of the water and then cast away again. Followers could sometimes be teased into striking a lure by stopping and starting it. When trolling for lake trout while holding a rod, we have often felt the spoon or plug being bumped by a trout, then caught the fish either by dropping some line back and then resuming trolling, by quickly retrieving a few feet of line, or by jerking the rod tip to dart and falter the lure. Jerking or pumping sometimes elicits a strike even when fish haven't bumped the lure. This entire phenomenon makes us wonder just how many near misses are had by lake trout trollers who keep their rods in a holder all the time or who don't affect some periodic change in the swimming behavior of their lures.

Changes in boat speed, turns, and manipulative boat operation momentarily change the swimming pattern of a lure, and these are often factors that cause a lake trout to strike. This is an instance where an electric downrigger that automatically oscillates a lure at regular intervals can trigger following lakers to strike.

A time-honored rod-holding, trolling tactic, employed by lake trout and landlocked salmon fishermen who primarily use light spoons and streamer flies, is to hold the rod nearly parallel to the water and jerk it backward from time to time. The lure speeds up momentarily, then flutters, and this behavior draws strikes. So important was this to some New England trollers that automatic devices were fashioned from windshield wiper motors to achieve the same affect, and now one prominent manufacturer recently started producing a more sophisticated version of this gadget for national distribution.

It's important to realize, however, that it isn't the faster speed of the jerked-back lure that draws strikes as much as it is change in behavior. Lakers basically like a slow presentation, quite slow, in fact, compared to salmon and other trout.

It is because of the laker's preference for slow-moving lures that the most successful lake trout tactic on the Great Lakes is to run a small plastic wobbling bait (called a Peanut by some) about 12 to 18 inches behind a dodger or cowbell attractor. Some spoons and small diving plugs are also worked in this fashion. In areas where there is a sandy bottom and when fish presumed to be lakers are spotted via sonar on the bottom in deep water (maybe 100 to 150 feet in summer), you can literally set your line by dropping the down-rigger weight till it hits bottom, then raise it up a turn. The lead from weight to lure needn't be long. (Some bottom-trollers like to use a banana-shaped downrigger weight for this, incidentally, dragging it right on the bottom.)

Not all lake trout fishing is done by trolling, however. We have had some excellent jig fishing for lakers. One nice thing about jigging for lake trout—besides feeling the strike and having a little better play of the fish—is that the lure has a single hook, which makes removal easy. You can also press the barb down and make unhooking, right in the water without having to handle the fish, easier still. This is particularly advisable in places where there are size limits or closed seasons on lake trout.

Light jigs can provide exciting small lake trout action in north-country rivers, and large jigs are occasionally as or more effective than trolling spoons or plugs in places where lake trout are abundant.

This sounds patently obvious, yet this differs vastly from trolling, wherein you cover a lot of territory looking for lakers while you are fishing for them. Jigging is not a way to cover much ground. Generally it's best to restrict jigging to fishing known reefs, fishing for bottom-hugging trout that are spotted on sonar or fishing in places where you've previously (or recently) caught lakers. In north-country locales, it's worth jigging at river mouths, to the side of heavy current where a major tributary dumps into a large lake. You can also catch lake trout by casting and retrieving small spinners and spoons, streamer flies, and plugs, primarily in northerly locales. Try this with some moderately light line and then see how well a lake trout can fight.

CHAPTER EIGHT
TROUT IN RIVERS

This chapter will focus on brook, brown, and rainbow trout, the three fish that provide most of the trout fishing in North American rivers and streams.

Brook trout are probably the Crown Prince of these species, certainly inspiring the most sentimental interest. A North American native, and actually a member of the char family, brookies are the most beautiful of the stream trout. In fall spawning color, the male fish radiates lime green, orange, red, purple, and inky black colors which are seldom matched in any other freshwater species.

Unfortunately, native trophy brook trout have all but disappeared from their once vast range due to the influences of civilization. Fishermen must travel far off the beaten path, usually to fast-running wilderness waters, to find the larger brookies. A few waterways in Quebec, Labrador, Newfoundland, and northern Manitoba, plus a number of northeasterly flowing rivers in northern Ontario, remain the last strongholds of trophy-sized, native brook trout in North America.

This isn't to say that brook trout, which are also known as speckled trout, can't be found closer to home. From Minnesota to New England, small waters carry more diminutive fish. There, the average brookie is more hand-sized than net-sized; a 2-pounder is a trophy, and a 12-incher is a big fish.

There are also certain sections of Montana and northern Idaho where native brookies can be found, but these are limited. Brook trout are distributed throughout the entire Great Lakes system and, in recent decades, have multiplied dramatically. In lakes such as Michigan, where brook trout were once an oddity, they have now become a standard catch for local anglers, who find them most available during November and December near warm-water discharges.

Stocking has played a major role in the availability of speckled trout. Where fishing or environmental changes have depleted the natural fish population, hatchery-raised brook trout have been planted. (Hatchery fish are easily identified. They appear less colorful and a bit fatter than native fish. Plus, stocked fish will likely have a clipped or damaged pectoral fin. Often, when caught soon after being planted, stocked trout have a liver-like taste, which comes from the commercial food they are raised on and which takes a couple of weeks in wild habitat to dissipate.) Even so, in most areas, there are fish enough to carry on a remnant of a native brook trout population. Stocking has played a major role in the availability of brown trout and rainbow trout as well.

Brown trout are not a North American native, having been imported here from Europe in the 1880s. They have been planted extensively, however, and, as they have

A black and white photo can't do justice to the beautiful coloration of brook trout.

a greater tolerance for warm water than brook trout, they are relatively abundant and popular. They grow extremely large in some lakes and reservoirs, as well as in certain rivers, though they do run smaller in most rivers and streams. River brown trout sport a great deal more color than their lake brethren and tend to make much better table fare.

Browns are a late fall/early winter spawner. It is not unusual to find brown trout on their nests in late December, although in many places you can't fish for them — or brook trout — in the latter part of the season. Like all trout, browns spawn over gravel/sand pockets.

Brown trout tend to lie in slower and warmer waters than brookies. Typical brown trout water is a deep, dark-colored slow-moving, stream that winds for miles through woods and farmland. Here and there, a dark 10-foot-deep hole is found just downstream from a shallow rippling area. Brown trout are also found in faster, wider water, and shallow water, too. Many rivers that possess rapid-flowing areas support good numbers of brown trout, especially in the pools and slicks.

With browns, for the most part, only small fish can be taken during the day, especially if it is warm and the sun is bright; overcast days are often better. It often takes late evening and darkness to bring out the larger fish. Browns are notorious for feeding at night, and while there is merit to fishing then, relatively few anglers do so in rivers. Dropping a gob of night crawlers under an overhanging bank and allowing it to drift with current is often the only way of drawing out those little-seen lunkers from undercut bank holes in the daytime in hot months.

Rainbow trout and their steelhead (anadromous) kin are found in numerous waterways throughout North America. Steelhead exist chiefly in large Western flowages and Great Lakes tributaries. These fish prefer fast water and are a hard-fighting, spectacular-leaping fish. They thrive in intermediate-temperature water, somewhere between that preferred by brook and brown trout in the 50- to 60-degree range. Unlike the others, they spawn in early spring, often after migrating up rivers or streams (in the case of steelhead that migration may cover a great distance). Also unlike the others, they will feed heavily on the eggs of their brethren; as a result, eggs or things that imitate eggs are used quite successfully. Nymphs, crustaceans, minnows, insects, and leeches round out their diet. Flies, worms, and salmon eggs are the most popular offerings generally. But in some environs, kernel corn and baby marshmallows are favored bait offerings.

In early spring, rainbows spawn in rocky, fast-flowing waters. A spawning area is usually located within the confines of an eddy created by a bottom-hugging rock where current rushes up and around. Fishermen drop salmon eggs (singly or in a sack) and worms directly in front of the fish in this locale. When not here, they are situated in deeper, main-flow water. Spring rainbow spawning runs can be an interesting hunt-and-fish adventure if you are able to search for and find fish, then work for a specific fish. Spawn bags, which are a cluster of eggs in fine nylon mesh, on a No. 2 or 4 short-shanked salmon egg hook, with a couple of split-shot up the line, are basic fare during this time for bait anglers, while fishermen work brightly colored streamers or sponge flies, drifting the offering across and directly in front of the fish repeatedly.

Rainbow trout are often found in pockets behind rocks, and it's smart to fish every pocket in fast-water areas. A Muddler Minnow or a streamer on a No. 10 hook is an especially good offering, as are small (No. 1 and 0 sizes) spinners.

A great many brook and brown trout are caught by fly fishing. Fly anglers usually use a light outfit (7- or 8-foot rod for 4 to 7 weight line) in order to fish small streams,

This dark steelhead was caught in April during spawning time; notice the milt dripping from the fish. Salmon eggs, worms, flies, and wobbling plugs are among the preferred offerings.

using perhaps an outfit on the upper end of this range for larger or more open waters and/or places where big fish might be found. Leader length should be about 7 feet long for small waters, slightly longer elsewhere (equal to the length of rod is often a normal measurement), tapering to a 2X or 3X tippet. Flies must be selected according to the type of minnow or aquatic insect that needs to be imitated.

Spring and summer insect hatches particularly attract river trout. In the spring, these hatches may occur during the day, but then, and later in the season, they may be most evident around sundown and last long into the night. Trout, especially browns, will feed on meatier forage in the night as well. Shiners, chubs, and other small fish are preyed upon, usually in a long, shallow, gravel flat above a deep pool.

There is an enormous assortment of dry and wet flies, nymphs, and streamers to use on trout, depending on the circumstances. Small spinners and minnow-imitating plugs are possible river brown trout catchers, as is bait. Bait may include many items, such as worms, chubs, or clipped crayfish.

The typical river brook and brown trout is a scrappy fish in all sizes. The larger fish put up a particularly good fight. Unlike rainbow trout, a brookie seldom jumps. He is a stubborn fighter, preferring to dig down and bore into the deeper, heavier water and employing a series of twisting, running rolls. It is during these heavy rolls that an angler with a limber, forgiving fly rod has an advantage over another angler with a shorter, stiffer rod. A fly rod gives, providing leverage and constant pressure on the hooked trout. The brown trout will, however, not only dig deep, but also jump, sometimes often.

Fly fishing tactics vary, of course. Nymphs must be retrieved in short jerking movements and at an angle downstream. Streamer flies, which represent minnows, are retrieved at a steady pace across or upstream in rivers. Dry flies are cast upstream and float naturally downstream while the angler gathers line rapidly. To work a fly across stream or retrieve upstream causes your offering to drag or move in an unnatural fashion, and fish will seldom strike a fly presented this way. In a very slow pool or a midstream beaver pond, a dry fly should sit motionless and drift with a breeze if there is one. Give the dry fly enough slack by mending line so it drifts without line pull. Pick an open area for your fly when a heavy hatch is on.

Some of the better brook trout flies are stonefly, caddisfly, and mayfly larvae imitations in nymphs; Mickey Finn, Royal Coachman, and Black Dace in streamers; and duns, caddis, mayflies, and bivisibles for dry flies. The Muddler Minnow can be used in all aspects by varying hook length and fly size.

Spin fishermen have a lot of success with river trout also, using small spinners, spoons, and sometimes minnow-imitation plugs, as well as night crawlers where bait fishing is legal, and large spoons and spinners in big, swift-flowing waters. Spinning equipment should be light or ultralight, with lines ranging from 4- to 8-pound strength. In some smaller streams, you might use 2-pound line and a 5-foot ultralight rod. Line capacity and drag is seldom a factor with reels used for spinning for trout, though they should balance well with the rod used. Where big steelhead are to be encountered, line capacity and drag are more crucial.

There are a number of different size flowages in which brook, brown, and rainbow trout are taken, and portions of these can be extremely fast or dramatically slow. There are some excellent trout-holding areas which can be found in nearly any flowage, and we'll discuss major ones in regard to fishing presentation.

A fly rod, a floating line, and a dry fly are the epitome of river trout fishing for many anglers, though all types of flies have merit at different times.

Slicks.   Fast, hard-flowing areas are known in trout-angling circles as slicks. In the summer, they are probably the best places to find trout.

Slicks are most often found downstream from an eddy or pool. It's the portion of the tailrace where water is running hard with little surface disturbance, and appears relatively deep. The width of these places varies with the flowage, perhaps being just 5 to 15 feet across or covering nearly the entire breadth of a river. There is little surface disturbance in slicks. They are smooth-surfaced and give the appearance of being difficult to fish because the water flows very strongly. The water may only be 2 feet deep, but the appearance of strong movement baffles many anglers, and they often don't present their offerings properly, getting poor results. Sometimes it's necessary to take measures to get down deeper. This may mean using a faster-sinking fly line or increasing lure weight.

Anglers also need to slow down their retrieve when presenting a lure in a cross-stream or upstream fashion in a slick. This keeps lures (especially spoons and spinners) from turning or running too rapidly and gives bottom-hugging trout time to determine that the lure now traveling above looks like something they would eat. Trout in such fast-moving water tend to hold longer, perhaps to make sure of their target. This does not hold true when fishing remote, seldom-fished waters, as the fish there are usually less cautious.

The most successful presentation comes from casting upstream and retrieving with the current or casting across-stream and drifting your offering downstream (see Diagram 1, page 105). Direct, cross-stream retrieves with some lures also work well in slicks.

Casting just slightly upstream across from the target area and retrieving at a moderate speed may be very effective, particularly when jig/spinner combos are used. Maybe this represents a darting minnow attempting to swim across hard-flowing water. Keep your rod tip high and allow your lure to "float" as it moves across the current. This helps prevent snagging on the bottom and allows the lure to swim effectively.

The selection of lures for fishing slicks depends on the size of river and the average size of the trout it holds. Where small native and stocked brook trout are present, small brown, black, or gray jigs work well, as do small spinners and spoons. In the larger rivers of the far north, use 1/4- to 1/2-ounce black jigs with undersized spinner blades (No. 0 or crappie size), crankbaits, and medium-size spoons.

A different type of slick exists in other sections of rivers. This is directly between, and slightly upstream of, a pair of sizable rocks or rock outcroppings in a river (see Diagram 2, below). Here, as before, the current appears to be strong, the surface is undisturbed, and water depth varies. The main difference between large slick areas and this locale is the presence of exposed large rocks, and the fact that this slick is much narrower and constricted. Normally there is a slight 2- to 6-inch bulge of surface water just above the rock obstructions; this causes the slick effect between them and is visible from a low angle. The best such slick is one with no surface water disturbance and a depth of at least 3 feet. Trout will hold directly between the rocks or just upstream a foot or so.

Diagram 1

Diagram 2

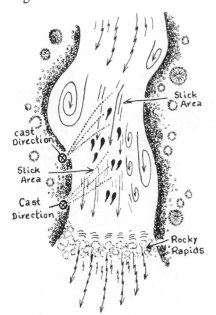

When fishing a slick, make casts slightly cross and upstream, as shown here. Don't overlook the small slick that exists just above a pair of rocks, as trout will hold just above them.

You must fish this area from above or slightly above and across stream, perhaps using a little heavier lure than you might elsewhere. Fly fishermen may find this area ideal for working a streamer in a slow, steady retrieve. Add tiny split-shot or use lead-bodied flies if necessary.

Upstream waterfall breaks, or lips.   These are especially good trout-holding areas on fast and moderate-flowing trout streams where rock gravel or clay is found above rapids or a falls. Few fishermen work the dark, swift water just above the falls or rapid drops. Yet trout, particularly large brookies, are found here.

In this spot, there are often large flat rock beds that create a dishpan shelf across the river. Current is forced up and over such structure, resulting in rapids or waterfalls below. At this place, trout wait for struggling food that gets caught in the forceful current.

Fishermen should stand well above the drop and cast directly out into midstream, holding the rod tip up at a 90-degree angle. Make the retrieve slow and allow the lure to float downstream toward the lip with the current flow, keeping it just off the bottom. Once the lure is about 10 feet from the drop, lift the rod tip up to a 12 o'clock position and hold steady. Don't retrieve line or let it out. Hold the lure stationary for 5 to 15 seconds. If a wary trout is going to strike, it will do so within this time frame. Then retrieve about 10 feet of line and hold the lure stationary again, letting it settle toward bottom. This action may entice those trout that are situated further upstream from the drop and behind bottom boulders.

Casting down toward the lip and rolling your lure just above the drop will also work. With this technique, an angler must make sure that he doesn't allow the lure to carry on over the drop. Just enough line should be retrieved to keep the lure positioned some 10 feet above the drop as it is gently worked across the current.

Above a rapids or falls is a good, and overlooked, place to catch trout.

Most fishermen work such areas from shore. From a boat, anchor to one side of the main flow and simply cast as you would while wading or fishing from shore. Increase lure weight if necessary to get down; use a faster-sinking or sink-tip fly line if fly fishing.

A fish hooked here will try to race down toward the drop in the rapids or falls if you exert too much pressure on it. Once a trout becomes embroiled in the downstream torrent, the chances of landing it are greatly reduced. Fish are very aware of the location of the rapids or falls but become disoriented by line pressure from above. Therefore, when first fighting a hooked trout in this situation, ease up on the pressure, and the fish will begin to head upstream against the current. Once this occurs, the less pressure applied the better. A looped line (as happens when current sweeps it) will provide downstream pressure on the hook and on the fighting fish, so, instead of pulling downstream with the current, the trout seeks to run upstream. Don't worry about slack line. Forceful river currents don't create slack.

Falls backwash. Beneath every waterfall, there is an area where white foam and churning water hide a trout sanctuary. This sanctuary is often recessed into the rock base of the waterfall. Cascading water here has created slow erosion backward into the bedrock over the years, creating a hard-to-reach pocket. The surface water above the pocket usually churns violently. Mid-depth waters may be extremely fast or turbulent and unswimmable, adding further protection from intrusion. This pocket is not only well-protected from predators but also provides excellent relief from the sun. However, food is continuously swept over the waterfall. Most food, such as hellgrammites, minnows, drowned insects and larva, and more, is caught in the backwash here and becomes easy prey for waiting trout. Getting at such a fishing spot is difficult. Many fishermen fail to work this area or do so in a half-hearted way. Turbulent waters churn so hard here that a lure placed within its confines soon is thrown back to a disgruntled angler.

Your presentation to the pocket below the falls (as indicated by the casting direction in Diagram 3, page 108) should start above the targeted area that you intend to fish. Getting an artificial or natural bait to wash down into a sanctuary pocket can be very difficult. Usually it can only be done by casting far above and upstream from the target area. Once a lure or live bait hits the water surface, you should allow it to carry down into the descending torrent. Don't retrieve until you're certain that your offering has dropped into the sanctuary pocket; this is normally sensed by a slight hesitation in line movement. Descending line will lose its momentum for perhaps 3 to 5 seconds before being caught up with the rest of the current. While the lure is in the pocket, lift the rod tip upward. Obviously the longer you hold your offering in this pocket, the better your chances of attracting fish. By moving the rod tip about and allowing back currents to work the floating bait, it may be possible to keep your offering (depending on what it is, of course) circulating a good deal longer.

Some flies and lures work in the backwash, but not reliably. Live bait such as night crawlers, sculpin minnows, larva, and leeches work very well in these backwashes. Fish these with a small split-shot, 12 to 18 inches up the line. Shot weight is dependent upon the strength and depth of the flow. Don't worry about feeling a strike. Under such conditions, trout tend to chomp down on their food and hang on.

In looking at the accompanying illustration of a typical river falls, you'll note that there are also trout directly beneath or downstream from the floating foam on either

Diagram 3

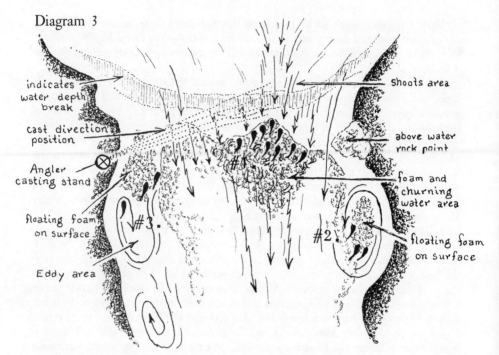

A tough place to fish is the sanctuary below a falls. Note suggested casting direction here and also the positioning of trout below and to the sides downstream.

side of this area. Often brook trout or brown trout that tire of holding directly beneath the foaming and churning areas move to the sides. Here they can be easily caught. These fish are eager to feed and have come to this position because it is easier to do so. The area beneath these side eddy pockets of foam is ideal for working flies and small lures. The slow eddy water near the floating foam allows for good fly or streamer presentation. In most northern rivers, a replica of the native sculpin minnow, such as the Muddler Minnow, works best. Make sure the fly is weighted a bit if it is bright out and fish are deep. In overcast or rainy conditions, a dry fly may do the job. Retrieve lure or streamer slowly.

Spring holes.   Spring holes are a good place to find trout in the warm months, though they are often ignored by the average angler. The colder water and its influence on surrounding environs is often conducive to attracting trout. Though a river's temperature might be near 65 degrees, for example, an upwelling spring may enter with 40-degree temperature. The merger creates a long tongue of cold water which trails downstream to eventually meld into the main river temperature. The length of these cooling zones depends on current speed, river and spring temperatures, and the volume of entering water, so the size of the area that will be attractive to trout varies.

Below-water springs are often found by wading anglers. If the temperature of water brushing against the legs drops dramatically, an angler immediately knows he's near

In the low water of summer, you may find trout at or near springs, which usually bring some cooler water into the main flow.

a cold-water spring. Another way to detect such springs is to look for an opening of tan sand which appears to have a slight dig-out on its upstream side and a mound of loose, white sand downstream. These sand patches can be found on mud, rock, or silt bottoms and normally have a circumference of 3 feet or more. Trout will hold about 6 to 8 feet down from the spring and trail downstream for as long as the cool water lasts. Under normal circumstances this will be about 50 to 75 feet.

Another type of spring is more visible. This is an above-ground spring that flows overland into an established river, stream, or creek. Look for soft, silky, bright green moss with ice-cold rivulets running down the bank as you travel downstream. A finger test will tell you whether such water flow is a spring or just runoff. A shorter distance of main current will hold trout below the entry area.

Beaver dam locales. Don't overlook the flooded upstream water above a beaver dam for trout. Beaver dams most often occur on small streams in low, willow-bottom country. There, it is easy for beavers to plug up the flowage with their wood and debris dams. Many fishermen work these areas from the shore or by wading, and some fish from a small canoe and find pleasant trout fishing.

Fly rods are a favorite tool in these generally mosquito-ridden locales. Dry flies or semi-submerging flies, such as a Muddler Minnow, work well. Because of their loamy, black-dirt bottoms, these backwater dam areas produce hordes of insects. This same black-dirt bottom absorbs the sun, which in turn heats the water and causes much of the trout population to feed late in the evening or just after sundown. This is so even where cold-water springs run into the backwaters.

Key places to fish here include weeds and lily pads, the outer curves or bends (where water is deepest), and short stretches directly below bends where the depth decreases.

Most beaver dam-influenced flowages appear dark or tainted. This is a tannin effect from upstream cedar swamps and black loam ground in nearby bottom country. Trout in these places are richly colored as a result. Good-size fish are found here, too. Most brook trout coming from beaver dam waters, for example, average 10 to 14 inches, with an occasional 2-pounder taken.

Fishing in flowing water for trout is an activity with many nuances, not only because of the different trout species, but also because of the varying types of water and conditions that are faced. We've tried to present some broadly based information here, but it is worthwhile to focus on a few other things that are particularly noteworthy. These include some tidbits on bait fishing, angling in spring, and a method of river trout fishing from boats that evolved in the Pacific Northwest and has spread to Great Lakes and Eastern waters.

Slipping/backtrolling.   Steelhead, rainbow, and brown trout are big-river targets for a non-casting method of presentation that is somewhat akin to trolling or a controlled method of downstream drifting. In some quarters, this technique is referred to as backtrolling (although different from the form of backtrolling on lakes as practiced by walleye anglers); in others, it is called Hotshotting (which is a derivative of the West Coast technique of using a Hotshot plug for steelhead and salmon) or pulling plugs, and in others, slipping.

Whatever you call it, the idea is to have your boat pointed bow upstream, using motor or oars to control the downstream progression of the boat. The boat moves very slowly—it actually drifts—downstream and at times remains stationary in the current (some boaters anchor once they have caught fish in a spot), while lures are fished at 50- to 80-foot distances behind the boat. The lures dangle in front of fish that the boat has not yet passed over, and this is a big difference compared to upstream trolling, where the boat passes over fish and alerts them to your presence, possibly spooking them. Additionally, lures that are slipped downstream ahead of the boat approach the head of fish, instead of coming from behind them and swimming past their head. Lures are usually fished in the channels and deep pools where bigger fish lie and waver in front of fish for a much longer period than they would if cast and retrieved or if trolled upstream and away. The fact that trout have a better chance of being undisturbed and of seeing a more natural presentation (a small fish, for instance, struggling against the current and being slowly swept downward) makes this a highly effective river fishing technique.

Most of this downstream drift-trolling is done with diving plugs or bait; winter-run steelhead, for example, are caught with pencil lead-weighted spawn sacks or single-hook salmon eggs. Many different attractions, including plugs, spoons, spinners, flies, and bait, can be used in slipping, depending on the circumstances.

When slipping, it's important to manipulate the boat properly in order to maintain precise lure position. The location and depth of your offering is critical to river fishing success. The lure must be on or close to the bottom, so you need to use the appropriate amount of weight or design of lure that will achieve this.

Pools are the major locales fished with this technique, and often the boat needs

Drift boating for river fish, especially steel-head, is a very effective big-river angling technique; these boats are also used to access hard-to-reach areas, then fishing from afoot. This angler got out of an anchored drift boat to catch and release this steelhead.

to be positioned far enough upriver so the lure slowly works from the head of a pool down through the tail of it; it's not good enough to boat down to a pool and then hold position, as the fish you seek may have been located at the head of the pool. When working from side to side across the river, you should realize that it takes a while for a trailing lure to catch up to the boat position; when you sweep close to a bank, for instance, hold that position because it takes time for the lure to get over to the bank. If you were to sweep in and out quickly, the lure wouldn't get as far to either side as you might like.

Another point to remember is that you want to slip backward in a slow, controlled fashion. When you stop rowing or throttle the motor back, a floating plug rises, a spinner doesn't spin, weights sink, etc. This is because there is now less pressure against those objects. Slow, controlled slipping keeps lures working best and draws more strikes. Boat control is maintained with oars, especially in rafts, johnboats, and river drift boats (McKenzie River-style dories), or with small tiller-steered, outboard motors.

Spring fishing. Spring is a season associated with mild days, budding leaves, and newfound greenery, and, while that may characterize the month of May in many regions where trout inhabit flowing water, it often doesn't typify much of April, when trout anglers are likely to dust the cobwebs off their gear and get in their first licks of the season. The early part of the spring sees a lot of attention from both casual and avid anglers because of the challenges presented and the opportunities for fun and success. Stocking is heavy at this time, and there are a lot of people who go fishing for trout only in the beginning of the year and once, if at all, later in the season. Because of the high interest in trout at this time, we thought it would be suitable to devote some attention specifically to trout fishing in this season.

Though the first few days and weeks of April may technically be part of spring, northerly anglers who brave swollen streams, bone-chilling weather, rain, and sometimes snow, think of this time as being more like late winter. Not surprisingly, early season trout fishing conditions are often unpredictable. For stream and river anglers, thawing weather, the amount of winter snowfall, and the amount of spring rain influence water levels significantly and thus have a major bearing on fishing opportunities and success. When forecasters predict great opening-day angling and excellent stream conditions, they do so when water levels are low to moderate and when temperatures have been unseasonably mild. In normal years, many trout streams are high, fast, and turbid in the early season, making fishing hard but not impossible.

Such conditions don't make for picturesque textbook fishing necessarily, but that doesn't stop too many anglers. It may make fly fishing fairly difficult, and perhaps not as effective an angling technique as other means of fishing, though no less enjoyable. Nymph and streamer fishing with sinking lines may be the way to go for the dedicated fly-rodder at this time, but even so, it is hard to cope with the torrent of early season water. Thus, the spin fisherman is usually the one who is best able to adapt to these conditions.

No doubt the most effective and time-honored, early-season stream trout bait is a live worm. It is fished on a small hook, perhaps a size 6 or less, with split-shot 8 to 12 inches above the hook. Most of the time it is critical to fish the worm just off the bottom; fast-flowing water makes bottom-bumping very difficult, so anglers have to use weights that are heavy enough to achieve this objective. Failure to keep the offering down deep in the current is often the principal reason for poor fishing results under early spring conditions. This is true for those using bait, lures, or flies.

The favored early-season trout lure is a spinner. This is easy to cast with light line and light tackle and features a revolving blade that attracts the attention of trout as the lure whisks by in the current. It must be worked deep and slowly enough to make the blade barely turn.

Fishermen will find it best to work upstream, casting their offerings up and across the flow and allowing them to drift down. The best cast is one that sends the lure quartering across the stream. Reasonably accurate casting is often necessary to effect

A fairly turbulent flow often characterizes early spring trout fishing on all waters.

a presentation that drifts the offering past boulders, through pools, into eddies, and by any other place that might serve to funnel food past the snout of a trout.

In many small streams, there isn't much opportunity to make long casts and drifts. Here anglers resort more to making short flips and dabbling their baits, lures, or flies, being careful to get into the most advantageous position before making a close-quarters presentation.

Early-season stream anglers should be mindful not to get so caught up in the chase that they overlook the hazards of spring trout fishing and neglect safety. Wading in fast, icy waters is particularly dangerous, and reasonable precautions should be taken. Also, special regulations exist on some area waters in the beginning of the season, and it's important to know on what waters fish must be released, or if the use of lures other than flies, or bait, is prohibited.

Bait. Live bait continues to be favored by many river trout anglers, and on that subject here are a few parting thoughts.

There are some good natural trout offerings that often go overlooked: crickets and grasshoppers. These tidbits naturally fall into flowing water and become easy prey for trout. They differ from other live bait in that they can be fished both on the surface and below it.

In fishing with these, use a short-shanked, light-wire hook in size No. 10 or 12, and hook the bait directly behind its collar. With the right hook, the insect will still float when impaled; add split-shot 12 to 18 inches ahead of the insect to make it sink. The bouyancy of these creatures will make them rise up above the weight, so they will float off the bottom while the weight bounces along it.

Other baits, such as leeches, minnows, hellgrammites, and grubs may work, too, for river trout, depending on the time of year and watershed. Still, live worms are the foremost natural bait for catching river trout, especially early in the season and

Drifting or anchoring and still-fishing bait is a popular river trout tactic in some areas, especially in the tailraces below impoundments.

in cold water. They are primarily fished on a light, small hook, with split-shot up above the hook.

Bait fishing, however, results in a fair deal of mortality for trout because the fish often become deeply hooked. In many cases, the objective when fishing with bait is, of course, catching fish with the intention of keeping them for food. In hatchery-supported, put-and-take fisheries (this includes small flowages as well as Great Lakes tributaries), one can't really quarrel with this. However, in areas with a high-quality fishery, native trout fishery, special size regulations, and/or fragile population, it makes good sense to fish with artificial lures rather than bait, and to judiciously limit your take of fish. Artificials allow you to catch and release more fish without harming them, provided you take good care in the release procedure. We suggest that bait fishermen weigh the conservation aspects of using lures (notice we are not suggesting that it is more or less sporting to use either), rather than bait.

CHAPTER NINE
WALLEYES IN LAKES

Like many fish species, lake walleyes were once predominantly a river creature. Time and circumstances over countless generations have changed this. Today, this once-migrating, river species has permanently ensconced itself in most areas of the country in numerous lakes and reservoirs, some of which are part of river systems and some of which are not.

The walleye is an extremely adaptable species in terms of its spawning and location. Spawning in lakes, for example, can occur in water ranging from 42 to 56 degrees. While walleyes are known as a bottom-oriented fish, in lakes they will easily suspend at any depth (some walleye have been caught in 85 to 90 feet of water over a total depth of 150 feet). On the other hand, at times this species is taken in less than 2 feet of water. They will feed over gravel and rock, holding close to bottom, or they will suspend a yard or so off bottom over silt when nymphs are emerging. It also isn't unusual to find walleyes working their way through a maze of fern-type weeds at midsummer in water depths ranging from 6 to 16 feet. That's adaptability.

Though walleyes are minnow feeders, their food selection is as diverse as the number of minnows and small game fish available. Darters, shiners, perch, shad, stickleback, and suckers all are ingested by growing walleye fingerlings. As lake walleye surpass the 1-pound mark, they'll consume young drum, ciscos, alewives, mooneyes, and black crappie. When water temperature rises into the 60's, walleyes may change their diet to crayfish, hellgrammites, frogs, and snails. Once water temperature drops back below 60 degrees, they seldom forage on these and revert to feeding on minnows and small game fish. River walleyes, by comparison, will spend much more time during peak summer season preying on crayfish than will lake fish.

The first places to look for lake walleyes are points, reefs, sloping bars, and underwater ravines. Lake walleyes are notorious for being deep (15 to 25 feet) and working up into structure to feed. During early summer and fall, feeding forays occur at any time during daylight hours. In the heat of summer, walleye will run up and onto the bars and points, but mostly at night or during fading light conditions. The total time consumed by these foraging streaks varies, depending on the amount of food available and time of year. Some feeding movements last but 30 minutes while others carry on for hours.

Drawn by old river-directed instincts, lake fish gather at the mouth of any stream or creek where it enters a lake or reservoir. This is most apt to occur in spring during and directly after spawning and in the northern-most walleye waters throughout the season. If it isn't the reproduction instinct that brings walleye here, it's the enormous

Once mainly a river species, walleyes have adapted well to lakes and reservoirs and grow large in those environs.

amount of bait fish these tributaries provide. Look for fish to locate within channel areas of the entering waterway as it winds out into the lake's deep water.

In spring, when no entering streams exist in a lake system, look for walleyes to gather and spawn in gravel or sandy bays, off shoreline bars where sand and gravel persist, and atop open-water gravel flats. Water depth will vary from 3 to 12 feet. Lake walleyes primarily spawn after dark and in shallow water. A certain amount of wave washing is needed to work the eggs prior to hatching, and this can only happen in the shallows, particularly where there is a sharp slope to the bottom.

To illustrate, imagine a bay where there is gravel and rock some 50 feet from shore with no more than 20 inches of drop. At that point, a sharp 18 inches of drop occurs. From here the bottom slopes off 8 feet, with more gravel in evidence over the next 100 feet. It would be just below the 18-inch drop that walleyes would spawn. Here they obtain a proper amount of backwashing wave action to facilitate hatching the eggs. Having spawned, the walleyes move into 8-foot-deep water. A period of nonfeeding adjustment occurs, and then they become active.

Look for spawning bays to have a good facing to the main lake, so the prevailing spring winds can readily enter. What may be difficult to fish may be an excellent place in which to find spawning walleyes.

Water temperature is the controlling factor in walleye spawning (45 to 50 degrees being prime), with some fish discharging eggs at 45 degrees and others as the water temperature increases. Not all walleyes will spawn at exactly the same time, so a given lake's walleye population may spread reproduction out over a two- to three-week period.

In the spring, walleyes migrate up lake tributaries to spawn, or congregate in gravel and rock bays in lakes without a tributary.

Spring walleyes are fairly easily caught. Find an entering stream or river, cast a jig, crankbait, or live-bait rig, and take fish in 3 to 10 feet of water. If this doesn't work, look for an open bay where the prevailing wind enters, and drag one of the same baits over any hardpan gravel structure. In spring, it's nearly that easy because walleyes are vulnerable until after spawning. At spawning time the males will hit anything that gets near their spawning areas. If the bait is dragged slowly enough, you may land a lazy trophy female.

As the water warms, walleyes move further into bay waters. If there is still a gravel and rock bottom, the fish will go deeper into 12-, 15-, 20-, or even 30-foot depths. Once again, water temperature and food availability govern this retreat.

While this movement to normal summer environs is in progress, walleyes are attracted to various structures, including an island, hump, reef, or deep-water weed bed. Walleyes stay there until forced into deeper water to suspend or to hold along an extremely deep rocky structure. However, for this to happen, the lake must have depths exceeding 60 feet. Often, much of a lake's open water has depths of 35 feet or more. This is good, and the more reefs and islands there are, the better. Water temperature has a great deal to do with where lake walleyes are located. When the temperature exceeds 65 degrees, walleyes are less accessible; they go deeper then, preferring to be in water temperature that is closer to 60 degrees.

The easy fishing for walleye in the spring primarily lasts a few weeks. Angling gets progressively tougher as walleyes move further out and down. Fishing during the balance of the year requires several things. First, you should have some type of sonar to determine depth. It isn't necessary to locate fish with this, but it's an enormous help in finding hard bottom and drop-offs. Also, you must be able to drift, troll extremely slowly, anchor, backtroll into the wind, and/or steady your boat for positioning while casting, as each of these techniques comes into play at various times and circumstances.

Since a lot of walleye fishing involves the use of bait, you should also have a decent device in which minnows can be kept alive. A flow-troll minnow bucket, an oxygenated livewell, or an aerated styrofoam bucket or cooler will do. Take block ice along on hot days; it will help if you're using the styrofoam bucket or cooler.

For bait, most walleye fishermen employ hardy minnows or chubs. In cooler weather, shiners or one of the darter species are preferred. No matter what the live minnow is, its size should average about 2 1/2 to 3 inches long when used strictly as bait or a little shorter when used for tipping a jig. To tip a minnow on a jig, run the hook point through the minnow's forehead and out its throat, which places pressure on the minnow's bony forehead, not on its soft throat. If pressure is placed on the throat, the minnow's body will tear off directly behind its gills at the slightest jerk or touch.

Live bait rigs in the form of small No. 1 and 0 spinners, snelled with No. 4 or 6 hooks, work well for drifting and trolling. Ahead of these, a small bottom-walking sinker is attached. Weight varies with depth fished and speed at which presentation is made, ranging from 1/4-ounce up to 1 ounce.

The tackle used in lake walleye fishing varies greatly. Some anglers stick to traditional level-wind bait-casting outfits; others rig a fly rod with spin-casting reel; and some use the same ultralight spinning tackle they would devote to crappie fishing. Most ardent walleye fishermen, however, prefer one of the following two outfits. The most popular one is a spinning rod and reel and 8- or 10-pound line. The rod, preferably graphite, is 5 1/2 to 7 feet long and has a fairly stiff tip, which helps to set the hook when a long length of line is trolled deep behind the boat and is good for detecting delicate strikes. Walleye often strike very lightly, so strike detection is important. The second most popular outfit is a spincasting one, 5 1/2 to 6 feet long, also with a sturdy butt and stiff tip, and equipped with 8- or 10-pound line.

Tackle needs aren't terribly sophisticated for walleye fishing, with light- to medium-duty spinning and spincasting tackle most popular.

There are some basic lake structures that will always hold walleyes. One of these is a rock or gravel point where water drops fairly consistently into an average lake depth of about 40 feet. (For a reference, see Diagram 4, below.) Here we have placed an angler on shore to simplify matters and to show better how such a point is structured. Notice that walleyes are within casting distance, even though their holding depth is about 20 feet, and that the point is aligned with an island some distance offshore. Somewhere between island and point is where this school of fish will be when not feeding. Once the urge to eat takes over, they will migrate up and onto structure. They go where the heaviest concentration of bait fish is found. During most of the summer, this would be on the mainland point. Only during the hottest days of summer (about two to three weeks) would they travel up onto the island point, as the water temperature out toward the lake's center will be slightly cooler then.

In this instance you could fish from shore using live bait (on sinker rigs), jigs, or truly deep-diving crankbaits (Mann's 15+ and 20+ plugs are examples). Work the point starting from one side, casting to the other side continuously until you have covered the entire structure.

This point can also be worked by backtrolling with spinner rigs and walking sinkers and is easily drifted across if you have the right wind direction. In early summer, walleyes would be in depths between 10 and 20 feet; in midsummer, look for them 15 to 30 feet deep. Clear water requires deeper fishing. The reverse is true if the water is muddy or the location of the lake is far to the north.

In northern walleye waters, including Canada and our northernmost states, walleyes will work points such as those found in Diagram 5, page 120 at the location marked A. If the water has a brackish tint, as many northern lakes do, then fish in late spring and early summer will be at or around 10 feet deep and slightly deeper if the weather is very warm. Unlike lakes in the central region of the continent, these bodies of water are much cooler, and walleye are located shallower throughout most of the season.

Diagram 4   **OPEN LAKE**

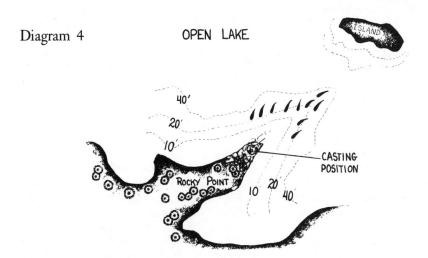

A rocky point may attract walleyes for feeding; depth will vary depending on season.

Diagram 5

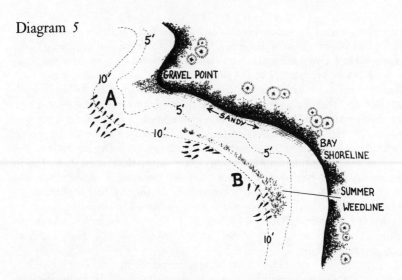

A gravel point, as shown here, may not be as pronounced but will attract walleyes directly off the point and along the nearby weed line.

Besides gravel points, cooler waters host schools of walleyes close to or directly in the weeds. Look for cabbage weeds first, coontail weeds second. If the weed bed is directly on the edge of 10-foot water, in a bay in close proximity to a point (as indicated in Diagram 5), it will be particularly appealing to walleyes.

These fish are best worked from a boat while backtrolling, drifting, or casting down along the weed bed. Use live bait rigs as you might on rocky points or jigs tipped with live bait. Crankbaits can be very effective along cabbage if you are able to work them.

Along the Canadian border, anglers will speed-troll through cabbage weeds in mid-summer to entice large walleye to strike. This is a somewhat unknown and seldom-used technique. When 1/2- to 1 1/2-pound walleyes are being taken out of 25 feet of water along sunken reefs, an angler can score on fish averaging 3 pounds and over by running a yellow Five-O-Diamonds Dardevle spoon through cabbage. It's a simple method. Add enough weight (sinker) ahead of your spoon to keep it submerged, troll at 5 to 8 mph, and weave your way in and out of the weeds.

It's possible that walleyes in the cabbage believe the rapidly trolled yellow spoon is a perch. Remarkably, however, once a walleye is taken from a clump of cabbage by speed trolling and the angler returns to jig the spot, his effort always meets with failure. But resume fast trolling, and another fish is often taken.

If water depth at the cabbage exceeds 10 feet, this method won't work. However, if a school of fish is found in 6 to 7 feet where cabbage grows, it's a deadly weapon. Remember to move your rod tip from side to side, thus avoiding any visible cabbage weeds. Try this method from late July to early September.

In many lower-latitude lakes, walleyes leave shoreline structure in favor of deep-water reefs or island points during hot summer days when the water temperature along the shoreline exceeds the fish's comfort zone. To better understand how such structure produces fish, refer to Diagram 6 on page 121.

Diagram 6

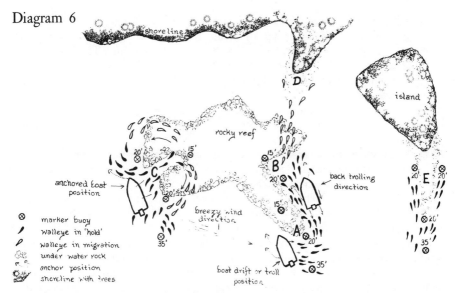

A deep-water, rocky reef is a prime lake walleye spot. Use marker buoys to identify the key locations. Drifting, backtrolling, and fishing from an anchored boat are also possible approaches here.

Once the deep-water reef is located, it's a good idea to identify the most fishable parts with marker buoys. Every dedicated walleye hunter should carry four to six small, brightly colored markers. They can be commercial models, made from a bright orange or yellow plastic, or just ordinary plastic bottles with string and discarded sinkers. Markers are noted as circled Xs in the illustration.

After surveying the rocky reef, begin at location A. A point here juts out toward open lake the farthest and is most likely to hold fish first. One marker is placed at the point's very end in about 20 feet of water. Another goes farther out in 35 feet of water where the rocks of the reef still persist, but fish may not. Next, a marker is placed directly atop the reef's point at its shallowest spot. You have now established two channels through which you may fish. Finally, place a marker just off the reef in 20 feet of water along its right side, one at location "B" where the inner bend on the right side angles away and out. This is a holding spot for fish that work up and along the structure from A to B. Most likely, they would turn back or veer left and migrate up and over reef structure, retreating toward A once again as deep water is reached.

To approach the fish at A, an angler can anchor and jig, though it is usually better to drift a live bait rig across and between the marker in 35 feet and one in 20 feet. Drifting will depend on wind direction. Those fish between "A" and "B" are best taken by back-trolling or anchoring atop the point and casting a jig into deep water, retrieving it into shallow water.

Conditions allowing, there may be a migration of those fish located at the bend near position B. These fish will head up and across the reef and head toward location D, which is a normal staging area for lake walleyes. Such a migration comes during the late evening hours and only lasts a short while.

Where a deep, narrow cut in a reef occurs, such as the one found at location C, walleyes will have a different type of feeding pattern. These fish will migrate much faster and are apt to be on this portion of the reef a shorter time. They come from fairly deep water, go into shallow water to feed, and return. This is an ideal place to use a jig tipped with bait. Anchor so you are able to cast and retrieve directly down the slot.

An open-water reef point is shown at location E. Here, as with every point-type structure, a school of walleyes runs up on the end of the structure, divides and migrates up along either side. Marker buoys were placed to register just such a feeding migration.

In all of the structures presented in this illustration, the depth of the walleyes vary depending on the geographic location of the lake in which this type of situation is found. Although the depth at which these walleyes exist may vary, the actions they take will not, so the principles of fish movement and angling approach will remain valid. Look for best results on such structure late in the day or early in the morning.

You should realize that wind plays a major part in how successful you will be as a walleye angler. You have to realize how wind affects bait fish and walleyes on various types of structure. Using a small island structure as an example, realize that, as the wind increases, bait fish on the upwind side are washed and jarred from their shallow holding areas near the shoreline and begin to work their way around either end of the structure. Walleyes in open water away from the island will be attracted to points as bait fish migrate around and into the protection of the structure. If the wind pressure isn't too strong, the fishing at either end of such an island will be good throughout the blow, though of shorter duration if the wind picks up strongly.

To take advantage of this, you should be on the downwind side of the island behind the points. There you can cast into the current flow created by the wind-swept waters and achieve natural presentation by retrieving your offering in the same direction as the oncoming bait fish. Obviously your boat is also protected from the wind here. This is just one example of how you can utilize the wind's effect on structure to find and catch walleyes, but it also shows how it is important to do so.

Over the years, experience has proven to us that west, southwest, or south winds are best for walleyes. A 3 to 4 mph breeze is about perfect for properly drifting walleye structures. But an 8 to 10 mph wind out of the southwest will help you take more fish in the same spots, though you'd think that this would be too rough a wind in which to fish.

Let's refer to a situation in Diagram 7 (page 123) to better understand the scenario. Walleyes are holding in locations E, F, and G. There isn't any wind, and it's a hot July day, around 4:30 in the afternoon. Two anglers in a boat work the normally productive points of their favorite island with no results.

Slowly the wind begins from the southwest. By 5 o'clock, it has increased to 7 mph, and two fish are taken. Things are looking up because the wind has created a shift in bait fish location. Wind-driven waves beat down on the island's exposed points and bait fish cannot hold there. The exposed shallows on the island's western and southern sides have become too rough for these schools of bait fish to stay in. They must drop off into deeper water. Walleyes that were located in the holding areas near the island sense this and come to meet the outward-moving food.

Disregarding their normal caution for shallow water (which is something they normally won't do at this time of the year), walleyes move up into 5 or 6 feet of

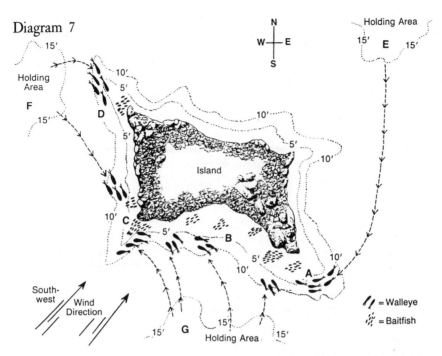

Here's a projected scenario for taking advantage of the wind when fishing around an island. Note that walleyes will move from deep-water holding areas into the shallower, wind-disturbed area.

water where the bottom typically starts to drop off (often called a breakline). Anglers working crankbaits or minnow-tipped jigs can have a lot of success by casting into the shallow, frothy water and retrieving out toward deep water. Holding a boat in such water is often hard, but not impossible.

Taking advantage of the wind is a rather elementary thing to do. Use your common sense and picture what might be happening to bait fish or other foods as wind-driven waves pound on likely walleye habitat. Your first instinct about what might be happening will probably lead you to fish. Keep in mind what rough water does to all the aquatic creatures involved, and you'll be successful.

As mentioned earlier, lake walleyes may not always be on or near the bottom. They will suspend just about anywhere there is deep water, a lack of structure, the presence of food, and a need to follow a proper water temperature. In South Dakota's massive Lake Oahe, for example, walleyes were first detected in suspension many years ago; they adapted to this behavior when food along the steep reservoir slopes gave out, and they followed the rainbow smelt out into the open lake. In central Ontario's Kagagami Lake, walleyes suspend with lake trout 65 feet down off deep rocky reefs.

Food is the drawing factor, as an overpopulation of small ciscoes fans out at that depth in water that is over 150 feet deep. And in Lake Erie, tens of thousands of suspending fish are caught each year.

In many reservoir waters in central portions of the continent, walleye will suspend at depths of 45 to 60 feet. Food is a factor but not always the determining one, as a lack of good bottom structure or the need for lower temperature and greater depth is sometimes the reason. Walleyes will suspend deep enough for water temperature to be adequate for their requirements.

When walleyes suspend, there are a couple of ways to fish them that work well. Vertical jigging, using a lead-head jig tipped with bait, is a preferred method when fishing for suspended walleyes in depths exceeding 40 feet. Use a 1/4- to 1/2-ounce jig, perhaps even larger the deeper you fish.

In water shallower than 40 feet, a modern "slip bobber" and live bait is good. A slip bobber, as its name indicates, allows your offering to slip down to the depth at which the fish you seek are holding. By attaching a small thread knot to your monofilament line (one that is reeled up onto your spool), an angler governs just how deep his offering will go. The bobber runs up the line till reaching the knot, and then it stops there. A suitable-weight sinker is attached just above the bait to ensure that proper downward thrust is placed on the bait. Once in position, the slip bobber works just like any other float.

Suspending walleyes have one characteristic that is seldom seen in any other species. They will hold a yard or so apart and stagger their location up and down by 18 to 36 inches. Thus, suspended walleyes are easily distinguishable, via sonar, from

Jigs that look like bait fish are good lake walleye lures and are often tipped with a minnow.

other species that tightly group. Also, walleyes will always hold within a 36-inch, up/down, staging pattern. Once again, water temperature is critical, even to a walleye's suspension.

TROLLING

Trolling is another method of catching suspended, deep-water walleyes, and some methods of trolling have taken hold in walleye fishing that were not used until recent years. These are applied not only to deep and suspended fish, but to shallow, bottom-holding fish as well, and you should be aware of ways in which you can be successful in trolling, too.

There are several types of trolling techniques that can be used for walleyes. Backtrolling, downrigger fishing, and weighted or unweighted flat-lining are the most prominent, and we've alluded to some of these methods earlier. Side-planer board fishing is increasing, and we'll say something about that in a moment.

Trolling is essentially done with live bait rigs, weight-forward spinners, and various plugs. Walleye foods provide a good clue to lure sizes, at least where plugs are concerned. Natural forage includes yellow perch and small fingerling-size fish such as chubs, minnows (including fatheads), and various shiners. Walleye trolling plugs are 4- to 6-inch minnow imitations, 2- to 4-inch crankbaits, and 2- to 6-inch banana baits. The latter are trolling lures per se, while the others can be cast as well; all are floating/diving products.

Minnow imitators have shallow-running, medium- to deep-diving, and sinking versions. Shallow runners for walleye angling include the Sisson Minnow-Mate, Bagley Bang-O-Lure, Rebel Minnow, Rebel Fastrac Minnow, Rapala Minnow, Smithwick Rogue, Bomber Long-A-Minnow, Cordell Redfin, and others. These lures will dive 6 to 8 feet deep on a long (150-foot drop-back), light line, but since it's hard to maintain precise positioning with long lines while trolling contours for walleyes (and long lines aren't usually needed anyway), 50- to 80-foot lengths are employed, and the lures run a bit shallower. Sinking minnow imitators are typified by the Rapala Countdown minnow; this type of plug can be good for cast-countdown-and-retrieve fishing for suspended walleyes, but it is not particularly effective for slow-trolling near the bottom because it invites debris pickup and bottom snagging.

Diving minnow imitators include the Rebel Spoonbill Minnow, Mann's Stretch 20+, Bagley Diving Bang-O-Lure, LeBlanc Swim Whiz, Drifter's Believer, and Smithwick Deep Rogue. This is an overlooked bait type that is particularly good for big walleyes. It's the favorite walleye lure on Greer's Ferry Reservoir in Arkansas, where monster walleyes are caught on them every spring by trolling or casting the tributaries. In addition to fishing them for Arkansas walleyes, we've used them on hard-fished and wilderness, walleye waters to search for lake and river fish. The Spoonbill Minnow, for example, is a good choice for short-line flat-lining when prospecting for fish. That bait will dive 9 to 10 feet on 12-pound test line with just 75 feet of it out, so an option is to use a shorter length of lighter line to achieve at least the same running depth and maybe get the lure a little deeper. Not all walleye trolling lures reach the same depth, however, so you need to know their capabilities if you'll be switching between brands.

Diving minnow-imitation plugs are a good big-walleye producer.

Crankbaits for walleye trolling may be the typical, bulbous models prominent in bass fishing, particularly such lures as the Rapala Fat Rap, Storm Wiggle Wart, Storm Hot 'N Tot, Sisson's Ticker, Norman N series lures, various Rebel crankbaits, Mann's 10+ and 15+, and others, but are slightly better in the longer and slender versions that are sometimes called "shad" baits. These are typified by Sisson T-Shad, Rapala Shad Rap, Bagley Bass 'N Shad, Rebel Deep Shad, and Lindy Shadling lures.

The so-called banana plugs are those with curvature of the spine. They include the Helin Flatfish, Luhr Jensen Fireplug, Dura Pak Lazy Ike, Heddon Tadpolly, and Bagley's Smoo, among others. These slow-trolling, wide-wobbling lures don't achieve much depth and are often fished with a weight ahead of them.

There are many colors that have merit, but a perch pattern is a favorite with many anglers, followed by silver and gold. Dark tops with light sides/bellies are very effective; bright fluorescent colors may do the job in muddy water, silver in clear water, and gold in stained water. Use this merely as a guideline, however, and don't be afraid to experiment.

The key elements in the successful usage of these lures are: proper speed to get maximum lure action; a knowledge of the diving abilities of each plug based on speed, line size, and length of line trolled; and selection of the right lure to get to the necessary depth. In most situations, plugs can be worked at slow speeds as well as near the bottom, and in many lakes it is necessary to do so. However, fishing them off the bottom and at faster speeds sometimes is effective, especially in a body of water like Lake Erie, so don't assume that there are always hard-and-fast rules at work.

On a big lake like Erie, walleyes often suspend, and while casters use a countdown method to put weight-forward spinners at the right level while drifting, trollers can cover a lot more territory with plugs they know will run at the appropriate, nowhere-near-bottom level. On smaller natural lakes, too, suspending can be midsummer, midday

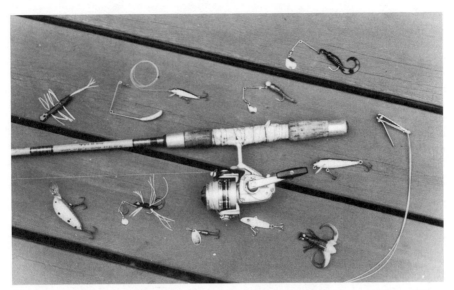

Jigs, plugs, jig/spinner combinations, and plugs or bait fished behind a bottom-walking sinker are among the foremost lake walleye attractors.

behavior for some walleyes. These fish will often be situated not far from shallower bars and points. In the evening, those same walleyes will move shallower to the edges of the bar or a rock or gravel point that break sharply to deep water. Using plugs that dive to 8 or 10 feet deep, troll from deep water to the point, then go along one side and work along the edge. Another approach is to pick a specific contour level, such as 10 or 12 feet, and keep your lures in that contour as you troll parallel to the edge of the structure.

If the lure you'd like to use won't achieve the necessary depth on an unweighted flat line, then you need to weight it in some manner. Minnow imitations and banana plugs are often weighted. Rubber-core sinkers or pinch-on split-shot, placed about 18 inches ahead of the lure, are standard, but you might want to try a small, swiveling, bead-chain sinker. A bottom-walking sinker is a very good option here as well, especially when fished with a minnow imitator set back on a 20- to 30-inch leader. The key is finding the right amount of weight to use. Split-shot and rubber-core sinkers are also used to troll with weight-forward spinners and spinner/bait combinations.

These are flat-lining techniques, of course, and some walleye fishing situations can be met by using other trolling methods, as well as flat-lining. Downrigging, for example, is gaining a foothold in walleye trolling circles, especially on large lakes, and now that anglers see they can still use 6- and 8-pound line with downriggers, they are giving it a go. Advantages to downrigger fishing for walleyes include the ability to run more lines (by stacking two rods per downrigger, or by using second-line, slider rigs); to cover a wide vertical range of water; to put any lure at a specific level; to appeal well to suspended walleyes; to get down to walleyes that are deeper than normally fished; and to overcome the problem of drift-fishing when there is no wind. When fishing in deeper water, you can set lures just 6 to 15 feet behind the downrigger weight; for shallower fishing, put them 40 to 60 feet back.

Drawbacks to downrigger use for walleyes include the fact that you can't tell if a lure has picked up debris, such as weeds, and isn't working well. You have to be careful about running depth and may have to check lures periodically to see that they're running clean. Sometimes, small walleyes take a lure and don't exert enough force to trip the downrigger release, so you drag them around for a while. Because of this, you need to be precise about release tension; some trollers employ light rubberband releases and, if a small walleye doesn't break the rubberband upon striking the lure, it will usually bounce it enough to jiggle the fishing rod or downrigger cable so you know there's a fish on and can take the rod in hand and snap the rubberband yourself.

The use of side-planers is also coming on in walleye fishing, particularly on Lake Erie. While side-planer boards may never be a super hot item on smaller inland lakes (if for no other reason than that the waters sometimes are crowded and people are drifting or anchored in places you'd want to troll these boards), they can have merit in such a place, particularly when you don't know the lake well, don't have an idea where to fish, and are scouting for relatively shallow spring fish. In those shallows, side-planers can help you get a lure well off to the side of the boat, if you have reason to believe that shallow boat passage might spook them.

It is not, however, a particularly easy chore to run a side-planer board 60 to 80 feet off to the side of your boat and keep it next to an irregularly contoured submerged weed bed; your boat is over open, deeper water, and you can't define the edge as well when you're not fairly close to it, meaning that you may often run your board too shallow or over the weed bed instead of along it and foul the lure. When you

On big lakes, walleye trolling encompasses the use of downriggers and side-planers for trolling, as well as conventional still-fishing and drifting techniques.

know the territory well, this is less of a problem. Keeping the side-planer closer to the boat, say 30 feet away, is also a way to deal with this. When you aren't fishing such narrowly defined structure, however, such as when trolling for suspended walleyes in large lakes, by running several lures off side-planers, you have the advantage of covering a broad horizontal distance and potentially putting your lures in front of many more fish than if you were strictly flat-lining directly behind the boat, drifting, or downrigging.

While plugs are particularly useful for side-planer board fishing and downrigging and may be used most often, they aren't the only way to go. Spoons work fine on downriggers, of course, and light spoons that don't attain any depth may sometimes be preferable to plugs because they run at the level you set the weight (you have to account for the diving ability of any plug when set behind a downrigger, in addition to the depth at which the weight is set). The same is true for light, weight-forward spinners that are tipped with bait. Many of the points previously mentioned about trolling for walleyes, particularly locations and depths to fish, are also applicable when these lures are used.

With weight-forward spinners (among which are the very popular Earie Dearie and Mepps Lusox) and spinner/bait rigs, however, flat-lining, with and without sinkers on the line, at a slow speed is the best trolling technique. These and bottom-crawling, live bait setups, such as the Lindy Rig, are probably the all-time favorite walleye lures, often fished by drifting, which, in a sense, is lake trolling, but slower. Backtrolling with such lures—using a tiller-steered outboard motor in reverse or a transom-mounted, electric motor (with lower unit turned so that the stern goes back when the motor

Backtrolling, a method of moving a tiller-steered boat slowly in reverse to carefully work structure, accounts for many walleyes.

is technically in a forward position)—by moving very slowly, stern first, to maintain precise position around points, reefs, weed lines, sandbars, and along drop-offs is a premier small-boat, walleye tactic. The transom acts as a slowing agent. Trolled lines extend out past the bow as the anglers back away, looking toward their trailing lines. This is one walleye fishing presentation in which anglers can slow their boats to a complete stop if desired.

By using some type of sonar unit, a backtroller can maintain position along specific depths, nearly hover over selected spots, and maneuver his boat to use whatever wind direction is present to position his boat in such a way as to keep his following bait in the proper place. This is especially true when a school of walleyes are packed into one area, a spot that may be no larger than a small room.

An ability to keep your boat and lure in productive water is absolutely essential, and controlled boat operation for precise lure placement is something that not enough walleye trollers master. This, and speed, are the vital factors in trolling weight-forward spinners, spinner/bait combos, and live bait rigs.

Trolling speeds with the aforementioned lures tend to be on the slow to super slow side. Super slow is just barely moving. But this isn't always the case, and speeds can change from day to day, although with weight-forward spinners, spinner combos, and live bait rigs, you seldom move fast, and with plugs you seldom move as slow as a crawl. Determining proper speed takes some experimentation and observation. When you troll for fish that you have not located and whose depth you are unsure of, it's best to maneuver your boat in S and zig-zag patterns, watching your sonar to spot fish that are large enough to be walleyes or bait fish, which might mean that walleyes will be nearby, and then concentrating on that depth. Work different speeds until you catch a fish; you can maintain the same speed if fish continue to strike. If they don't, it may be that you caught one particularly aggressive walleye out of a school and need to go slower in the same area to appeal to the other fish.

The various types of trolling have application throughout the walleye season but are particularly useful for anglers who are unfamiliar with a body of water and need to do some searching and fishing at the same time, as well as for summer fishermen.

In the fall, walleyes revert to spring and early summer habits. Shallower water and rocky structure are the keys then. Food turns to an all-fish diet as they fatten up for the winter. In fact, when you open a fall-caught walleye, you'll observe rows of yellow fat along its intestines. In late fall, walleyes drop off into a bit deeper water. They seem to follow food and temperature for the most part. The average depth in which winter walleyes are taken through the ice is somewhere between 20 and 30 feet. They continue to feed, however, throughout the winter season, providing thousands of ice-bound anglers with many happy fishing hours, but that's a subject we'd prefer to leave for another time, as we have much more to say about walleyes—this time in rivers—in the following chapter.

CHAPTER TEN
WALLEYES IN RIVERS

There are many people who think that a river walleye is just like a lake walleye and is fished much the same way. Not so. River walleyes aren't anything like their lake cousins and must be approached differently, which is why we're devoting a separate chapter to angling for walleyes in river environments.

The differences between the two are noticeable even as spawning commences. Many lake fishermen, for example, believe that river walleyes spawn during late March and early April. In reality, walleyes in many waterways have already begun their spawning run at the start of the new year. River walleyes, which return to their birthplace to reproduce, don't wait for warm water to spawn like their lake brethren, and they prefer nighttime spawning.

River walleyes spawn when the water temperature is between 42 and 52 degrees, 46 being ideal. A severe drop in temperature, especially if brought on by a sudden snow melt upstream, will cause female walleye to abandon spawning beds, and if

The river walleye: similar to the lake walleye, but with different habits.

the temperature doesn't come back to a suitable level within ten days, the female may not spawn. Ninety percent of river walleyes lay their eggs during darkness, primarily in one night. No nest is built, and eggs are laid promiscuously over gravel or creviced bottom structure. Depth depends on water temperatures, though most spawning occurs in less than 8 feet of water.

After spawning, the bigger fish, which are mostly females, begin to migrate. Most river walleyes only travel short distances to return home, although in a river system that is connected to a large downstream reservoir, these fish may migrate 10 to 20 miles. They may travel even further, but in any case, by summer, river walleyes have returned to their normal habitat. There, they prefer water temperatures that range between 56 and 65 degrees. As summer advances, they may be found in slightly warmer water, 70 degrees being tops. At this time, they will stick within 3 to 4 miles of home base.

Most anglers think of walleyes as bottom feeders, with their favorite food being minnows and small game fish. This is generally true, although at times they can be found at nearly any depth. In reservoirs, walleyes may suspend at depths ranging from 20 to 85 feet. But in rivers, walleyes have little need to suspend (although they may do so at frothy rapids or beneath heavy waterfalls, where they can take advantage of backing water currents and circling subsurface eddies). River walleyes are primarily located on the bottom. This is because that is where their food is usually obtained. No matter where walleyes are found, they are there because the area houses food.

TECHNIQUE/TACKLE/LOCALES

Slipping

Perhaps the most critical aspect of river walleye fishing is proper bait or lure presentation through boat control. The technique we use is called "slipping," and it is also useful in river fishing for other species besides walleye, although it is especially significant where walleyes are concerned and is a small-boat technique that should be described early in this chapter because it relates to fishing the places that might hold walleye and to the types of lures used, both of which will be described shortly.

In its simplest form, river slipping is a method of moving slowly backwards downstream while in complete control of your craft, in such a way as to allow passengers and boat operator to fish at ease. Slipping is used to work a shoreline by casting lures, as well as to get down to bottom-hugging walleyes in mid-river pools and channels. The key to its success is presenting lures in a proper manner.

To "slip" running water, point the bow of your boat upstream and accelerate the outboard motor in forward gear. With the bow placed into the current, throttle the motor down to a point where your boat has begun to move backward downstream. The thrust of the motor is not enough to keep you going forward, and your boat slowly slides backward, stern first. When the boat begins to slowly back downstream while the motor is thrusting forward, you are "slipping," using the best method of boat control possible on running water. Realize that you are moving very slowly, sometimes almost imperceptibly, and that you have precise control over your position and rate of descent.

This boat control must be maintained, of course. To test yourself, accelerate forward a bit and drop off a couple of times. You'll find that, although you are moving forward and backward, boat control remains easy. The reason for this is that you've found a pivoting point. Were you to steer or manuever your boat from a center, or upstream, spot in the boat, the pressure exerted on other portions would overpower the point of pivot. When this happens, the whole boat swings sideways or at least is set into side slips that are difficult to work out of. Thus, the person running the motor spends most of his time fighting the current.

When slipping, as you turn the motor sideways, the boat moves laterally, but the bow does not turn to the side, as you might expect. Because your pivot point has no downstream pressure on it and is at the farthest spot downstream, the bow slides to the side with the entire craft following suit.

Turn the motor so the propeller thrust pushes toward the direction you want to go. Once your boat begins to slip sideways, immediately turn the motor in or out to correct side drift. You may note that this sideways slippage feels similar to the power steering of a car. It doesn't take much turning of the handle to set a slightly different course and, with a little correcting, to maintain that course. You now have accomplished the two most important functions in river slipping: backward movement with the motor in forward thrust, and sideways movement without having to realign your bow completely. Everything else in river slipping is just a matter of adjustment and practice.

Realize that rivers which flow at a rate under 2 mph are somewhat hard to manuever in, no matter what technique is used, because they flow slowly. When slipping here, you'll need to put the motor in neutral more often to compensate; otherwise you'll be moving slowly upstream even at the lowest forward throttle setting. Another thing to keep in mind is that you should plan to start your fishing well above the area you expect to slip.

Slipping, a method of maneuvering a river boat like this johnboat, allows you to move slowly downstream and completely control the placement and speed of your presentation.

The easier form of slipping is fishing along a bank or shoreline. When selecting a river shoreline to practice slipping, pick one where the contour juts out into current, then recedes inward to create a series of points and eddies. Surprisingly, the boat seems to follow a similar path created by the current break coming off the upstream point. With the motor at a steady forward thrust, the boat backs downstream with ease as you cast and retrieve. When situated close to rocks and rapids formed by a small descent into land structure, cast upstream toward shore and retrieve slowly downstream. Upstream casting allows you to present lures in a manner similar to the movement of natural bait in current. The boat stays an even distance from shore as it slips downstream. Continue casting upstream and retrieving downstream. The bow of the boat is always pointed into the current. It is a position easily held, providing you don't allow eddies and backwaters to entrap your boat.

In the main river, anglers don't cast, but use a trolling-like form of activity when slipping, in order to fish hard-to-reach areas such as slicks (which are areas below pools where water smoothes out), center-channel structures, and spots where deep-water hardpan exists above fast water. To accomplish this style of fishing, cast your lure out behind the boat and allow it to work backward as the boat slips slowly downstream. To keep lures or live bait from fouling on the bottom, lift the rod tip occasionally, which allows water to elevate the line, then lower the rod tip so the lure sweeps on downstream. This also gives you a natural movement that simulates live bait being swept with the current. Hair jigs with spinners or plastic-bodied jigs work extremely well under these circumstances.

When slipping like this, you needn't work a straight line backward constantly. Move sideways as often as necessary to position your lures in many locales across the breadth of the river. By moving back and forth as you descend with current, you can cover a lot of area and be more effective than when casting.

Incidentally, you don't have to worry about motor noise when slipping. In medium-to large-sized rivers, the volume of water will defuse the sound and vibrations created by the motor, usually without disturbing fish. Even if there is some disturbance, river walleye recover quickly, unlike lake fish.

Tackle

Before we discuss places to fish, let's review the equipment used for river walleye angling. Tackle here is generally lighter than that used on lake fish, except when working very large waterways and connecting reservoirs. Spinning rods from 5 1/2 to 7 feet long in medium action, and reels filled with 8- to 12-pound line are standard. Lure weights vary from 1/8- to 5/8-ounce and include spoons, spinners, jigs, minnow-style plugs, and crankbaits; live bait rigs are also used. Lure colors vary seasonally as they do with lake fish, with light colors popular in spring and fall and dark colors in midseason.

Jigs are by far the most effective lure that river walleye anglers can use. They work close to the bottom and well represent minnows and crayfish, which are the favorite foods of river walleye. Jigs that dig deep and walk along a rocky river bottom without becoming snagged are especially useful. Small and shallow rivers generally require 1/8- to 5/8-ounce jigs. In fast water you should increase weight; for example, use a 1/8-ounce jig in medium-fast rivers when depth averages 4 feet, but a 1/4-ounce jig in very fast water of the same depth.

A jig, barely visible in the mouth of this netted fish, is the top lure for river walleye fishing.

Fish jigs with the current. There is no need to jig them. A slow, rolling action is preferred in rivers, as current irregularity creates all the jig action needed. When casting across current with jigs, allow them to float along while raising and lowering your rod tip, keeping the jig just off bottom.

When selecting jig color, keep in mind that walleyes prefer minnows in spring and fall and crayfish during midsummer. In spring, use white, yellow, chartreuse, and silver colors. In fall, use the same colors as well as blue. In midsummer, select brown, black, green, or a combination of orange and brown.

Live bait, of course, is also quite effective and popular. A live-bait rig, 1/4- to 1-ounce in weight, rigged with 20 inches of dropback leader and a No. 2 short-shanked, turned-up-eye, bronze hook, is standard. Minnows, night crawlers, leeches, water dogs, salamanders, and crayfish are used. Preferred minnows are fatheads, stone rollers, shiners, river chubs, red-tailed chubs, and emerald shiners. Sinker style can be split-shot, rubber core, egg, Lindy, or Bait-Walker.

The third most effective river walleye catcher is a silver spinner. Sizes No. 0 through 3 are used, accompanied by a couple of BB-size split-shot for weight. Attach a short piece of white pork strip to the spinner's treble hook. This combo should be worked very slowly, often with the current, to be effective. Also productive at times is a small (2 1/2-inch-long), shallow-running crankbait. The best color is a crayfish pattern, but yellow or chartreuse are also effective. These are best used in moderate flows and, unless current is practically nonexistent, not in large-lipped, deep-diving versions. Strong currents cause deep divers to work erratically, running with abandon off to the side when cast.

Crankbaits (and minnow-imitating plugs) are also used effectively in combination with a trolling sinker. This is mainly a trolling rig, although it can be cast if a short (14 to 20 inches), dropback leader is used. These plugs work well behind 1 1/2- or 2-ounce, bottom-walking sinkers and are particularly useful when trolling center channels or working wing dams, so plugs get down deep on bottom without snagging or twisting.

No matter what lure you use, work it slowly, keep it on bottom, and, when possible, work it with the current; in other words, effect a downstream presentation so that lures and live bait come before walleye in a natural fashion. This is very important. Considering that most food comes with current, it follows that duplication of that presentation will catch fish. Minnows swept away from a slow-moving holding area, for example, though facing into the oncoming current, will slip downstream. Crayfish cannot swim upstream into currents and are forced to float with them or to crawl painstakingly upstream along the rocky bottom. Hellgrammites and grubs don't have a chance against oncoming currents, nor do leeches and earthworms. When current speeds reach 1 mph or more, these natural baits come downstream, so it is logical to present your offerings that way.

There are exceptions, of course, as there always are in fishing. Bait fish and large minnows (such as 3 1/2- to 5-inch-long red-tail chubs, shiners, and suckers) can maneuver up against fairly heavy current. They do so in a manner similar to sculpin, by darting from one bottom rock to another. Fathead minnows and several species of dace, especially those smaller than 2 inches, are unable to accomplish this and inadvertently are swept away by the current.

No matter what lure is used, you must affect a natural presentation in order to entice big river walleyes.

One way to capitalize on this downstream movement of natural food is to use either a jig tipped with live bait or live bait by itself on a single hook. Jigs should be tipped either with a minnow or a bit of night crawler. There is no need to keep the minnow alive. Embed it through the tough, bony part of its head, running the hook through the forehead and out its throat so the point of pull remains on the minnow's head. A tipped minnow will stay on much longer when hooked in such a manner. Tip a jig with a minnow in the spring and fall and with crawler pieces throughout the summer. Use just a *piece* of night crawler or you'll retard the action of the jig. The crawler is only there for scenting purposes.

Keep your rod tip high as you begin a downstream retrieve after casting your jig up above a likely fish position. It is easier to retrieve this way and to detect a strike. The strike of a river walleye can be difficult to feel until the fish turns and the line tightens at the rod tip. During that moment between strike and turn into current, you need a little insurance to help the fish hang onto your offering. Tipping provides this.

To present a tipped jig, keep your rod tip high and reel slack line up to keep pace with the current. Add very little motion, just a slow rolling, to your rod tip. The current will add enough action to the presentation to entice fish.

Live bait is used in a downstream presentation in much the same manner as jigs, although you have to pay close attention to sinker placement. Put split-shot generally within 6 inches of the hook, sometimes as close as 3 or 4 inches. With a live bait rig, use a 12- to 15-inch dropback leader. Minnows should be hooked through the lip, frogs and salamanders through the nose, leeches through their cupped mouths, and crayfish through the tail. Cut off the crayfish's claws to prevent him from grabbing onto the bottom.

Jig and sinker weights are determined by river depth and current force. A downstream presentation requires half the weight normally used in other forms of river presentation. With live bait, you might use as little as two No. 00 split shot or as much as a 3/8-ounce egg sinker. In shallow, fast rivers use 1/16- to 1/4-ounce jigs. In deeper, big rivers, use 1/4- to 1/2-ounce jigs.

Locales

Now that we've talked about methods and offerings, let's review the prime places to locate river walleyes.

Current cuts. Though current cuts may not be the No. 1 structure for river walleyes, they do contain the greatest variety of gamefish, including significant numbers of walleyes. A current cut, or edge, is that place where one current meets and passes another, for example, where an upstream surge of 2 mph eddy current butts against a 4 mph downstream main current. It is also where mainstream current brushes up against circulating, restless currents created directly behind and downstream from a bridge abutment; where main-river water pours around a wing dam; and where incoming small tributary current pushes its way into a larger, heavier flow. In essence, wherever two currents with different speeds (regardless of direction) meet, a current cut, or edge, is formed. Diagrams 8 and 9, on page 138, illustrate one example.

Diagram 8 shows a typical current cut created by a shoreline point and its circulating shoreline eddy, while Diagram 9 shows the water depth in that situation. The same type of structure may be created in much deeper water, perhaps double or triple the depth shown here.

Diagram 8

Diagram 9

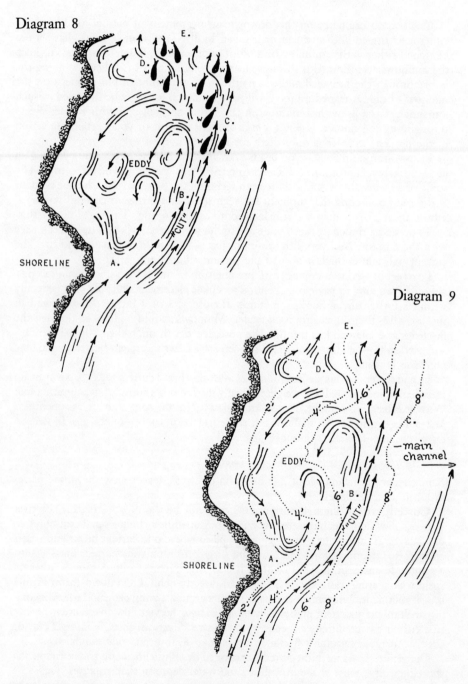

This current cut shows fish placement (left) and relative depth (right) in a typical, river walleye environment.

Contrary to popular belief, walleyes are seldom found in the upper areas of any eddy/cut structure. In the vicinity of location A of the accompanying diagrams, you may find crappie, northern pike, and smallmouth bass, but seldom walleyes. The only time that walleyes are found up near the head of the pool is when they are on the prowl, feeding.

It is also highly unlikely that you will find walleyes at location B, although this is an area that does attract smallmouth bass. Walleyes spend most of their time in an area along the cut, such as at location C. They will be just upstream from here a short distance from the eddy's end and will string out along the cut till it fades off toward shore. Note that walleyes hold directly along the 8-foot mark, which is the deepest they can locate within the cut's influence without falling off into heavy mainstream currents.

Note that at location D there are four fish that are holding directly under an area called a "slick." This is a smooth, heavy-flowing area where the surface shows disturbance. In most cases, the slick flows over a lift in the bottom. Walleyes that normally would hold along the cut drift up into this area to feed.

This situation and information holds true no matter how long a shoreline eddy is. When fishing such a structure you should approach it from downstream. Position yourself at location E and cast up along the inside of the cut to location B. You can fish from above it, too, by placing your anchor at point A or thereabouts, casting your offering downstream along the inside of the cut just past B. From here, while anchored, you can still-fish with live bait or retrieve a lure in slow, rolling motions.

The primary walleye food found along these eddy cuts are minnows, hellgrammites, and crayfish, which you can duplicate by using jigs, live-bait rigs, or crankbaits. Remember to fish a current cut from its inner, slower-moving side. This will minimize the effect of drag on your line.

River Islands. Though the area around river islands isn't considered top walleye grounds, it is one of the most widely fished structures and one that holds hordes of walleyes and their sauger cousins.

At locations A and B in Diagram 10 (page 140), schools of walleyes hold along the cut and mingle slightly into the inner-circulating waters in search of food. Directly behind the island, up from point A, a shifting school of fish rotates with the eddy current, undecided which cut area they will hold on. They will only stay there a few minutes. While there, if bait fish are available, the walleyes will feed.

Directly behind the island, walleyes may be taken on crankbaits, minnow-style plugs, or jigs. This is not a good area for live bait presentations. The fast and oft-repeated movement of lures through this spot is better. Walleyes come and go in this spot too fast for live bait to be continuously effective.

During early morning and late evening hours, points C and D hold the majority of walleyes that locate near this structure. Often these areas are 150 to 250 feet downstream from the island in big, slow rivers. In fast, rocky rivers, this distance is cut in half. Fish the area as you would any current cut at this point where main and secondary currents meet.

If sauger are available in the river system you fish, they will be found at locations E and F. Their movement in and out of these giant eddies is part of their natural search for food. They do not stage along a current cut nearly as much as walleyes do. Jigs tipped with bait work well at these spots. Work lures extremely slowly, directly on bottom.

Here are the places to look for walleyes
below a river island.

Diagram 10

If you fish on a large, slow river, walleyes will often hold at location G during
daylight hours, though they don't feed here nearly as much as they do in the other
regions described. However, live bait, such as shiner minnows, fatheads, crawlers,
or crayfish, will work when presented on a live bait rig. Water depth at this point
varies. In some rivers, it will be less than 10 feet; in others over 20. Adjust lure and
sinker weight accordingly. For best results, anchor and still-fish from an upstream
position, leaving live bait directly on bottom.

During late evening and after sunset hours, walleyes may migrate up to location
H. Here, they work shallow water along the current cut, feeding on schools of bait
fish. Often the water depth at H is less than 6 feet, sometimes only 2 feet, over rocky,
erratic terrain. Use small spoons, crankbaits, and spinner-jig combos here.

Hardpan Lifts. This is the premier structure for river walleyes. Wherever river bottom hardens, becomes rocky, and builds under layers of shale or gravel, you're apt to find walleyes. It is here, *upon the hardpan lifts*, that walleyes seek and feed upon bait fish, hellgrammites, and crayfish.

What is a "hardpan lift?" Where do you look for such structure? Every river system has its hardpan lifts. They can be found jutting out from points and bends, where surface rippling occurs, where frothing rapids are found, and where shorelines pinch together, creating a narrowing in river structure.

The key to discovering these lifts is looking for a disturbed river surface or rocky shoreline structure jutting out into a river's mainstream. When you see a swirl, boil, ripple, or surface bulge, there is a form of hardpan lift below it. Rock, gravel, shale, or stone are the materials remaining after riverbed waters have swept away all the mud, silt, and soft sand, and they make up the majority of river lifts. To understand why fish hold around and over these places, remember that walleyes in rivers are bottom-hugging fish that seek protection from current behind rocks. Currents coming down and around the rock create an eddying effect behind it. By nosing in behind an 8-inch rock, for example, a 10-pound walleye is able to hold stationary with little or no finning effort. The holding fish literally allows his chin to touch bottom in behind the rock. Rocks also provide excellent holding areas for bait fish, crayfish, and hellgrammites, which become an easy target for walleyes. All a hungry walleye has to do is open its mouth and scoop up the food. If a rock is large enough (1 to 2 feet in diameter) it may hold a school of walleyes. If it is just 3 to 4 inches in diameter, a fish up to 3 or 4 pounds could hold behind it. This explains why shallow, rocky riffles or rapids hold dozens of hungry fish.

Many anglers prefer to anchor and present live bait downstream into hardpan structures. Others troll slowly up and through them with heavily weighted lures. Still others cast cross-current and retrieve. All will take fish, but a downstream presentation is most productive.

To work hardpan lifts by casting, you must place your offering in a proper position from a proper angle to best imitate natural bait and successfully reach the target rock below. Start from below and to the side of the structure, casting above and slightly across the current. The closer you are to being straight below the structure, the better. Hold your rod tip high, retrieve rapidly, and float your lure over the bottom. Primarily use jigs, or jig-spinner and jig-bait combos. Though it may seem to be a rather fast presentation, that doesn't matter; hungry walleyes have an easy time catching fleeting downstream meals. The further you are situated from the side of this structure, the more you can use live bait rigs in addition to jigs or even diving plugs or spoons.

With a basic understanding of why fish are able to hold on these hard-textured structures and how they should be approached, let's examine a hardpan lift in more detail, referring to Diagrams 11 and 12 on page 142. These are identical, 11 being an overhead view and 12 a cross-sectional view.

Where rough water exists (locations 1 and 2), there is a pair of typical river hardpan lifts. Shorelines pinch inward, bottom hardens and rises upwards, and surface waters become rough. Both areas are excellent fish producers.

Location 3 always provides larger walleyes during the summer and fall seasons. Only during and just after the spring spawning run does location 1 provide big fish.

Diagram 11

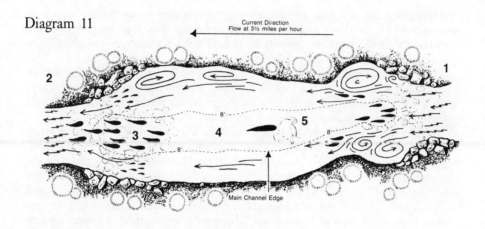

Diagram 12

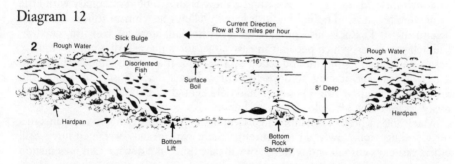

The hardpan lift described in the text is shown above in an overhead view (Diagram 11) and below that in a cross-sectional view (Diagram 12).

For the most part, small fish are to be found on the downriver side of hardpan lifts, and a lot of them can be caught here.

The area that particularly interests every river angler is in and around location 3, which is a prime river walleye hole. The best holding site for walleyes here is that spot between the beginning of the uplifted area and the end of the bulging slick. Here, hungry walleyes wait behind rocks for food to come to them. Schools of bait fish, frightened by the compression of water atop the shallow, rocky area, become disoriented. They arrive here after being forced downstream by current, and they flee in a disorganized fashion back upstream or toward river bottom, becoming an easy target for holding walleyes below.

The exact spot at which large walleyes hold is where the river begins its upward bottom lift back toward an area just below the disoriented bait fish. Smaller walleyes will hold in an area below the disoriented bait fish, extending to where rough water begins.

As seen in Diagram 11, most walleyes locate in the river's center-channel region in the 8-foot-deep section. This is especially so in late summer and fall; however, walleyes will spread out into shallower areas above a hardpan lift during early spring and midsummer days. Food availability governs these actions. Late in the season, bait fish tend to locate near the river's central channel area, while earlier in the year they spread out over the entire upstream region above the lift.

Anglers who haven't fished this river structure are advised to look for a bulging slick on the surface. This is atop each hardpan lift. A bulging slick is a section of smooth, flat water that appears to lift up on the surface just ahead of shallow, rough water. You must make your presentation above and upstream from this.

You should realize that although it appears to be a short distance between the two hardpan lifts in these diagrams, perhaps as much as half a mile may separate them. With this in mind, you can better understand why small holding rocks, such as those shown at location 5, are so important for the angler to investigate. These illustrations, incidentally, show a more open view of the single-rock structure that attracts large walleyes. The structure lies between locations 4 and 5.

Hardpan lifts do not always appear as represented in these illustrations. They may take the form of rock wing dams; gravel bars on small streams; shale ledges in deep, slow-moving rivers; hardened granite walls in far northern rivers; or stony bars on a mountain waterway. In each case, there's a good chance that more and bigger fish will be taken from the upstream side of these hardpan lifts than from the downstream side of them, a fact that many river walleye anglers don't realize.

There are numerous other areas to look for walleyes in rivers, too. For example, look for large, single boulders that protrude just above the current. Here, walleyes

River walleyes are found in various places in rivers; they are primarily located on the bottom.

will always be downstream from the rock at a point where the current cuts join and there is a smooth slick.

In the spring and fall, river walleyes will locate at the mouths of large and small tributaries. In the spring, they are drawn by spawning needs; in the fall, it's bait fish. Here, too, current cuts and hardpan lifts should be worked.

When working a river that has rocky waterfalls, some of the best walleye fishing is just above a waterfall, not below it. Once again, walleyes take advantage of disoriented bait fish that become frightened by the waterfall behind them. In some cases, walleyes hold a mere 10 feet from where the falls drop off and down. Casting upstream and retrieving downstream is the most efficient way to entice fish here.

In large river systems, many walleye anglers work close to dams. This is alright during winter and early spring (spawning time). However, it is often better to work deep waters off wing dams, island channel cuts, deep-water bridge abutments, and center channel edges. All of these spots require the use of stout tackle, heavy sinkers, and live bait. Look for walleyes in July and August to locate along a river channel that has considerable depth, where the bottom drops from 20 to 40 feet. Fish here will be situated where there is an indent in the channel wall at about 23 to 28 feet deep.

If there is one, almost-guaranteed-action place to look for walleyes in large rivers, we'd have to say it was at riprap just as the sun sets. This is especially true if there is deep channel water close at hand. You'll also encounter smallmouth bass here, but if the waterway holds walleyes, they'll come to this spot to feed on its enormous population of minnows and crayfish. Start by using a crankbait, and if this doesn't produce, go to a jig.

River walleyes, incidentally, shouldn't be overlooked for sporting traits. They can be scrappy devils, much better fighters than their lake cousins. One way in which they are like their lake relatives, however, is in edibility. That makes them doubly tough to beat for angling enjoyment.

CHAPTER ELEVEN
NORTHERN PIKE

The evil-eyed, spear-shaped northern pike is a fish that might well have been named "water wolf." Indeed, it is often likened to the notoriously vicious barracuda of saltwater. Although disparaged by a few fishermen who catch pike while seeking other species of fish, the pike is a worthy angling quarry, one that grows fairly large, fights well, and accommodates sportsmen often enough to be of substantial interest to a lot of anglers in the areas in which they are found.

The distribution of northern pike today ranges throughout Alaska, across river and lake systems in the central and southern half of Canada's Northwest Territories, down into Wyoming, through the Missouri River waterway, across northern Kentucky, up through Pennsylvania, and into the province of Quebec. They have been stocked in impoundments elsewhere, including such states as Texas, New Mexico, Oklahoma, Tennessee, and Alabama, where they have attained a 10-pound average in just over three years, but have a relatively short lifespan. Northern states such as Minnesota, Wisconsin, Michigan, and the Dakotas host pike in nearly all their water systems. Trophy-size pike, however, which were once widely available, now are primarily found in the northern regions of Canadian provinces, while an occasional big fish (over 18 pounds) is taken in other waters. Impoundments on the Missouri River in North and South Dakota still produce a good number of such fish.

From the day they hatch, pike eat their way into larger territory. They first kill off brood brothers, an instinct that stays with them always, as later 10-pound pike will eat 1- and 2-pound pike and 20-pound pike will eat 3- and 4-pound pike. They will, of course, eat just about anything—ducklings, mice, squirrels, muskrats, turtles, snakes, a range of fish species, and birds. Blackbirds, for example, especially bold and aggressive males, fall victim to pike during spring when brush and wooded areas are flooded as they dance inches above water on overhanging limbs. The gluttonous aggression of pike is actually a trait that endears them to a legion of anglers.

Northern pike begin their spawning ritual when water temperature reaches 50 degrees. Spawning may occur at lower temperatures further north. Pike spawn when possible in heavily weeded cover; the more growth available, the better for the highly adhesive eggs.

Born in weedy waters, pike spend much of their life in similar habitat, holding motionless in the vegetation, camouflaged for suddenly striking passersby. Menacingly, the northern pike waits in ambush for a moment of attack.

Key habitat structures in lakes include weedy bays, river inlets where weeds are plentiful, shoreline points with beds of cabbage weeds on their open-water sides, reefs

Northern pike are aggressive gluttons, which makes them a good quarry for anglers.

with coontail weeds, marshy shorelines, lily pads, and reedy pockets along sandy and rocky shorelines. There are many others, but some form of vegetative structure obviously holds a major portion of the pike population.

In rivers, again look for weeds. Try areas where small rivers and streams merge with the main flow. Always try the small eddy beneath a beaver lodge. Try downstream from islands, shallow backwaters, shorelines just below riprap or wing dams, the inside of large eddies, the back side of bridge pilings, under docks, and where brush and slow water meet. River pike are lazy fish. They, too, establish an ambush position. There is no better place to accomplish this than where still water and passing river current come together. Look for pike in the still area and present your offering along the edge of the moving water.

If you were to take a poll to determine which lure is best for northern pike, seven out of ten people would name the red and white Eppinger Dardevle spoon. This is a good, traditional, lure choice, but that is not the only thing that will take pike, even though some anglers fish practically nothing else.

Other highly effective lures include a fluorescent, orange-bladed spinnerbait or bucktail spinner; an orange and yellow-backed minnow-imitation plug; a yellow, Five-O-Diamonds pattern spoon; a black bucktail with a single fluorescent spinner; and some crankbaits in gaudy metallic colors.

Good pike lures tend to be brightly colored and flashy and to work erratically. If two anglers were to troll a yellow spinnerbait and a black spinnerbait through pike and bass waters, the yellow one would take pike and the black one would take bass 90 percent of the time. This should tell a first-time pike hunter something: select lures that have pizzazz.

Lure types and the techniques used to present them vary greatly for northern pike, although many would-be pike catchers stick to the simplicity of casting spoons in and around weeds. Casting weedless spoons directly into a mass of shoreline vegetation and retrieving outward can have merit, of course. The Johnson Silver Minnow is the most popular spoon for this, primarily being used in silver, but also in brass, black, and multi-pattern colors. Nothing represents a darting, foraging minnow better in heavy vegetation. Some anglers deftly cast non-weedless spoons (such as a Dardevle or Doctor) around cover for pike with some success, as well as such plugs as the Creek Chub Pikie, Cisco Kid, and Rapala.

While all of these lures catch many fish in wilderness waters, just casting a flashy spoon or plug at a clump of weeds may produce a pike, but it isn't always the answer or the only option. It often takes a little more effort to dupe pike in heavily fished environs, meaning that some other lures and techniques come into play.

Large jigs, with and without spinners, for example, are becoming more of a pike angling tool, although jigs are not normally a lure used for fish that reside in and around vegetation. Many new pike jigs, looking like plastic eels, are brightly colored. Some are constructed of natural hair, most of synthetic material, while others are molded from plastic. Most measure 10 to 14 inches in length, with oversize lead heads, and a single, long-shanked hook that protrudes upward 4 inches back along the eel's body. During hot summer months, use an eel jig without a spinner. In spring and fall, add a silver, 3/0-bladed, jig-and-spinner combination.

If there is an exception to the gaudy lure color rule, it can be found with this product. Eel jigs are manufactured in a variety of natural finishes, including perch, sucker, shad, and pike, and are found in the standard pearl, fluorescent yellow, and two-tone orange/black colors, all of which can be effective.

Some anglers slow-troll these big jigs along the deep edge of weed beds, slowly lifting and lowering the rod tip as they go. Others cast them to the outer edges of cabbage and reed clusters. Casting directly into the heart of a cabbage weed patch and jerking this jig rapidly toward you in 3- to 4-foot sweeps works best. The jig hook seldom attaches itself to the weeds and, when it does, it loses them on the following jerk.

Surface plugs are lures that are generally not considered pike catchers, though some work well at times. In the spring, just after ice-out, is one of those times. Then, minnows flood black loam bays in northern lakes, drawn by warm shallow water to spawn. Pike are attracted by the gathering and stalk the minnows in packs.

Spotting such an event is easy. Look for dozens of surface-breaking minnows as they frantically flee near the surface. At times there may be several dozen silvery minnows above the surface at a time. Between noon and 2 P.M., in the warmest part of the day, is prime time. By casting almost any silver-plated spoon, you can hook plenty of fish, but for a great thrill, try small floating plugs that have a rear spinner or propeller.

Pike seldom strike a surface lure that is more than 3 inches long at this time of year; most of the minnows you are attempting to represent are shorter than 3 inches, and duplicating the look of these bait fish is of utmost importance. Watch for a surface explosion of bait fish followed by a series of swirls and boils, then cast into the immediate vicinity. Allow the bait to rest a moment, twitch it ever so slightly, hold, and twitch again. If there isn't a strike by the time a third twitch is made, retrieve and cast again in the direction the minnows were running. Often, if the water is clear enough, you can see a pike race up under the bait; the fish waits until the lure is again twitched, then charges up to ingest it.

Fishing jigs along the edge of deep weeds or in the midst of cabbage weeds can produce big pike.

Obviously, feeding pike mistake such a surface lure for a crippled or floundering minnow and see it as an easy meal. Address your presentation accordingly, but don't overwork the lure. Leave enough time between rod-induced lure movement so the fish below believe it is a dying, crippled minnow struggling periodically on the surface.

This type of surface plug can also be used during calm days along shorelines when there is no obvious feeding spree going on and at the mouths of stream confluences. It may catch springtime, northern pike of all sizes, but during lazy summer days, you will seldom take a fish over 5 pounds on it, in part because most larger pike retreat into deeper water near weed beds then.

Spinnerbaits have come into their own in the last decade among the pike-fishing fraternity. Bright colors seem to work best most often, although during late July and throughout August, a jet-black skirt and fluorescent orange, willowleaf blade really produce.

Spinnerbaits can be used with or without a trailer hook or trailer skirt, though rubber skirts add some appeal and hold up better than marabou or vinyl versions. To further improve a spinnerbait's pike appeal, add a curl-tail body to a trailer hook or to the spinnerbait hook. This should be of a contrasting color. Single-bladed models are preferred over double-bladed ones, and the willowleaf shape is better than the Colorado.

Fish spinnerbaits through weed beds, around timber, up against stumps, in and about brush, and across rocky points. They work exceptionally well in the spring when pike stage in extremely shallow water during spawning and post-spawning periods.

A spinnerbait with a trailer hook is a particularly good spring lure.

Obviously shallow, visible weeds are pike haunts that can be worked with several types of lures, but anglers should recognize that they must move to deeper weed beds in warm weather to find the mid- to large-sized northerns. Deep-water cabbage weed beds hold midsummer pike, and this structure is found in most northern lakes. To locate this weed, look in water that exceeds 6 or 7 feet in depth and goes down to 15 feet. This is the common depth for cabbage weeds, also known to anglers as "pike weeds." This vegetation begins producing fish the moment its growth reaches half the height of the depth in which it grows.

During early summer days, pike migrate to this structure where it has grown in 6 to 8 feet of water. At this time, the weeds are 3 to 5 feet tall. As summer progresses, fish continue their migration into cabbage weeds that grow in water that is 8 to 12 feet deep. By midsummer, the cabbage has reached maturity and can be spotted just under the surface. Cabbage, or pike, weeds never grow above the surface or lie on the surface. In late summer, their seed pods will cluster a few inches under the surface but will not touch the surface. If you see weeds that grow to the surface and out along it, if only a few inches, they are not cabbage but a variety of coontail. This type is not apt to hold pike as well as cabbage will.

In cabbage weed beds, single plants are spaced 18 to 24 inches apart while sporting willowleaf-shape tentacles 6 to 10 inches long. The shorter the leaf and the closer plants grow to one another, the fewer pike such an area will hold. Small pike tend to stage in great numbers in cabbage weeds that grow 6 to 8 inches apart but seldom will these fish have much weight, the average being 3 to 5 pounds.

Big pike, from 10 to 25 pounds, hold in larger cabbage, which grows in deeper water. Look to the outer edge of this, in 10 to 14 feet of water, for trophy fish. Pockets or indentations in the cabbage are especially notable. Here, trophy pike lie on either side of these openings, waiting to ambush the smaller fish that swim out of the main weed bed. If you can find a large patch of cabbage where shoreline weeds lie in approximately 6 feet of water and outside weeds lie in approximately 14 feet, you've found ideal pike country.

Lures that work in cabbage vary greatly. They should be large if you seek trophy-size pike. It is above cabbage weeds that many pike anglers switch to musky-size surface baits. Giant Jitterbugs, imitation muskrats, lengthy jerk baits, large minnow-imitation plugs, and huge poppers can all be used. No matter which surface lure you choose, it must be worked very slowly. Give it plenty of time between twitches or jerks. One lure that you can work fast, however, and be successful, is a large Mann's 1 Minus crankbait, which makes a lot of noise and runs just below the surface.

Large spoons, both weedless and standard, are also used around cabbage. One of the favorites is a 12-inch-long number that comes from Norway called a Piker spoon. Dardevles, Johnson Silver Minnows, and crippled bait fish imitation spoons are likewise productive and work best in oversize versions.

But, if we had only one lure to work cabbage, it would be a large black (yellow is a good second choice), musky-style bucktail spinner with fluorescent orange blade. Day in and day out, this bait will take more pike off cabbage than any other lure. It is a bit difficult to cast because of its bulk and a tendency to hold water (which makes it heavier), but it is worth it. Surprisingly, these large, treble-hooked lures can be cast directly into the cabbage without becoming tangled in weeds too often, provided you don't let them sink too far after they enter the water. And, with the deeper cabbage weeds spaced as they are, you can guide your lure through them by moving the rod tip from side to side.

Although casting for northern pike is the preferred method of presentation, many anglers find trolling rewarding. Northerns are a fish that easily fall victim to a lure trolled at a rapid speed. Their lack of caution and vicious attacking style makes speed trolling feasible. To do this, for example, using a 14-foot aluminum boat and 10 h.p. motor, the throttle would be set nearly at half speed. Sometimes the throttle might be set nearer to three-quarter speed, but 6 to 10 mph is the range.

Spinnerbaits make excellent rapid trolling lures. If their wire arms are aligned prop-

Weeds, both shoreline and submerged cabbage, are the hallmark of pike terrain.

erly, the lure won't spin, and the rotating blade thumps a constant signal to nearby pike. You may have to add weight to the lure to keep it beneath the surface (depending on boat speed); attach weight 18 to 20 inches up the line. Sometimes, however, a lure that breaks the surface every now and then works better.

Spoons can also be effective in speed trolling, provided they don't twist your line (using a good quality swivel will counter that). Flashy spoons in fluorescent orange, red, or chartreuse normally get the nod. Spoons in the 3- to 4-inch range normally are chosen, but larger 5- to 8-inch-long models can be used as well. Large jigs with an oversized spinner, some plugs, some in-line spinners with ball bearing swivels, and even a few surface baits will work for speed trolling. If the water is shallow, a propellered surface lure that is long and tapered can create a great deal of excitement.

Use a rather long line when speed trolling for pike. There must be a fair distance between the lure and the passage of the boat, so 125 to 150 feet of line is recommended. This is not the occasion for light tackle, incidentally, as the shock of the strike of an attacking pike can be hard on equipment. Bait-casting tackle is preferred, with fairly strong line.

Lures aren't the only pike attraction, of course. Bait, in the form of dead smelt, sucker strips, live chubs, suckers, and perch (where legal) are part of the repertoire. They can be suspended beneath a float or cast, and they can be retrieved or left stationary on the bottom.

In large western reservoirs, frozen smelt are affixed to hooks, cast from shore, and allowed to rest on the deep sloping reservoir bottom. A dead bait rig, combining a large single hook (3/0 to 5/0 size), a wire leader drop-back, and a 2/0 short-shank, treble hook, is used. The single hook is forced into the mouth and out the smelt's forehead. The leader is then pushed up through the gill cover and attached to the single hook. Finally, the treble hook is snapped to the leader's loose end, and one of its barbs is forced into the smelt's tail. The lead weight used on the rigs varies from a mere 3/4-ounce (just enough to force the frozen bait to bottom) to as much as 4 or 5 ounces. Slip sinkers are preferred, with an egg sinker used most of the time.

These dead bait rigs are used in small bays, casting the smelt so it reaches the bay's midway point when flung from one of its shorelines. This same rig can be used in many hard-fished waters across the northern regions of the United States and Canada. Preferred bottom conditions are sand or gravel. There can be some scattering of cabbage weeds, but the bottom should be devoid of fuzzy weeds or moss.

Sucker strips can be used in a manner similar to frozen smelt but are most effective when trolled or cast. The bait is fashioned by cutting a long, belly meat strip, including the front bottom fins, from a 1- to 3-pound sucker, or by filleting either side of a sucker. Fillet strips should be cut thin, with the skin intact. Like the frozen smelt rig, a large single hook is embedded through the skin of the thick head end. With a belly strip, make sure the hook is embedded ahead of the bait's pectoral fins, otherwise the bait's action will be cut considerably, diminishing its effectiveness greatly.

By rigging a strip of sucker meat (some anglers put a spinner blade ahead of it) behind a proper sinker rig, you can troll the outer reaches of weed beds or deep-water areas where suspended pike lie. Run the bait behind a keel sinker, bead-chain sinker, or Bait-Walker rig; these don't create twist whereas pinch-on and snap-on weights often do. There should be at least 36 inches between strip and sinker. Sinker weight varies depending on the depth at which you intend to troll; try 1 ounce of lead for every

8 feet of water depth desired, considering that a high speed is being trolled. Pike like fast-moving baits in shallow water and a bit slower-moving bait in deeper water.

Because pike tend to strike a rapidly moving bait at its middle, the use of a treble-hooked stinger is believed to help catch fish. But a greater number of fish are lost when hooked by a treble stinger on the first strike. Therefore, use only a large, single hook. Once a strike is felt and the fish has firmly attached itself to the bait, drop the rod tip, open the bail or put the reel into free-spool, and cut the motor. Retrieve any slack line and gradually work the fish toward the boat. If he lets go, a couple of soft jigging motions with the bait will generally cause the fish to return. This time, he will attack the bait at the head end, an act that will see him hooked in proper fashion.

If a strike is felt and the fish is lost, try increasing trolling speed immediately. This may cause the pike to strike the bait higher up and be impaled on the large single hook. As you may have gathered, northern pike like the feel of soft fish flesh and are not easily discouraged away from strip baits.

To cast bait rigs, shorten the length of line between sinker and bait; 20 inches is about right. For casting, use a treble-hooked stinger. With the rod in hand, you have an opportunity to set the hook hard on the first strike. Work the edges of weed patches, rocky drop-offs, and lily pads for best results while casting dead bait rigs.

Live baits, including large chubs and suckers, can be presented a number of ways. These work well when suspended beneath a bobber. Use an appropriate size bobber, perhaps 3 to 4 inches in diameter, which is determined on the water by trial and error. A healthy sucker should just be able to sink the bobber to which it's attached but not so much as to keep it under more than a second or two.

As with fishing lures for pike, a steel leader should be used in live bait fishing, since the sharp cutting teeth of pike are no match for monofilament line. If live bait is suspended less than 4 feet beneath your bobber, all the drop line should be wire, preferably fine monel. Fifteen-pound test monel is adequate, unless the fish you work are unusually large.

Hook size depends on the size of your live bait; the bigger the bait, the bigger the hook. Normally, 3/0 and 4/0 hooks are used. Just enough sinker is used to hold the live bait down. Hook the bait behind the dorsal fin, allowing it to balance ever so slightly forward. Such positioning affords the bait a better leverage for swimming, and the livelier it is, the better.

One of the most productive areas to fish suckers and chubs under bobbers is in holes in lily pad patches. Here pike lie in wait along the pad's outer rim. Another spot is thick reed edges where water depth holds at 3 feet. Success depends on how close you place your live bait to the reed's open-water edge.

Live suckers and chubs can also be free-lined. During the peak of summer, some pike retreat to deep water along cabbage weeds, off rocky points, and along deep-river channels. Suspended, they wait for the arrival of perch, bluegill, suckers, shiners, chubs, and smaller game fish and are vulnerable to a free-lined sucker or chub.

Rigging bait for this is simple. Hook the bait halfway between the tail and dorsal fin, being careful not to touch its spine when running the hook point through and under the skin. If you fish shallow water, there is no need for a sinker. Your wire leader and hook provide enough weight to sink the bait slowly. In water deeper than 8 feet, add split-shot or sinkers to force the bait down. In many cases, a lively bait will seek the shelter of deep water on its own.

Approach from a deep-water position. Cast your offering in on structure (use a soft, two-handed cast which arcs your bait toward the target on a 45–degree angle), allow it time to swim deep, and gradually work the bait toward deep water.

Regarding tackle, bait-casting, spin-casting, and spinning gear are all suitable, though bait-casting is most preferable where large lures or bait are used. Line capacity is not a big factor with reels in pike fishing. Rods should be 5 1/2 to 7 feet for lure use, with a stiff butt and midsection and rather fast tip. A good live bait rod is stiff and longer, up to 8 feet in length.

Most pike fishermen prefer heavy line, with 12- to 17-pound-test favored. There are many who chase northerns in a more sporting fashion on 6-, 8-, or 10-pound lines. The one difficulty with light lines is the heavy weeds in which these fish are found. Pike tend to make long, steady runs through the thickest of weed beds. When this happens, lines lighter than 10-pound-test may not withstand the pressure. To compound the problem, that same hooked pike will make two or three hard dashes in the opposite direction through the same weed bed before he's finished. As a result, we think 12-pound line is a good medium, even where big fish are concerned, although we recognize that there are times when even a 25-pound-test line may not do the trick. When spawning in the upper regions of small, flooded creeks, for example, hooked northerns often dash in and about flooded timber. It takes a strong line to stand the wear and tear of such action.

Subduing a pike, be it large or small, is good sport, however, no matter what the conditions. Some pike do little fighting until brought close to the boat, when all hell breaks loose. Others, especially large fish, give you a battle from the moment they are hooked. Those that strike a lure suddenly, right at the boat, are the most startling, but this all adds up to a lot of fun.

Line capacity isn't usually a concern for reels used with pike, but rods should be fairly sturdy.

CHAPTER TWELVE
MUSKELLUNGE

Musky fishing really isn't like any other kind of freshwater fishing. Muskies aren't like any other freshwater fish. Either you love to fish for muskies — no doubt through some quirk of human behavior — or you don't want to bother with them at all. Because of the unpredictable nature of the quarry, musky fishing is one activity in which you needn't feel disappointed if you haven't succeeded by the end of the day, which ought to tell you something about the level of dedication needed to be rewarded in this endeavor. The fact that musky fishermen are proud to note that they have simply seen a fish — called a "follow" — and that "close" counts in musky angling as it does in horseshoes also tells you something.

Let's state right up front: muskies *are* tough to catch. Tougher, probably, than any other freshwater game fish. But they aren't as tough as the 10,000-casts-per-fish theory has it. Indeed, there are anglers who are able to do far better than the common catch rate. In part, that is because some fishermen who call themselves musky anglers are quite casual about their musky fishing; they fish for muskies as an afterthought while primarily pursuing such species as walleye, or pike, or bass. There is a distinction between catching the elusive muskellunge and fishing for them, and most anglers go equipped more with hope than with expectation.

If constant action and numbers are your game, muskies aren't for you. On the other hand, if you rarely see a musky, let alone catch one, you're probably doing something wrong. The road to success begins by acquiring a fundamental understanding of the fish and its habitat. Muskies are primarily caught near some specific form of cover. It is arguable whether they always inhabit that particular locale or merely visit it frequently to feed. In some waters, especially those that are shallow, small, and without great areas for muskies to wander, these fish will take up a station that is conducive to their feeding, security, and body comfort requirements, and stay there until late in the season. In other waters, particularly large lakes and rivers, some fish will stay in one locale while others will spend most of their time in deep-water sanctuaries, migrating to desirable locales (which could be shoals, weeds, points, etc.) strictly to feed, then returning to deep water.

It isn't particularly necessary to determine which of these conditions holds true where you are fishing for muskies, unless you'll be spending a great deal of time on that water and want to establish patterns of behavior to narrow down productive fishing times. What is important is to be able to identify and find the places that are likely to hold feeding muskies, particularly in the fall, when the best musky angling

Muskies are probably the toughest freshwater fish to catch; besides being able to identify musky habitat, you have to be a dedicated, persistent angler.

of the year is usually experienced, and particularly where there is an opportunity to catch really big muskies.

Muskellunge do not roam in search of food. They lurk in or by places where food is abundant and where they can lie relatively concealed to pounce on appropriate-sized forage. The angler seeking likely musky lairs should determine if prospective areas are conducive to good feeding opportunities. Veteran anglers refer to such musky feeding stations as ambush points. When trying to locate muskies, think in terms of the available forage and its habits and a musky's predisposition toward ambush points.

Muskies often seem to have preferred forage in every body of water, though it is sometimes hard to quantify this. Walleyes are undoubtedly one of their preferred foods, and you don't have to search hard to find an angler who has had a musky attempt to steal a walleye that was being brought to boat. Ciscoes, suckers, perch, golden shiners, and bass are also prime musky foods, and other species of forage and game fish enter into the equation in various areas. I am told of a taxidermist who mounted many muskies and reported finding bullheads in the stomachs of a lot of the muskies he prepared.

It is unlikely that muskies will consume a lot of small fish to make a meal or to chase abundant, open-water prey such as shad or alewives, but muskies may take such tidbits if open-water prey wander near their ambush stations. Muskies do strike big lures, perhaps because they are prone to eating big fish. There have been many instances documented of muskies consuming fish that are up to a third of their own length. A 15-inch walleye, for example, really isn't that big to a 40-inch muskellunge.

It seems reasonable to assume that after a musky consumes a big meal, it will be fortified for a day or several days and may not need to move into an ambush spot to feed. It also wouldn't need to follow bait fish to constantly be near a food source.

Realistically, this all adds up to a generally site-specific fish that utilizes certain places to feed because it attracts prey large enough to make an ambush attack worthwhile. Type of cover, depth, and the presence of current will determine which places are better than others.

Submerged vegetation is a primary musky lair. Small muskies relate heavily to cover and, in the case of vegetation, may lie in the midst of weed beds; bigger muskies don't seem able to move within that cover well enough to forage, so they are attracted to the edges of that cover at the breakline where weeds end and deep water begins and at the corners, pockets, or other irregular contour features.

Another important musky locale is a point of land. Points, whether they extend from the contiguous shoreline or from islands, are natural impediments to fish movement and attractants to prey and predator alike for migration, home-area identification, and security. The most attractive points are those that have a long, underwater slope and are adjacent to deep water, especially if they break sharply from 10 feet off to 20 or 25, those that have some form of heavy vegetation around their perimeters, or those that have rock piles on the underwater breaklines.

Yet another prominent musky lair is an open-water shoal. Underwater mounds or islands, sand bars, and gravel bars are roughly the same thing. These locations may be rocky or boulder-strewn, or they may be sandy with moderate weed growth, but they attract small bait fish, which in turn attract such fish as perch, smallmouths, or walleyes, making them favorable feeding areas for muskies.

This shoal, with weeds nearby, is a likely musky lair, especially if it is close to deep water.

There are, of course, other places where muskies can be found, places that hold feeding opportunities for a particular reason. In some musky waters, for instance, there are warm-water discharges in areas that may not otherwise seem to be top musky locales. In the fall, the immediate area near such a discharge is affected and may be attractive to forage fish and muskies. A feeder creek that is cool in the summer or one that is warm in the fall (both offering slight water temperature changes in the immediate tributary area) can spur feeding activity and thus be a good place to fish.

Current is also a big factor. A point or shoal that is washed by strong current is a prominent place to find muskies. A locale where strong current can bring bait washing by, or which retards the movement of weak, crippled, or wounded fish, is another. Back eddies, slicks, and current edges are more good spots. Where a secondary tributary meets a major flow is also a promising locale, especially in summer when the secondary tributary may be dumping cooler and more oxygenated water into the main flow.

Finding and catching muskies, then, requires attention to lake or river conditions. The person who motors his way around a musky lake without regard to the type of water conditions he faces will most likely be unsuccessful.

Muskellunge are said to prefer a water temperature that ranges from the mid-50's to low 70's, which covers the usual water temperatures from late spring through early fall, and they seem to adapt to the higher and lower ends of that range as local conditions warrant. They spawn in very shallow, near-shore water in the spring, usually before the fishing season is open in northern states, stay around in the near-shore shallows for a while after spawning, then move out to deeper environs. Deep, however, is a relative term.

Most muskellunge are caught quite shallow throughout the season, usually in less than 30 feet of water and primarily under 20 feet. This is as true on the most reknowned muskie producers, as well as on hundreds of smaller waters, although in the summer on southern highland impoundments, muskies may suspend in deeper water over river channels and sharp drop-offs. Most muskies caught by casters are taken in 10 to 20 feet of water as well, in part because these are the depths at which most fishermen are proficient.

Casting is the foremost method of pursuing muskies on most bodies of water, in part out of tradition, in part out of practicality (heavy vegetation on small bodies of water hinders most trolling efforts), and in part due to law (trolling for muskies is prohibited in some bodies of water, particularly in Midwestern states). Casting can provide not only the thrill of feeling a strike and setting the hook, but also the sighting of fish. Trollers don't see fish that might follow their lures, but casters often do. Being curious creatures, muskies will follow a boat and eyeball a lure up close. They'll pursue a cast-and-retrieved bait right up to the boat, occasionally striking at boatside, more often slinking off into the depths.

A following fish sometimes can be caught by repetitive casting to the same area, but it is much more likely to be taken right at the boat. It is said that 70 percent of all musky strikes—for casters—occur right at the boatside. Not all fish that follow a lure are noticed, but veteran anglers watch the water behind their lures carefully. Most musky casters make a frantic, figure-eight motion with their lure by the boat when they see a following fish, and some do it every time they bring their lure in, whether they see a fish or not. (In clear water, it is possible to see a fish from a fair distance away, but in dingy water, you may not see a fish until it is right under your nose.)

To accomplish the figure-eight retrieve, stick the rod tip a few inches into the water and, with 6 to 12 inches of line out beyond the tip, make a furious series of figure-eight patterns in the water with the rod. This makes the lure move frantically, perhaps like an alarmed, fleeing prey, and sometimes triggers a strike from a following musky. Maybe the fish simply are stimulated by the frothy, water-beating activity. We may never know, but the point is that sometimes this catches fish. Just hold onto your rod and be sure the drag control is set properly on your reel.

Just as mysterious as the question of why muskies do what they do is the matter of what lures muskies will strike. A bucktail spinner is the premier muskie-catching lure among casters, but one can legitimately ask if this is because more people fish this than any other type of lure or because bucktails are truly the lure preferred most by muskies. There's no simple answer.

Bucktails, which are weighted, in-line spinners heavily dressed with bucktail hair over one or two treble hooks, are of primary use in shallow- to mid-depth casting, over the top of submerged cover, and along the edges of shallow submerged cover. The Mepps Giant Killer, Blue Fox Vibrax, and Eppinger Buhl Spinner are typically popular muskie bucktails. These lures are found in a host of color combinations, some quite gaudy, but black is the top producer, hands down.

Diving plugs, shallow-running minnow-style baits, jigs (1/2- to 1-ounce versions with hair and soft-plastic, single or twin-tailed bodies), and jerk baits are the other principal types of musky lures. Jerk baits, which are a form of lure peculiar to musky fishing, are quite popular. They are large wooden plugs, 6 to 10 inches long, that are very buoyant and that are fished in a pull-pause retrieve. Few jerk baits do anything more than slip inactively through the water when pulled and bob up when paused.

Bucktail spinners, jerk baits, diving plugs, and an assortment of other lures make up the musky angler's repertoire.

If ever there was a "do-nothing" lure, it is the jerk bait, yet there are times when this type of lure is the only bait that will get a rise from fish. Many jerk baits are homemade, some resembling nothing more than a broom handle. Perhaps the most effective of them all is the Suick, a flattened, rectangularly shaped, wooden plug with a metal lip and tail, which darts just a few inches below the surface when retrieved. Eddie Baits, Teddy Baits, and a variety of others have their own devotees as well.

Obviously bucktails, swimming plugs, and jerk baits are fairly shallow-running products, yet all of the various musky lure types can be used around the weedy habitat that musky casters predominantly work. Jigs and crankbaits are worked around the edges, of course, and sometimes are retrieved over the top of deeply submerged vegetation. A good tactic with deep-diving plugs is to reel them down till they hit vegetation, then stop the retrieve (which allows the lure to float upward), then reel it in a few feet till you hit vegetation, then stop, and so forth.

Muskies, as mentioned previously, do follow cast lures, and it is not uncommon for them to come well away from cover to trail a lure or to strike it, and there are often strikes that are in relatively deep water and well away from the main site (weedy point or reef, for example) that you might be casting to. This happens with jerk baits and bucktails as much as with deep-diving plugs. Deep-diving plugs, however, are better than other lure types for fishing reefs, points and quick-current edges that don't have vegetation on them.

With all these lure types, fishing presentation is a vital element. How you fish for muskies—the way you use your boat and equipment to cope with the fishing conditions—can be a main factor in your success. Running up to a large weed bed, for example, then drifting over it while making a cast or two is a sloppy way to fish. Better to drift along the side, rather than through the prime habitat, which allows you many casts over the cover without alarming any fish that might be there. Even better would be using an electric motor. The musky caster can use an electric motor as much as the bass angler, primarily for boat control and positioning benefits. The main concern is keeping your boat in the proper position for the time required to fish an area thoroughly and properly.

Working a visible straight line of vegetation is an example of how it may be worthwhile to fish close and parallel, rather than perpendicular. However, when the vegetation is punctuated by cuts, channels, pockets, and the like, it is advisable to keep the boat out a bit and cast in, concentrating on the irregular features and the holes in the interior of the salad. When casting around points, three basic boat positions—on either side of the point and straight out from it—should be taken, and a range of casts should be made from each location. If you have a depthfinder, you should watch it as you work around the point; concentrate on the break area where the point tapers off to deep water.

A depthfinder can be a substantial aid to all musky fishermen anywhere on a lake, regardless of the type of boat they use. In most cases, proper boat positioning over areas likely to hold muskies but not visible to fishermen can only be accomplished through the use of a depthfinder. By watching this instrument and following the contours of a promising spot (such as a mound, rock pile, deep grass bed, etc.), you can keep your boat on the fringe of the likely area and your lures in the appropriate zone.

Sonar is even more important in trolling, as is depth control and positioning, but more about those points in a moment.

Because they are useful at slow to fast trolling speeds, exhibit plenty of action and are well-fished at relatively shallow depths, floating/diving plugs are the primary trolling ticket. This particularly includes deep-diving plugs but also shallow and intermediate divers, depending on the strength of line to be used, the depth of water to be fished, and whether sinkers, weighted lines, or downriggers are utilized.

Five- to 8-inch–long plugs are customary for this, preferably in single- or double-jointed versions, but also in unjointed models. Such lures include Bagley Deep-Diving Bang-O-Bs, Drifter Tackle's Believers, LeBlanc's Swim Whiz, Bomber Water dogs, and Cisco Kids. Magnum Rapalas, Whopper Stopper Hellbenders, and Mann's Deep 20+ and 30+ plugs can be useful, too. Creek Chub Pikie Minnows, in single- and double-jointed versions, have been perennially successful trolling plugs, and the former numbers the all-tackle world record among its accomplishments. Lure colors include black; black and white; chartreuse; silver and black (or "shad" pattern); perch, walleye, largemouth bass, and musky patterns; and yellow with red or tiger stripes.

Some people troll bucktails over weed beds that come to within 2 feet of the surface, but we've never tried this and don't see how it can be done without motoring through the weeds, a tactic that may stir muskies up but which does no good to the habitat or to your motor (weeds that cling to the intake will prevent water from entering and will cause an outboard to overheat).

Large spoons, incidentally, were once a prominent trolling and casting bait for muskies, but they have fallen into general disuse for these fish in deference to the more representative and active plug. This may have to do with the public's increased awareness of the need to control depth (which is hard to determine reliably with

---

These two muskies were trolled from the same lake on the same morning by flat-lining plugs along a mid-lake drop-off.

a spoon) and also the general population decline of muskellunge. Nonetheless, as with bucktails, there are some anglers who troll spoons over weed beds.

For flat-line trolling (using lures without downriggers or heavy weights), you must know how deep your lures are capable of running with the line you use, speed of boat, and length of line out. The general rule is the lighter the line, the longer the length of line, and the slower your boat speed, the deeper a diving plug will run. Within the aforementioned group of intermediate and deep diving plugs, however, there is a considerable difference in depth attainment. For instance, on a comparable line size/length/speed basis, Mann's 20+ and 30+ crankbaits run the deepest, with Bang-O-Bs not too far behind; Pikie Minnows and magnum Rapalas, on the other hand, run the shallowest. At a moderate speed and with 75 feet of 12-pound line employed, for example, Mann's 20+ will achieve over 25 feet, a Bang-O-B will dive about 18 feet deep, the magnum Rapala about 10, and the Pikie a little less than the Rapala.

You do have options, however. You may be able to get a plug to run 14 feet deep when trolling with 75 feet of 12-pound line. But suppose you want to use heavier line (most musky anglers do). To get that plug to the same depth with 30-pound line, you might have to add a 1-ounce (or heavier) weight or let out twice (or more) the length of line. Obviously you have to take several factors into consideration to determine the depth you want to achieve.

These lures are fished, incidentally, on short lines. There is seldom much reason to put out more than 75 feet of line, although there are some special-tackle trollers who do so. Muskies are not spooked by boat noise, and some midwestern trollers catch them right in the prop wash, within 10 to 25 feet of the boat and just a few feet below the surface. The prop wash apparently attracts or excites the fish. Except for prop wash trolling, line lengths normally vary between 40 and 75 or 80 feet.

Lures that won't achieve the desired depth on a flat-line troll need to be aided with keel or bead-chain sinkers. Some prop wash fishermen use 4- to 16-ounce lead weights to get lures down quickly, and such heavy weights are needed because of the turbulence behind the boat and the fast speed (up to 5 mph) at which the lures are run. Others, trolling further behind the boat, use lighter weights. Arthur Lawton, a St. Lawrence River troller who caught many large muskies, including the all-tackle, world record, used 2- to 3-ounce weights with Pikie Minnows, let out 50 to 75 feet of line and trolled on average at 2 to 3 mph, but no more than 4 mph. If you're trying to get down in that 10- to 17-foot range, you can do so with several of the aforementioned, deep-diving plugs without weights, unless you use rope for fishing line.

Downriggers are becoming more of a tool for muskie trollers, as well they should. Downriggers allow you to fish very heavy line without affecting the depth of the lure being used and without having to use lead weights on the fishing line. They make short-line, prop wash fishing easier. They also make it practical to troll spoons or spinners at precise depths and to use shallow-running plugs, such as 6- to 8-inch minnow-imitations (like a Rapala, A. C. Shiner, Rebel, or Bagley Bang-O-Lure), at specific depths. Downriggers keep you from having to check your lures often to see if they're clean (when flat-lining, especially near weeds and when leaves are dropping in the fall, you have to check your plugs often to see that no debris has gotten on them). When trolling at 12- to 20-foot depths, downriggers allow lures to run shorter

An old trolling system for muskies — wire line (right) — has given way to the new: downriggers.

distances behind the boat (or weight), which makes turning and boat manipulation much easier.

However, hook setting while using downriggers can be a problem. Releases should require a lot of tension before they free the line, not only because the diving plugs being trolled pull hard, but also because of the difficulty in setting the hook into the mouth of a musky under any circumstance. Only the best releases — ones that will handle heavy line and which have adjustable tension settings — should be used, and it's a good idea to test the striking force needed to spring them. Those muskellunge that attack a lure sideways, which is what they usually do to a fish, clamp down with extraordinary, vise-like pressure and may never get firmly hooked. This is an endemic musky fishing problem that is made even tougher by not setting the hook directly, but rather indirectly via a downrigger release.

This is not to say that hooking muskies is significantly easier when flat-line trolling. Essentially the rod, resting in a holder, sets the hook. When a musky strikes a trolled lure, get to the rod immediately and set the hook by hand. If the boat operator has enough presence of mind to think of this, he can aid hook setting immediately after a strike by speeding the boat up for a moment, then throttling back as an angler grabs the rod (big-game, saltwater boaters do this). Your tackle must be stout enough to handle this, however. And this still doesn't guarantee that you'll sink the hooks into a musky's bony, toothy maw. Muskies are hard to hook when casting or trolling.

The same is true for those who might attempt using side-planers for musky trolling, to get lures over weed beds or right along weed edges, close to various shore structure, and near river locales that prevent boat passage or where it wouldn't be prudent to troll your boat. With side-planers you can run relatively short drop-back lines as well. However, hook setting might pose difficulties.

Few musky trollers presently use side-planers, but we mention this subject because these devices add another dimension to your presentation abilities. Presentation is especially critical when musky trolling, as any pass by an ambush point or feeding area must bring the lure along a specific contour and path of travel. Boat position and speed must be precise, and, for this reason, line lengths are fairly short. Where turns and frequent S-trolling maneuvers are necessary, short lines may make boat and lure manipulation easier. Anyone who has trolled the contours of weed beds, points, reefs, or islands appreciates this maneuverability aspect of getting your lures in prime position.

Lure placement and arrangement while trolling is an important aspect of presentation and should be carefully thought out. The more people in your boat and the more rods you fish, the more important this becomes.

On Lake St. Clair, big boats and open water are the order of the day, and a guide boat might be arranged as follows: two to three rods may be run in the prop wash; one will be directly behind the motor, running the lure about 6 to 10 feet back and a few feet under the surface; a second rod will be in a holder on the port side of the stern, facing out the stern and angled slightly toward the wake; the lure on this will be 15 to 20 feet back; a third rod will be in a holder on the starboard side of the stern, facing out the stern and angled slightly toward the wake; the lure will be 30 to 40 feet back in the wake. Depending on how many anglers are aboard, another one to three or four rods might be fished. On both gunwales, slightly ahead of the stern, a rod is angled about 20 degrees away from the stern, with lures 10 to 20 feet back. Further along both gunwales, near midship, a rod is perpendicular to the gunwale, running a lure 40 or more feet back.

A small, Wisconsin guide boat fishing three lines might be arranged like this: a stern rod is placed in a transom rod holder pointed directly at the prop wash, with 25 feet of line out and a lure that runs 6 feet deep. A port rod is placed in a holder and lays perpendicular to the boat, with 60 feet of line out and a lure that runs 12 to 15 feet deep. A starboard rod, also perpendicular to the gunwale, has 80 feet of line out and a lure that runs 10 feet deep.

A traditional St. Lawrence River wire line troller running three lines would set up as follows: port and starboard rods will be at 90-degree angles to the gunwale, running between 100 and 150 feet of wire line and a jointed diving plug. A high line of nylon monofilament will be placed in the middle of the stern, running 200 to 300 feet back with a lure that dives 10 to 15 feet deep. (We mention this system since it diverges from the usual short-line trolling and also because it illustrates wire line trolling. Most St. Lawrence River guides today are running nylon monofilament flat-line lengths between 75 and 200 feet for open-water trolling, in part depending upon the lure they're using.)

Many anglers don't have a musky trolling, rod-setting system to follow religiously, preferring to tailor rod setting and lure placement to the conditions. When trolling the edges of weeds, sandbars, shoals, and so forth, they might have a shallower running

Parcel post, the best way to ship your giant musky. Actually, this 42-pound fish was being weighed for certification as a possible line-class world record. It was caught while trolling.

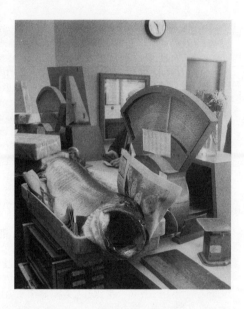

lure on the side of the boat nearest the edge, and a deep-running lure on the opposite side. When fishing two lures off the same gunwale, they may put a deep runner on the inside rod on a short- to medium-length line and a shallow runner on the outside position but on a longer length of line (it might get as deep as the other lure but be further back to avoid tangling and also aid fish playing and hook setting). Or they might try using a lure on a short line behind a downrigger plus a flat-lined plug set back on a long length of line. There are plenty of variations to try. You just need the right equipment, good rod-holder placement, a knowledge of the depth you're trolling, and good boat maneuvering skills.

One of those skills involves turning. Turns are important in all forms of trolling, probably because the change in bait movement triggers following fish to strike, but especially in musky fishing. This stands to reason. If muskies follow cast-and-retrieved lures to a boat—and strike—why wouldn't they follow a trolled lure a modest distance? Might not the behavioral change of a lure when a turn is made (rising or falling, increasing or decreasing speed) cause a following musky to pounce on the lure?

You can achieve similar lure behavior change in other ways. Speeding up or slowing down the boat for a few seconds is a good tactic. Using an oscillating downrigger is another. Keeping a trolling rod in your hand and either ripping the lure forward momentarily or pushing the free-spool button momentarily will serve to speed up and slow down a lure for a sudden change of pace that might make a following musky think its prospective prey is attempting to elude him.

Sonar equipment, of course, is vital to musky trolling efforts. Not only do you want to know the depth below you, but also when you are encroaching shallow water, a reef, or weeds in time to be able to do something about it and to keep lures from getting snagged. Except in deep open water, you seldom find muskies on sonar, but you find places, define underwater terrain, and maybe locate smaller fish schools that might attract muskellunge (in which case you should troll around the school, not through it).

As for basic tackle, most musky anglers, whether they cast or troll, arm for monsters. Twenty-pound line is viewed as light, anything less as ultralight and foolhardy. Twenty-five to 40-pound line is standard musky line, and some use even heavier. There are still a fair number of musky anglers using braided Dacron instead of nylon monofilament for the no-stretch aspect it gives hook setting efforts. They use big, saltwater-size reels, and 4- to 5-foot trolling rods that you could beat the dust out of a rug with.

We fish 12- to 20-pound nylon monofilament or cofilament line and troll and cast even the hardest-pulling, deepest-diving lures with 12. Many big fish have been taken on such line. Lighter line makes plugs dive deeper and swim with great action. You can get more of it on a reel, too, which means that you can use a smaller, and more comfortable, reel. Muskies rarely run like a big salmon, so a reel with great line capacity is not necessary. Reels that hold between 100 and 150 yards of 12- to 20-pound line are adequate. They should have an excellent drag system, however, and preferably a clicker. For rods, medium- to medium-heavy-duty 6- to 7-footers with a fast tip but lots of backbone are good, though many avid casters like a real shillelagh sort of stick. Keep in mind that you may be trolling hard-pulling lures and doing some high-speed trolling, so the rod has to have the strength to endure this, plus a hard strike.

Whether casting or trolling, you should consider using wire leaders with your lures. A 12-inch steel leader is standard; some trollers use up to 30- and 36-inch wire leaders because they fear having large, open-mouthed muskies roll on their line and cut it. Long leaders do hamper casting efficiency and sometimes fish control; we opt for 6-inch leaders where possible, sometimes fishing without a leader.

When you catch a musky, take particularly delicate care with it. What threatens muskies most is the mishandling and keeping of fish. That's one reason why we don't use, and didn't discuss here, bait fishing for muskies. When bait fishing, there is high potential for deep-hooking fish, which translates into greater mortality when you catch fish that you must, or want to, release. We believe that the only muskies that should be kept are outstanding trophies and that someone who already has a wall mount or two doesn't need another. Since muskies are not generally an abundant resource, we urge you to keep this in mind.

CHAPTER THIRTEEN
CATFISH

Whiskered creatures who travel close to the bottom of North America's waterways, catfish are indeed ugly; they do grow huge and fight hard; they do scavenge anything old or new to eat; and they are a favorite with many anglers. A high percentage of America's anglers, at some time during the season, fish for one catfish species or another. Most angle for channel cats; a much smaller percentage work blue catfish; and a select group seeks out flathead catfish. Each fish is approached a bit differently and has its own peculiarities.

One thing they have in common, however, is that not all catfish are caught only on rotten bait—and not all catfishermen smell bad, wear dirty overalls, and chew snuff. Today, a catfish angler might well fish from a high-powered bass boat instead of a rusty johnboat powered by a small outboard motor. His clothing might be a sporty cap and wind-resistant, brightly colored nylon jacket, patches and all. Catfishing really knows no bounds among anglers—nor should it.

CHANNEL CATFISH

The most popular quarry, channel catfish, is a river fish for the most part. Originally the channel cat roamed only in the southern two-thirds of the Mississippi and its tributaries, but now the range of this fish spreads from western Montana down to southern Texas and eastward, and it is found as far north as southern Ontario and Manitoba. It is raised in farm ponds throughout the land and is considered the premier freshwater table fish by a great many anglers and non-anglers alike.

Though most catfish species appear ugly, not so the channel catfish. It is less pot-bellied than the flathead and blue, and, with the exception of old, quick-growing channels from southern impoundments, it is less massive. When 12 to 16 inches in size, this fish is generally pale blue, olive, or gray with a silver cast and sports a host of nearly black dots or spots. Adult fish lose many of their spots and darken deeply across their back and flanks. Light blue becomes navy; pale olive turns greenish; and ivory bellies turn milky gray. Barbels (whiskers) turn dark black while fin tips often darken to blood red/black. Body color will vary with surroundings, confusing identification somewhat. Aged males, for instance, may darken to a point where they appear gray-black with ivory-gray bellies. In some southern environs, anglers turn up an albino channel cat mixed with a school of normal-colored channels.

This good-sized channel catfish was caught on chicken liver, fished behind a bottom-walking sinker.

Channel catfish spawn in late spring or early summer. The exact timing is regulated by latitude and water temperature, but the ideal time is when water temperature is between 75 and 85 degrees. Depending on habitat, channel catfish may migrate into rivers or current during spawning time. Look for spawning channel cats by overhanging rocks, pockets beneath stumps, the inner cavities of old logs, open pockets below bouldered rock structure, bank holes, log jams, and any other secluded, darkened, spooky places where the female might avoid the watchful eyes of predators.

Unlike their blue catfish cousin, channel cats prefer fresh bait. It isn't that they won't eat rotten bait or man-made stink baits. They do, but they seem to prefer fresh baits. Stink baits are best used in farm ponds. Natural food consists mainly of aquatic insects when channel cats are young, but encompasses crabs, mayflies, clams, minnows, varying mollusks, caddis flies, crayfish, water plants, and in some instances, land-bound creatures that have been trapped by rushing waters. In northern regions, sucker minnows are the principal minnow-style food, while in the south, shad are predominant. Frogs, though not in all catfish habitat, are considered a channel cat delicacy at times in the northcentral region.

Locating schools of channel catfish isn't really that hard. Look to current cuts in rivers, stream mouths, gravel and rock bottoms, deep-cut river banks, shallow ripple areas with a hard bottom, and river channels. Keep in mind that this fish always feeds into the current and takes advantage of his keen sense of smell. It is a smelling ability second to none, so catfish must always be approached in rivers from above.

In the spring and early summer, when water temperature ranges between 60 and 72 degrees, catfish are fairly easily caught. Their feeding habits are strong, fast, and positive then. Once food is inspected by the cat, he will ingest it immediately, turn back downstream, and be easily hooked. This is not the case when hot summer days settle in and water temperatures head toward 80 degrees. At this time, bait presentation is best done via "straight-lining" in running water, a technique we'll discuss in a moment.

A channel cat's ability to steal a bait is unequalled. Unlike blue and flathead catfish, channel cats have a peculiar way of approaching food, closing down on it, and backing off when engulfing it. As a result, most anglers miss 50 percent of their strikes. Detecting strikes is a critical aspect of channel cat angling, so let's review what happens so you understand how to react.

As we said, catfish primarily locate food through their exceptionally good sense of smell. We've seen cats swim a scent trail nearly 200 feet to get at chicken liver. A channel catfish approaches bait slowly, works his barbels over the target, then slowly opens his mouth and walks up on the bait. At this point, the angler usually feels practically nothing, although there is a slight lessening of line tension. It is so slight, however, that it's hard for the average fisherman to detect when current is tossing and churning his submerged fishing line.

Next, the catfish moves slightly (a few inches) up into the current, completely closes his jaws, and crushes his prey. By this time, he has detected, by taste, what he has inhaled. The angler's line has slackened off dramatically, but there is no indication that a fish has taken the bait. The angler sits, waiting for the familiar *tap-tap*. This is the ideal time to set the hook, but 99 percent of all catfish anglers fail to detect the feeding fish at this point, even though he's sucked in the bait and is gently mouthing it.

Satisfied that the chosen morsel is palatable food, the channel cat will now open his mouth about a third of the way, and gently walk backwards. This is when most fishermen feel what they think is the tap of a striking fish. The catfish has already begun to crunch and munch the bait. Anything soft, like shad, smelt, chicken liver, or dough-style bait, will immediately fall apart under such pressure. Eventually only the hook remains. If you allow the fish to munch long enough, he'll spit an empty hook out every time.

A catfish's movement backwards takes about 3 seconds. You have to be sharp enough to strike him prior to this. Even if you do manage to set the hook during that backward walk, you'll probably miss a hook-up. With the mouth partly open and the bait hook lying flat in his mouth, the chances of the fish having the bait jerked out of his mouth are 50-50. When you realize, too, that channel cats are extremely sensitive to line pressure, you can see how the hook-setting odds begin to tumble even more.

The trick to hooking this river bait stealer is catching him before he moves backward, when he has food in a closed mouth and is confirming taste. Remember the point about sensing slack line; it's the key to hooking channel cats consistently.

For channel cat fishing, many anglers swear by the use of egg sinkers, which allow catfish to run with the bait. There is some merit to this, as slow-water cats will pick up a bait and move sideways with it, mouth it a number of times before swallowing, and stay there, which presents good conditions for the use of an egg sinker. But where there is any significant current flow and when fish are very finicky, channel cats will move backward. Then, straight-lining is preferable.

Straight-lining is a catfishing technique in which you present bait directly downstream away from the boat or shoreline point on which you are stationed. There is no need for special equipment. Only sinker style changes. Instead of split-shot, egg sinker, or a conventional casting weight, use a wire-rigged sinker such as a Bait Walker or a similar sinker with weight on the bottom. This sinker's forward-fulcruming action is necessary to indicate slack line. Sinker weight will vary, depending on water conditions, from 5/8-ounce to 2 ounces. The deeper and faster the water, the heavier the sinker needed.

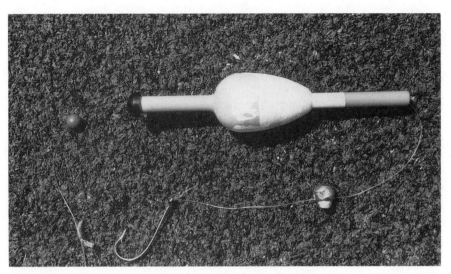

A slip bobber and split-shot is one of the setups used in bait fishing.

To implement the straight-line technique, you must be upstream from the target area. Behind your sinker, attach a 24-inch leader and a short-shanked hook. The sinker's upper wire arm will keep the leader and bait slightly off bottom.

Cast directly downstream to the selected target. Once the rig rests on bottom in proper position, reel slack line up, affording direct contact between sinker, trailing bait, and rod tip. Current flow shifts will lessen and increase pressure on the rod tip at times. The angler must keep constant pressure evenly distributed between rod tip and bait. This is done by lifting and lowering the rod tip as pressure decreases and increases.

When a catfish picks up the bait and moves slightly forward with it, a small vacuum is created in his mouth around the bait. Your rod tip now slacks off dramatically as the catfish crushes down. At this moment, drop your rod tip about 18 inches, reel hard, and set the hook.

Anglers disagree greatly on which bait best attracts channel cats. On each sector of major waterways, there is someone who makes a home-brewed concoction that native catfish anglers swear by. Generally these contain cheese, anise oil, sour mash, ground corn, crushed shad, and sometimes a bit of rotten chicken liver. Most of these homemade baits work, but fresh bait usually is more productive for channel cats.

First on the preferred list is frozen chicken liver and gizzard shad. Where shad are hard to come by, use sucker meat and Great Lakes smelt. Night crawlers, hellgrammites, shrimp, clams, and crayfish are popular baits, too.

Though treble hooks are used by many catfish anglers for live bait fishing, we have found that a single, short-shanked Eagle Claw Hook (1/0 to 3/0) with an upturned eye does a much better job. Both the upturned eye and the offset barb help when the hook is set by presenting the hook's point at an offset angle in the fish's mouth.

We recommend frozen, instead of traditional unfrozen or rotten, chicken liver as a primary bait for channel catfish. The latter are inadequate because of their poor attaching quality. If you've ever tried to put a piece of soft, unfrozen chicken liver, or rotten, sunbaked liver on a hook, you've found that they can barely be kept on the hook long enough to cast. Only frozen liver holds well to a single hook. It will stay on three times longer than new, unfrozen or rotten liver and will attract four times as many catfish. Biologists claim that freezing chicken liver breaks down acids within that create scenting. As frozen liver thaws, it exudes scent much more, making it more attractive to catfish.

There are two sections to chicken liver. Use one section at a time by thrusting a single hook in and out one time while the liver remains in a frosty, frozen condition. Keep livers frozen by placing a frozen container of them in a styrofoam minnow bucket filled with chipped ice. The container contents will thaw only slightly, and you'll have to dig each frosty liver out.

Many channel catfishermen prefer to use stiff rods loaded with rather heavy lines; walleye trolling rods with 20-pound line are their preference. Such precautions may be necessary when working waters that are filled with brush and logs or when there is a chance of hooking really large fish. However, many prefer a medium-weight bait-casting or spinning rod equipped with 10- to 15-pound line. For extra fun, use a 5 1/2-foot, medium-action spinning rod, ultralight reel, and 8-pound line. This outfit will probably give an angler the biggest challenge and the biggest thrill.

Channel catfish are a relatively clean-water fish. If pollution becomes too much of a problem, channel cats will disappear. Wherever you find this silky-skinned fish, you're also apt to find walleye. They inhabit similar territory in rivers and often feed on similar food. Cats have even been known to run down schools of shad or river shiners just like walleye. Anglers often are surprised to land a channel catfish on a minnow-style plug while angling for bass or walleye.

FLATHEAD CATFISH

If ever there was a truly ugly fish, the flathead catfish is it. With a huge mouth, puny eye, blotchy brown-and-gray color, and prehistoric tail structure, he is rather repulsive. The older and larger flatheads grow, the more grotesque they look. In many places, they sport yellowish bellies, mottled gray sides, and dark brown underskin. Unlike other catfish, the lower jaw on a flathead protrudes somewhat, like the jaw of a bulldog, and the upper head is notably flat.

Though less common than channel catfish, flatheads grow to larger sizes. It isn't uncommon, for example, to hear of 50-pounders being taken on rod and reel along the lower Mississippi River system. The largest flathead ever taken on rod and reel was over 100 pounds. Even in the north, where channel catfish average 3 or 4 pounds, it isn't unusual to hear of 35-pound flatheads. Nationally the average flathead may be about an 18-pounder, so you're dealing with a large, strong quarry here.

Flathead catfish relate best to slow, sluggish rivers, preferably large ones. They are a river species first, reservoir species second, and lake species last. Sluggish rivers provide a multitude of wing dams and navigational structures, and flatheads prefer to hold below these. Wing dams, in particular, are a favorite place for young flatheads. Most

Flathead catfish grow fairly large,
particularly in impoundments,
where this 25-pounder came from.

large adult fish, however, prefer deep, big-water rivers and lakes. Fish over 35 pounds are more apt to be found below a dam, holding below open, churning gate waters. Dead, stunned, and mutilated fish are easily snatched up by waiting flatheads here.

The flathead's diet consists mostly of fish and crustaceans. Anglers often take these huge catfish on deep-diving crankbaits, jigs tipped with sucker minnows, or large live bait left to lie on the bottom. Though flathead take just about anything, they prefer live fish. Small, 1/2- to 1-pound live carp and river suckers, hooked through their noses with a large, 4/0 to 6/0 single hook, work well. For trophy flathead catfish, try live hand-size bluegills, where legal; these should be impaled with a 3/0 hook directly behind the back fin and should flounder 3 feet behind a weight that is heavy enough to hold them on bottom.

Flathead catfish are not beyond eating their own kind, which includes smaller flatheads and especially stone cats. Many a walleye angler has been startled to feel the heavy pull of a flathead while fishing his favorite walleye hole with a live "willow cat." This 2- to 7-inch-long bait, actually a stone cat, is considered one of the best walleye baits along stretches of the upper Mississippi, Missouri, and St. Croix rivers. Stone cats thrive there and are also a top flathead producer. Flatheads sometimes chase a school of willow cats down in shallow backwater areas.

Be prepared for long periods of inaction when pursuing flatheads. Boring as this may seem, the wait is always worthwhile once you hook into this ugly brute. It will be a fight never to be forgotten. There isn't a freshwater fish to equal a flathead's tenacious, stubborn, deep-water battle, which can literally wear a fisherman out.

BLUE CATFISH

Blue catfish are probably the least understood members of the catfish clan. They are also fewest in number and are spread over the smallest area, but they grow as large or larger than flatheads.

Unlike channel and flathead catfish, the blue has no spots or mottling on any part of his body. The general color is pale blue on top with whitish-blue to gray on the belly. Blue catfish have a distinctive forked tail, an upper jaw that carries well over their chin, and a straight-edged, high-riding anal fin, all of which make them easily identifiable.

Blue catfish are found extensively throughout southern parts of the United States and even in parts of Mexico. Like most catfish, blues prefer rivers and large dam impoundments. This fish, however, is often found working the lower river estuaries and backwaters. His wandering may even take him far away from any current pattern and into lakes, where he easily adapts for permanent residency. Much of his habitat is inaccessible to the angler, as the blue cat wanders through some very shallow waters into hidden backwaters to obtain food.

Spawning occurs when water temperatures are in the 80-degree range. Like channel cats, blues reproduce in some of the roughest and toughest brush, log, wood, and rock structure around. Anglers seldom find their spawning nests. Tagged fish have been known to travel 100 miles to obtain a place to spawn.

This fish is often taken by anglers working below dams on large river systems. But blues tend to school like walleye or white bass. In some rivers, a feeding pod of blues can cover a large surface area.

Though blue catfish are noted for striking the worst of stink baits, their diet consists of just about anything. Minnows, crabs, vegetation, decaying matter, rotten flesh, insects, clams, snails, stink bait, strong cheese, and even sour chicken trails are on their menu. Some old-timers along major rivers use nothing but their own stink bait concoctions made from rotting chicken and fish parts. Others use dead and soured crayfish and crabs. Many of these anglers fish with rods as stiff as telephone poles, 80-pound line, and ancient, star-drag reels. Others use heavy pike or bass gear with 25-pound line. A really big blue does require stout tackle, especially around logs, timber, and other cover, but more conventional sporting tackle fills the bill nicely for most blue catfish angling.

Bait fishing techniques are similar to those mentioned previously for channel and flathead catfish. The bigger the fish sought, the bigger the hook and the larger the bait used. The use of a line-slipping egg sinker is recommended. A big blue must be given the opportunity to swallow his prize. Allow him to run till he stops, count to ten, and set the hook with all your might. You'll soon know how big he is; blues tend to run more than the other two species.

All three of these catfish species are found downstream from dams nearly at the exact same position on any of these structures. Downstream from each T.V.A. dam, roller dam, lock-and-dam system, etc., there is a "dig-out" area followed by a hump.

There are several places below dams that offer opportunities to catch catfish.

Constructed of hardpan material forced downstream with the current, the hump provides an ideal staging area for game fish. The hump may come within 6 to 10 feet of the surface before falling off into the depths downstream; there the water may be 45 to 65 feet deep. Most of the channel catfish will be found in this, as well as trophy-size blue and flathead catfish. The hump will vary in form, but most are egg- or oval-shaped. Look for channel cats to hold along the upstream sides. Flatheads and blue cats hold downstream from the hump where deep water and lifting hardpan come together.

Below many dams, there is an area of shoreline riprap that also attracts catfish, which spawn here in small pockets and swirling eddies. Here, in early summer, along the outer edges in 5 to 8 feet of water, catfish feed on crayfish when they shed their shells.

Along this riprap you can catch catfish with a technique normally reserved for walleyes. From shore, walk the riprap structure downstream while your floating bobber and bait drift with the current. Use a slip bobber, which allows the hook and sinker to drop just so deep and no more. For bait, use a black leech (spawning catfish love leeches) on a No. 8, short-shanked hook, with BB-sized split-shot, 6 inches above the hook. The leech hangs 3 to 4 feet below the bobber while drifting just off bottom. In some areas, where riprap literally runs for miles, an angler will walk his bobber three to four blocks before returning to his starting place to repeat the procedure. In the heart of summer, catfish move deeper off the riprap. Eventually they will be found at a point where rock riprap and soft river bottom meet, where they are best caught by normal angling methods.

Shoreline riprap is often found below river dams and is a good place to find channel catfish early in the season.

In rivers with wing dams, anglers can harvest many channel and flathead catfish around riprap near these structures. In spring they can be found directly below the structure and close to it. Later, in warm weather, catfish will move up and around the wing dam and position themselves upstream from it.

Wing dams are man-made structures placed in large river systems to divert current flow toward the center channel. They consist of broken rock and are formed like a solid rock dock bed. In most cases, water runs over wing dams all the time, being deeper in the spring. On all wing dams, one end is anchored to the shoreline. Channel cats and large flatheads feed at these wing dams immediately after sundown. The top sides of these hard structures are literally alive with crayfish and bait fish at sunset and during the first hour thereafter.

Deep holes or pools present a good river catfishing opportunity, too. Channel cats work up into shallow water to feed and move back into deeper water. Though some channel catfish are caught during the daylight hours directly from within a hole itself, they are best caught as they move into the shallower areas upstream from the hole. This movement, throughout most of the season, occurs just prior to sundown and lasts for an hour or so after dark.

Flatheads, on the other hand, may refrain from feeding throughout the day and then begin at dark. Unlike channel cats, flatheads venture only part way out of the deep hole to feed. If hole depth is 20 feet and the upstream hardpan is 12 feet, a flathead may only work into 16 feet of water to feed, whereas a channel cat will work into the shallowest upstream point.

Don't overlook fishing at night. On the whole, anglers spend as many hours working these species after dark as they do during daylight hours. In the south, night fishing

Catfish will move from deep water to shallow to feed, especially in rivers. During the day, catfish may be found below an exposed wing dam type of structure.

is a common practice, while in the north, more anglers work this fish during daylight.

Nothing has been mentioned about limp-lining, trot-lining, and jug fishing, all of which are intricate parts of the world of catfishing but not a portion of which share the exact sporting techniques required when rods and reels are used. Jug fishing proves that all of these catfish suspend at times when feeding. How else would catfish gobble up a bait hanging 24 inches below a jug and drifting in 14 feet of water? You might keep this in mind when angling for catfish, although bottom fishing is certainly most productive.

We haven't talked much about catfishing in still waters, where blue and channel cats usually are more abundant than flatheads. Pond channel catfish are readily attracted to cheese and stink baits. Here, plastic worms, threaded with a treble hook and dabbled in a favorite brown stink bait, work well. This isn't to say that fresh cut baits won't work, which they do, but stink baits seem to do best, especially during midsummer.

If ever there was a sit-and-wait situation, pond catfishing is it, for it takes time for pond cats to get to your bait. And when ponds have weed growth, the wait can seem forever. When weeds and moss cover the bottom, channel and blue catfish suspend above the vegetation and often circle in a migratory manner. Keeping tabs on their movement can be a problem for the angler. A slip bobber can be used to intercept these circling fish. The bait will suspend beneath the bobber just above the weeds.

To keep up with these catfish you might try an old trick used by Arkansas and Louisiana catfishermen. Once the first catfish is taken, by whatever means, it is impaled behind the dorsal fin with a No. 8 hook and attached via a short length of light line to a small crappie bobber and released back into the water. Follow the bobber as it moves around the pond surface. The released catfish will return to the school, and you work directly ahead of the moving bobber. This is an effective ploy, although you should check on its legality where you are fishing.

Catfish will take artificials, incidentally, but not nearly as well as some anglers might like, and lures are much less effective than bait. Flatheads are most susceptible to lures, with crankbaits being most productive. Channel cats are often caught by anglers who have tipped a jig with a minnow or a lively piece of night crawler. And some bass anglers, fishing with a large jig and pork-chunk combo, have latched onto catfish. But these incidents are not commonplace when you are actually seeking to catch catfish.

In large impoundments, anglers will catch some catfish while trolling plugs or jigging spoons or bucktail jigs, again usually while seeking striped bass. Even in impoundments, live or cut bait (shad or herring mostly), fished off the bottom, is the main ticket (using a 4/0 to 6/0 hook and 2-foot leader tied to a swivel, above which is a heavy egg sinker). In non-current areas of impoundments, look for catfish primarily along river beds and creek beds, concentrating on curves, bends, deep holes, and the junction of two creeks, as well as at breaklines where the bottom drops off deeply.

Catfish will suspend, as we've mentioned, but for the most part are a bottom feeder and must be sought near or on the bottom. Still-fishing and drifting with some form of bait is really the way to go.

In closing, we advise you to be careful when handling catfish, which have pain-inflicting, mad-tom spines near the front of each dorsal and pelvic fin. These spines can inflict ripping wounds. You can avoid any chance of sticking yourself if you approach with hand from the underside of the fish, placing your thumb against the back side of one pectoral fin and your index finger against the other. Grasp firmly with palm across the catfish's stomach. The fish will be securely held and can be unhooked.

CHAPTER FOURTEEN
ROUGH FISH

It's a strange thing that American anglers do when they use the term "rough fish" to refer to such a large portion of our freshwater species. Strange, perhaps, because the word "rough" has such a negative connotation. Why do we dislike carp, suckers, drum, gar, buffalo, bowfin, and such others? And why are some fish, but not others, elevated to a status far above that of "rough fish"? In Europe, Africa, or Asia, this situation doesn't exist. There, any fish that fights hard, is difficult to entice, and can be eaten is one worth catching, not disparaging.

The difference, of course, is that we are spoiled; we have so much good fishing that we don't mind ignoring certain types of fish, especially if they don't jump or take lures readily. We also have a lot of "pro" fishing fraternities who have placed excessive emphasis on a single species, such as largemouth bass, without having a balanced attitude of appreciating and pursuing a wide range of species. It is a common angler attitude that the less popular and less publicized fish are no good and not worth fishing for or bragging about.

Oddly enough, an angler can land a 20-pound carp on 4-pound line in a fight that lasts up to an hour, but be ridiculed, while on the same water at the same time, a bass fishing pro may catch a 3 1/2-pound bass on 20-pound line in 30 seconds and be viewed as a hero. This makes no sense. Someday, if we have depleted those species we call game fish, anglers may turn to rough fish species with a kinder attitude.

Among those rough fish species are some creatures that don't get much respect but do provide anglers with good fishing. Carp are probably the foremost of these.

CARP

Carp fight up until every last inch of line is retrieved. With a powerful sweep of its broad tail, this bronze devil is off on a surging run that will test the finest tackle. Several determined runs and many minutes later, he may flop onto his side to be led in. But that's not the end. Carp have a knack for rolling and flapping violently just as the net is swooping toward them. Many a fish has escaped at this moment.

Carp can be found nearly everywhere. They are easy to find, and, in many waters throughout America, still relatively easy to catch. Where normally an angler may find difficulty gaining access to a trout stream, landowners along carp-loaded rivers or lakes may welcome you with open arms.

The common carp that thrives in our waters is a giant member of the minnow family, the largest group of freshwater fish in terms of species and numbers. And they do grow large! There have been countless tales of 80- to 90-pound carp that were commercially netted or found dead along a shoreline. The confirmed rod-and-reel record, however, is 57 pounds, 13 ounces, a fish that was taken from the Potomac River in Washington, D. C. It is not uncommon to catch carp in the 10- to 20-pound range.

Carp move into shallow bays, stream tributaries, or flooded fields and marshes to spawn in mid to late spring or early summer. They spawn in these shallow areas with little concern for danger, and they are quite noticeable as they thrash about and roil the water. Often their backs are exposed, providing an obvious target for spear fishermen or bowfishermen.

Carp feed on nearly anything edible. Such aquatic morsels as insect larvae, crustaceans, and small mollusks make up a large part of their diet. With their vacuum-cleaner mouths, carp do much scouring along the bottom, often uprooting water plants in the process.

The carp is a hardy, durable fish. It can live in waters that will not sustain other fish species, and it can withstand extreme changes in water temperature. Carp require little oxygen and can live comfortably in warm ponds and sluggish streams. In stagnant, polluted waters they suck in the oxygen-rich surface film that has been in direct contact with air. They enjoy warm water, even though it may be too warm for them to feed. While carp have been caught in lakes fringed with ice, the first frosts usually mark the end of the carp season. In general, they do not feed in water colder than 50 degrees.

An increase in water oxygen content will increase their appetite. The amount of dissolved oxygen is influenced by temperature, water depth, and agitation through wind or rain. Other factors that affect the amount of oxygen in the water are weeds

Determined fighters, carp thrive in many environments and grow to large sizes.

that give off oxygen in the daytime and carbon dioxide after dark, and decaying matter that absorbs oxygen. There is less oxygen in very deep water than in shallow.

Let's follow carp in a small, shallow lake during a typical twenty-four hour period in summer, starting in the afternoon of a sunny day when the surface water temperature is very high.

At mid-afternoon, nearly all the carp will be at or near the surface. Most will be in the shallows, especially if there is very little wind. Many carp are gliding slowly back and forth, some raising a glistening back or dorsal fin above the surface. Others are almost motionless among the weeds. Few show a willingness to feed.

When evening arrives and the temperature begins to fall, carp become more active. Some begin to feed at the surface; others at the bottom. As the temperature drops, there is some leaping. A general movement toward the east side of the lake begins, as this side gets the last rays of the sun. If the sky is cloudless, the temperature may fall rapidly after sunset, and the majority of the fish will make their way into deeper water.

Carp are likely to feed in the shallows during the daytime if wind or rain keep the temperature in shallow water between 60 and 70 degrees and if there is an increase in the oxygen content of the water. If the temperature in the shallows drops below 60 degrees or thereabouts, the carp will tend to move into deeper water that cools more slowly. Most commonly, midnight finds most of the fish in relatively deeper water unless the night is exceptionally warm.

Just before dawn, the fish may begin to move to the edge of deep water nearest the west side of the lake, which is first to receive the morning sunshine. With first light, a few carp venture into shallower water on this side. This is something they often do out of habit, even when the temperature fails to rise.

With rising temperature, carp activity increases and some leaping occurs. No one knows exactly why carp leap. It seems to accompany changes in temperature, and the more rapidly such changes take place, the more fish seem inclined to jump. Possibly, leaping may often be a prelude to feeding. A further increase in temperature attracts the fish toward shallower water, especially on the western side, until by midday they will again be nearly all in the shallows and, if the temperature has risen too high, no longer feeding.

Open-water lakes, extensive reservoirs, and slow-moving back waters host a lot of carp. In all of these, the use of worms, corn, grubs, marshmallows, potatoes, or dead bait is recommended. Here, such bait works much better than it might in faster-moving water. In rivers where rapids, rocks, and gravel bars persist, an angler can use these baits, but often live crayfish and hellgrammites produce twice as many fish.

In faster streams, many carp are taken on artificial lures, particularly a small brown jig that is tipped with a worm. The brown color obviously represents a crayfish, and the worm tastes like a crayfish (or so we're told). Once in a while, a carp will snatch up a slowly worked, dark-colored crankbait.

For bait, however, some anglers swear by their own dough ball recipes. In most cases, the ingredients of these baits are similar. Their basic makeup is like this recipe from Gil Tucker of Coon Wash, Illinois. It includes two cups of corn meal, two cups of water, one-half cup of syrup (corn or Karo), one tablespoon of anise oil, and four tablespoons of vanilla extract. Mix and cook these ingredients in a pot over a low fire until they boil. Stir constantly after they've boiled and simmer for about 8 minutes. Remove it from the heat and let it sit and cool for about 25 minutes. Flour a baking pan and roll the mixture into small balls. The bait can either be kept in balls or under cover in a container in its finished form.

Gil adds one last touch to the dough balls, as do many anglers. Once they are rolled into the desired size, they are dipped in a secret watery solution. This has a dark red appearance, and we're told it contains bile ducts of catfish, soft honey, carp blood, and more vanilla extract. The dough ball recipe Gil uses is rather common among carp fishermen, but it must have been that reddish solution that helped make his dough balls work so well. In testing at later dates, it worked both ways, but those who dipped in the final solution seemed to produce more fish.

Many fishermen impale a dough ball with a treble hook, but we don't find this necessary. A single, offset Eagle Claw Hook in No. 4 to 2/0 sizes has proven best over time.

Look for carp primarily in shallow water. If you can find them on a sand or gravel flat, all the better, because they can locate your offering much easier. The weedier it becomes, the less apt a carp is to find your bait. In back waters, work narrow, open areas between deep-water locales. Carp funnel through these and hunt for food while doing so.

In rivers, carp are found at the head of pools, eddies, and slow-moving slicks, and beneath undercut banks. They also hold along bottom structures where there is some current relief. In big rivers they can be found en masse below dam structures where eddying currents rotate against lock-and-dam walls or roll off gate ends.

In running water, you'll know you've hooked a carp by the direction the fish takes on its first run. Carp head toward shallow water, shoreline weeds, or submerged bank obstructions immediately after being hooked. If you can stop that first run, generally the fish will be boated.

The tackle you'll need to do that will vary. Bank fishermen prefer longer rods (with long handles) so they can be used in conjunction with a forked stick for a resting forum. Boat anglers can use their normal walleye and bass fishing gear. The average line strength used for carp is about 10 pounds. If you fish for a trophy, then heavier line, say 20 pounds, might be worthwhile. If you want great sport and don't mind losing a fish or two, 6-pound line on an ultralight outfit will do nicely.

WHITEFISH

The lake variety of whitefish are found throughout Canada, Alaska, the northern regions of New England, and all areas bordering the Great Lakes, including northern Minnesota. Whitefish generally have a dark back and silver sides. The average whitefish caught by anglers is in the 1- to 2-pound range, with an occasional fish of 4 or 5 pounds and even some in the 8- to 12-pound class. However, commercial fishermen have taken much larger whitefish in gill nets. Though distribution in the United States is limited, this fish deserves a higher recognition than it presently enjoys, and it is the one small, sucker-mouth-like fish which can readily be caught by any angler who possesses just a little bit of fly fishing skill.

Whitefish are an insect feeder, although they also eat mollusks, leeches, fish eggs, fingernail clams, and amphipods. They are apt to be caught on nymphs or dry flies. Whitefish rise to the surface in large schools to devour adult mayflies, march browns,

The insect-feeding whitefish is a good candidate for fly fishing tactics in both rivers and lakes.

caddis flies, and black gnats. On summer evenings, when there has been a hatch of long-winged mayflies, whitefish porpoise their way across quiet surface waters in deep-water bays, where black bottom silt incubates the squirming larvae before releasing them upward. Whitefish consume these insects as they detach themselves from bottom, as well as the dying insects that cover the surface.

Pods of whitefish choose a single direction and a similar return pattern in which they feed in lakes. School size varies from fifteen to forty fish, all of which follow a leader. Their movement pattern covers a hundred yards or so, and other schools work similarly nearby. It isn't unusual to see two to four schools traveling the same pattern, one every 50 yards. This is governed by the number of insects available.

Whitefish rise gently when feeding upon floating insects. A fish glides to the surface, its mouth gently sucks in a fly, and the body rolls up and over. There is little water disturbance and virtually little of the fish to see, except for a part of the dorsal fin, which cuts above the surface and then disappears. The fish quickly targets its next meal and gently ripples the surface a few feet away. This feeding pattern may continue for some time, perhaps an hour, until the need for food is fulfilled.

An angler equipped with a light fly rod and a brown mayfly or caddis imitation on a No. 12 hook can capitalize on this feeding behavior and is in for a treat. By selecting an open area ahead of the oncoming whitefish school, he is virtually assured of a strike.

When the fish strikes, set the hook softly with a gentle rod lift. Whitefish have an extremely soft mouth, and if you set the hook too hard, you'll tear it away. When the fish is on, there is usually an immediate series of surface-thrashing head shakes, followed by a long, deep-diving run. From this point on, the hooked fish might break the surface like a rainbow trout, sulk like a walleye, race off sharply like a northern pike, or roll like a lake trout. Each fish is different.

For this angling, use a single-action fly reel, a 7- to 8-foot fly rod (the lighter the better), a 6 or 7 weight floating fly line, and a selection of high-floating, dry flies. An assortment of caddis, brown bivisibles, mayflies, march browns, and grey duns will suffice. Periodically, treat flies with flotant to make them stand up higher on the surface.

Whitefish can be caught in other manners, too, mostly by jigging a small dark jig, fished plain or tipped with a small insect. Once in a while, a whitefish will strike a spoon or small plug, though a jig is far more likely to be effective. Whitefish are found in rivers, too, incidentally. There they feed on insect hatches directly beneath waterfalls and along back-switching bank eddies, as well as in slow pools.

GAR

These fish, no matter which variety, are a fantastic fighter. Spotted, short-nosed, long-nosed, and alligator gar are fairly abundant in southern and midwestern lakes and river systems. Their flesh isn't particularly appealing, and their eggs are toxic, but they lack little in rod-bending, fighting action.

The diet of gar can be compared to that of most other fish that travel slow, weedy backwaters: frogs, crayfish, blue crabs, small fish, minnows, and shiners and, on occasion, more exotic fare. Like northern pike, they spawn in weedy, backwater locations, not building a nest but spewing eggs randomly above vegetation.

This long-nose gar fell to a crankbait.

In the south, gar hunters employ huge setups to pursue giant alligator gar, using large cans or jugs, strong rope, and a huge piece of bait that drifts freely. Obviously this isn't conventional sportfishing, but some of the gar they take nearly reach the 200-pound mark. It isn't unusual to take a 100-pounder.

The average sportfisherman, however, is apt to take much smaller gar when casting for northern pike or largemouth, smallmouth, or white bass. Long-nosed gar, for example, love to hang close to white bass schools below dams and rocky, wing dam structures. There they feed on the crippled, dead, and dying shad left by the vagabond whites, and it isn't uncommon to land a gar while pursuing white bass.

When setting the hook on a gar you have to hit it hard because of its boney snout and needle-like teeth. Getting a hook solidly into it is difficult. Gar always hit the bait with their bill first to kill it. Then they turn around and ingest it into their mouth. One lure that they particularly favor is a silver, mylar jig or jig-spinner combo; another is a silver-sided, minnow-imitation plug.

Look for gar to sun themselves a lot. They seem to enjoy exposure to the hot rays of the sun, though they become lulled into a sleep-like daze at times. Keep this in mind when approaching such a fish. It probably doesn't even hear or see you. You may have to make several casts just ahead of its nose to startle it into action.

STURGEON

The sturgeon is an anomaly. It isn't worthy of being classified as a game fish, but its eggs are nearly priceless. It reaches hundreds of pounds, spawns millions of eggs, grows to lengths exceeding 10 feet, and is a strong stubborn fighter; yet there is a general lack of interest in this fish, probably because so little is known about sturgeon and the dozen or so sub-species that comprise its family.

Sturgeon are a river fish. Their range covers most of North America when all the members of the sturgeon family tree are taken into consideration. The most common and widespread of these fish is the so-called lake sturgeon, which isn't the largest, though it can grow to 300 pounds and be 6 feet long. This fish is often hooked accidently by central-region walleye anglers. It usually succumbs to a gob of night crawlers left lying on the bottom. Most of these walleye-haunt sturgeon escape capture, leaving an exciting "monster-that-got-away" tale. This is understandable, since the equipment used for walleye is hardly strong enough to land the average size of lake sturgeon encountered.

To be properly equipped for a deliberate encounter with a sturgeon, you need a large-capacity levelwind reel and fairly stiff rod, one that you might use to cast for muskies. Line weight varies, with 25-pound-test the beginning point, and line of 80- to 100-pound strength used by those specialists who pursue really large (150 pounds) sturgeon. Hooks do not have to be large; 1/0 to 4/0, short-shanked hooks do the job. Sinkers are heavy, however, because much sturgeon fishing is done behind such river objects as a high falls or dam, with slip, three-way, or walking sinkers in the 3- to 10-ounce size preferred.

Sturgeon feed on such small bottom matter as fish eggs, mollusks, insect larvae, leeches, decapods, crayfish, and hellgrammites. Night crawlers apparently are effective because they taste like crayfish. Sturgeon often act like, and resemble, catfish. They

Sturgeon are primarily a river fish and a bottom feeder. Though over 40 pounds, this is a relatively small sturgeon.

have barbels for sensing food, and their mouths are without teeth, though they effectively crush their food.

When fishing for sturgeon, first work any large, deep holes directly beneath a waterfall or dam. Sturgeon also hold directly downstream from a shallowing in river bottom where a hardpan lift is apparent. If the shallows are 2 to 4 feet deep, fast and running over rock and gravel, look for sturgeon to hold about 50 yards down from the structure where surface water smooths out. Here, the water should be about 8 to 10 feet deep.

If you fish a slow-moving, mud-bottom river that has a number of slowly twisting turns, look for sturgeon to hold along the outside edge of a bend. Look for places that are at least 2 feet deeper than other areas in the river channel. Stick to the center of the river channel if the river does little or no bending. Where the river bottom consists of mud and loam, keep your bait slightly above bottom by using a floating jig tipped with a leech or night crawler or a tiny crappie float tied between sinker and bait. In fast river waters, fish channel areas with deep drops.

SUCKERS

There isn't any area of the United States that doesn't have one species of sucker or another. These fish are found in all watersheds, in creeks, streams, rivers, reservoirs, lakes, backwaters, ponds, and sloughs. They will eat just about any fresh, natural baits found in their locale and aren't crazy about artificial lures. They are a bottom feeder, and offerings should be presented on bottom or within a couple inches of bottom. A host of sinker styles do the job. Sizes seldom exceed 1 ounce unless heavy fast current is worked; common sizes are 1/4- to 5/8-ounce.

Garden worms and bits of night crawlers work on suckers better than anything

Suckers are also bottom feeders and found just about everywhere; shown is a redhorse sucker.

else. Don't put an entire night crawler on your hook; this is simply a way to feed these hard-to-hook creatures. Use about a third of a worm at a time and bunch it on the hook. A single, No. 2, turned-up eye hook with a short shank is a good hook for sucker fishing. There should be at least 24 inches between the hook and the sinker. In slow water, or no current, this may be shortened.

One of the biggest mistakes made by those attempting to hook suckers occurs at the first sign of a strike. Most anglers set the hook when they feel the initial tap, but they miss the fish. Let the fish tap your bait about three times. After the third time, point your rod tip directly at the fish and then set the hook hard. This way you'll hook nearly 85 to 90 percent of your strikes. Don't allow the tapping to continue too long, or you'll lose your bait, and the sucker will reject the hook.

When working river systems, fish the flats where current flows over rock and gravel. It is the same structure where you might find catfish or walleye. Try eddies, small pools below islands, currents behind stumps, pockets downstream from large rocks, holes below bridge abutments, and small-stream channel areas where there is a gradual slope into deeper water. Cast bait downstream and allow it to rest directly behind you.

Don't be surprised at the fight some suckers provide. Many a smallmouth bass fisherman has been fooled by the leap of a redhorse sucker that took his night crawler. Often, a redhorse will leap several times after being hooked. And there aren't many fish that can compare with a 12-pound hognose sucker as it doggedly fights across current, stripping line from your reel.

CHAPTER FIFTEEN
WHITE BASS, SHAD, PICKEREL

WHITE BASS

White bass have become something of a fill-in fish for anglers, being the main quarry for some, a substitute for others, or just simply fish that aren't pursued specifically but are enjoyed when a school is encountered while fishing for other species. Though very popular, their fame has never really achieved the level one might suspect of such a feisty adversary. Perhaps that's because the angling brotherhood did not know these fish until relatively recently, when the construction of reservoirs in recent decades resulted in a vast expansion of the white bass's range. Today white bass—also known as sand bass, sandies, silvers, and a few other terms—swim in nearly all mainland states and in nine Canadian provinces.

One of the reasons for being attracted to these fish is their voracious appetite and, thus, their willingness to strike lures. White bass, when found, are relatively easy to catch. As a schooling fish, they are found in good numbers, so the opportunity exists for a lot of action. Another attraction is their food value. White bass are good to eat. Most states encourage a high harvest of white bass because these fish are relatively short-lived and fairly prolific, so you needn't feel reticent about keeping a lot of the white bass that you catch. Although relatively small in size, white bass are primarily big-water fish, seldom being found in quantity in lakes under 300 acres in size.

White bass are a true member of the temperate bass family, which also includes freshwater yellow bass; white perch, which are a panfish found in brackish tidal water, saltwater, and some freshwater lakes and ponds; and striped bass, which are the giant of the group and a fish of saltwater origin that has adapted spectacularly to freshwater environs.

Unlike their striped bass relatives, white bass aren't heavyweight fish. However, their savage strike and vicious, darting fight surely place them in the middleweight division. A 5-pound, 14-ounce fish holds the current world record, indicating the top size they may attain, but a good-sized white bass is a 2-pounder and anything over 4 pounds is a genuine trophy.

If you were to categorize the white bass you might call him a gang fighter. His days are limited, not only because of actions but because of lifespan. Most white bass fail to live past their fourth year, though a few will live up to eight years. Growth is dependent on geographic locale, of course, plus food supply. Cold water and a lack of shad in the north, and warm water and abundant gizzard and threadfin shad populations in the south account for regional growth differences. Small fish make

White bass don't grow as large as their striper cousins, but they pack a lot of punch and eagerly strike lures.

up a large part of the adult's diet, which serves as a clue to appropriate lure size.

White bass do not consume much food in the winter, which virtually eliminates them as prey for ice fishermen. But their reluctance to bite during the cold disappears when the water warms and the spawning urge is triggered. White bass spawn from late March through June, depending on latitude. During helter-skelter spawning runs, they gather in amazing numbers in the tributaries of lakes and impoundments, as well as in rivers. In the latter, they especially congregate below obstructions such as a dam, sometimes so thickly that fishermen swear that they could cross the water on the backs of white bass.

When the water temperature reaches the 54–64 degree range (58–60 is ideal), white bass begin their spawning rituals. In a reservoir, they usually seek out tributaries and prefer spawning on gravel or rocky bottoms in shallow water. If a lake lacks tributaries, the fish select shoal areas to deposit their eggs. Like walleye, male white bass may begin their spawning migration well before females, sometimes as soon as the water temperature surpasses 45 degrees. Spawning activity generally lasts about two weeks, however, at any one locale, and the actual spawning process occurs both day and night, not on a nest, but in a transitory manner.

Except for the spawning period, white bass in a reservoir or river are constantly on the move, searching for suitable forage and/or comfortable, open-water conditions that usually conform to their needs and those of shad. They seem to prefer deep, open water but venture near the surface when avidly pursuing a school of bait fish. A school of white bass may slash into minnows or shad one minute, then vanish, traveling anywhere from a hundred yards to a mile before reappearing. They may not reappear at all, or they may appear out of sight (binoculars are useful for scanning the horizon to spot schools of fish or birds).

The whereabouts of white bass may be erratic, but they are always schooling fish, existing in packs that are sometimes enormous in number and breadth. In the most frenzied periods, huge schools of white bass that slash into bait have covered many acres of water.

In non-river environments, therefore, anglers watch the horizon for circling, feeding seagulls. Lake, river, and reservoir populations of gulls are always attracted to surface-feeding white bass. As a result of the marauding actions of white bass, the gulls have an opportunity to snatch bait or pieces of fish from the melee. When you spot working birds, instantly race toward them, throttle back upwind, shut the outboard motor off, and drift down through the surfacing fish. This is often referred to as "jump fishing," and can go on for hours as anglers chase feeding schools of white bass.

Most schooling/feeding eruptions last just a few minutes. Sometimes you can predict just about where the white bass will surface again. Watch the gulls as they drift off after the school disappears because they may lead you to the fish again in a short while. This action is often a late-in-the-day or early-morning proposition, especially in late summer and in the fall. The same type of activity can occur with striped bass or hybrid stripers, and occasionally the species will mix.

In deep water, white bass prefer to be over sand or gravel bottoms, but no matter where you locate them, they don't remain there very long. This constant swimming keeps white bass vigorous, which is translated into spirited fighting when caught on light tackle. White bass won't leap when caught, but they run in swift, diving circles. On ultra-light tackle, they are very sporting fish.

Usual white bass tackle includes fly, spinning, and spin-casting outfits, and even cane poles, although light or ultra-light spinning tackle is preferred and is most functional. Rods need only be in the 5- to 6-foot range, with ultralight, light, and medium actions all of value. Line size may range from 2- to 10-pound test, with 6 an ideal strength.

There really is nothing fancy or involved about the lures used to catch white bass. The most popular white bass catchers are jigs and spinner-jig combinations, in white, yellow, silver, and chartreuse colors. Any small lure that looks like a minnow or shad will catch some white bass when a school is located. Lead or metal swimming lures in light colors—like a Heddon Sonar, Mann's Little George, or Gapen Slip—are good choices, too; these can be cast a long distance, will work quickly, and have a good fleeing-minnow type of motion.

Other white bass lures include small crankbaits; spoons; minnow-imitation plugs; spinners; slab-style jigging spoons; and a number of propellered, surface lures. The topwater plugs that sputter (sometimes called "splash baits") are especially fun to use when white bass surface feeding activity is at a peak, and frenzied silvers will strike at the slightest commotion. The fish think the lure is an injured and floundering bait fish, and, in this state, they can hardly help but viciously pounce on the plug.

The key to the effectiveness of most non-surface lures used in white bass fishing is having flash. That is why spoons that have reflective tape on them, highly polished, nickel spinners, and even nickel-plated, ice fishing jigs work well. Many white bass anglers place two or more brightly reflective lures on their line at one time, especially jigs or jigging spoons, leaving an 18-inch interval between each bait. Some tie a light jig on behind a crankbait and use the plug to cast far and swim the jig down. Using these and other methods, an angler can sometimes catch two or even three, scrappy white bass at a time.

Lead or plastic swimming lures, which look like small threadfin shad, are among the leading white bass catchers.

Live bait is a possibility, of course, although bait is not used much for actively feeding, moving schools of fish because it is preferable to be mobile and pursue fish by casting to them. Shore fishermen, however, do not have that ability. Many of them use the well-known, Wolf River bait rig, which was developed on Wisconsin's Wolf River primarily for white bass fishing and which has become popular for white bass elsewhere as well.

The Wolf River rig consists of a three-way swivel with a dropper weight on a short leader and a hook attached to another leader about three times the length of the sinker leader. Small minnows are baited, hooked through the lips, and cast or lowered into the main stream of a river. The rig can be bumped along the bottom in current in an erratic manner, or it can sit there and be still-fished.

Few other baits take white bass as well as minnows, but that doesn't mean that garden worms, night crawlers, leeches, and certain grubs won't work, although, for the most part, they are more effective on slow, midsummer days.

The angling approach for white bass can be varied, obviously, and even includes trolling, a subject we haven't discussed here.

Since white bass are on the move so much, an angler who relies on one spot may be disappointed. In lakes and reservoirs, it is wise to pick out a dozen or so areas where white bass have been caught before and return to each one when you are pursuing these fish specifically. Other times, look for riprap on shorelines, rocky points, reefs off islands, old river channels, sand bars, sudden drops in water depth, and stony flats where water holds at a constant level somewhere between 10 and 16 feet deep.

Finding white bass in river systems is not very difficult. Look to those areas where streams enter, where bridge pilings disrupt current flow, above wing dams, along riprap,

Though they are most abundant in large lakes and reservoirs, white bass are also found in river systems, and the area below a lock-and-dam structure is one of the better places to locate them.

downstream from lock-and-dam structures, on rocky points, and where hardpan (see the river fishing section of the smallmouth bass chapter) lifts up off the bottom to disrupt surface waters. It is likewise a good idea to work any back eddies created by stumps or rock and to fish that area just upstream from a downed tree that lies crossways in river currents. Keep working an area where you've caught a fish or two, as others should be nearby.

SHAD

American shad are something of a marvel. Not just for their good size, strong fight, acrobatics, and fine-tasting roe, but simply because of the mystery of their being. In an age of intense interest in all aspects of fish life and angling, we have come to know the *minutiae* of many popularly sought game fish. But not the anadromous, coastal river-running shad.

We don't know, for example, what food sustains them through their lives, though the supposition is that it may be plankton or other miniscule sea matter. We don't know what forces guide them unerringly to find their natal waters. Because the stomachs of river-migrating shad are empty, we know that they don't eat when they return home to spawn; yet it's rather puzzling why they strike an artificial lure and yet aren't caught on bait, like such anadromous fish as steelhead and salmon. Such mysteries make shad a fish that we can marvel at, and it keeps them — and angling for them — on a relatively uncomplicated level.

American shad (*Alosa sapidissima*) are not to be confused with the shad (threadfin and gizzard) found in southern and western reservoirs, which are bait fish that provide good forage for such species as striped bass, largemouth bass, and trout. American shad live most of their lives in the ocean and then return to major Atlantic and Pacific Coast rivers to spawn, returning to the sites where they were born. They generally weigh in excess of 2 pounds, with 3 to 5 pounds common, and the occasional fish weighing from 6 to 8 pounds. The males (called bucks) are usually smaller than the females (roes).

One of the traits that make shad such appealing fish is their "here today, gone tomorrow" nature. In a seasonal sense, the shad run only lasts for approximately six to eight weeks. This feast/famine relationship also exists on a daily basis during the season, however, especially in the early stages of the run before the main body of fish has migrated through. Shad often move through a river in stages or waves; they are affected by water conditions, and they are often not present in the same locales on a day-to-day basis.

The elusiveness of the shad is part of its allure for veteran anglers, of course. If the fish were always present and receptive, it wouldn't be quite the sport that it is. And, speaking of sport, it's a wonder that shad haven't been accorded a loftier status in the annals of game fishing. With drag-screeching runs, broadside-to-the-current fight, and frequent, aerial maneuvers, shad are a spunky fish that are not outdone by any other species.

Perhaps the relative lack of attention paid to shad is due to the fact that the fish aren't much for mid-day activity. Often you can experience good shad angling in the evening, and early morning is considered prime time. The first two or three hours of the day may be best because shad migrate upriver at night, and there is a new

This good-sized American shad was taken in early morning, which is one of the better angling times for these fish.

wave of migrants in the morning and perhaps also because of the low level of light. Shad will move, however, during the day, particularly on cloudy or rainy days, and may migrate from pool to pool or even move around in a large, slow-flowing section of water during the day, being visible on or just below the surface as they cruise en masse. This is often seen when the fish are on their spawning grounds, and they appear to be daisy-chaining, much like tarpon.

Shad basically stick to the channels, preferring the deeper water to the swift, riffling, shallow sections. The primary place to fish for them is in the pools. This is slower, calmer, and deeper water than the rest of the river sections, and shad primarily rest in such spots before continuing upriver. You may find a large school of fish occupying a particular pool on a given day, or you may find few or none. Sometimes, when success tapers off in a given spot, you merely need to move slightly up, down, or across the river to be back in action. Having had success at the tail of a pool, when action slows, you might go to the head of the pool in deep water nearest the swifter channels.

Newcomers to shad fishing need only to know that a light-action, spinning rod, 6- to 8-pound-test line, an appropriate spinning reel with a good-quality drag, and a mixed supply of shad darts will equip them with the best of the veterans on the river. Darts, which are a lead-bodied, buck-tailed form of jig with a tapered body and slanted nose, are the perennially favored shad catcher, though some anglers have success with flies, small spinners, and tiny spoons.

Usually you must get your offering down near the river bottom, a task that is influenced by the depth of water, strength of the current, weight of your lure, and size of your line. Shad apparently strike out of anger or reflexive action and thus don't seem to go out of their way to chase a lure. Your offering has to get down in front of a fish's nose to be effective. For this reason, it's common to get hung up and to lose a fair number of lures in pursuit of shad.

Shore fishermen, waders, and those casting from anchored boats should cast across and upstream, allow their lure to sink to the bottom, then, with line tight, let the lure swing downstream with the current until the lure reaches the end of its sweep. Boat fishermen either troll into the current or anchor and still-fish their lures by letting them swing in the current. In either case, let out approximately 75 feet of line behind the boat, using a heavy enough lure (or weighting it with split-shot about 18 to 24 inches ahead of the lure) to get just off the bottom.

Darts range in size from tiny to 1/2-ounce. The heavier versions are used in early spring when the river is swift and roily, and it takes a lot of weight to stay down. But heavy darts are also large in size and may not attract fish even when they do stay down, so anglers often go to smaller sized darts with split-shot ahead of them; the extra weight keeps the dart down, but the smaller size dart is more favorable to shad. One-eighth to 1/4-ounce darts are most widely used.

A red-headed, white-bodied dart (with white or yellow bucktail) is the time-honored, favorite color and is a good fish catcher. But darts come in a host of colors and combinations, and it pays to have a selection of sizes and colors available. Black head/green body, green head/chartreuse body, red head/chartreuse body, and red head/yellow body have all been very successful colors for us. Some anglers have a preference for orange- or gold-bodied darts, and it often seems that what works is that which you have the most confidence in. Nonetheless, it's a good idea to switch colors frequently

Shad stick to the channels and deep pools and are caught on lures, either by trolling, casting, or still-fishing.

when shad fishing, especially when you know there are fish in the locale you are working, and they don't respond to your initial offering.

Very effective for trolling are tiny spoons — actually gold or silver willowleaf blades soldered on No. 6 hooks. A good shine is important, and the rig must have perfect balance to run properly, since action is especially critical. The spoon should twirl at a fast rate and look like a miniature propeller in action. It is fished in the same manner as trolled darts, though it is not necessary to put out as much line; 50 feet or thereabouts will do if the river section is from 8 to 12 feet deep. Use a swiveling, bead-chain sinker with these spoons, about 18 inches up the line; 1/4–ounce is a common size.

Flyfishing for shad is growing in popularity, though it is practiced more on the West Coast than in the East. Rods should be suited for 6 to 8 weight lines, and be 8 to 9 feet long. Sinking lines, fast-sinking lines, or floating lines with a sink tip are in order, depending on conditions. Some fly-caught shad are taken close to the surface, and anglers use a sink-tip line to keep the fly down a short distance while they retrieve it in short quick strips. Streamer-like flies, some with bead eyes to make them sink, are used.

In spinning tackle, a 6- to 7-foot, light-action rod is good. For extra fun, you might try light-lining with long rods; it's possible (and challenging) to land shad on a 12-foot-long noodle rod, using 2- through 6-pound line. Six- to 8-pound-test line is standard and very suitable to the size and fight of shad, though some anglers (particularly trollers) will use heavier line.

Besides being somewhat sensitive to light, shad are also sensitive to water conditions. A heavy rain, which raises and muddies the river, will not be beneficial to shad fishing, and they either retreat from locations they previously inhabited or become inactive till more favorable conditions prevail.

Shad begin to enter the lower reaches of rivers in March but usually don't appear in great numbers until late April, with the peak of the run between mid-April and mid- to late May. A lot depends on the level and temperature of the river. Fifty-five degrees is an optimum temperature for activity.

If early spring is colder than normal, the run may be one to three weeks behind schedule. Sometimes when this happens, fishermen think the run is over before it has actually commenced. In a cold spring, the good fishing may be compacted into a two- to three-week period, with success dropping off markedly once the water warms up into the 60's. Obviously, you have to put some time in to stay on top of the fishing, and you must be flexible to be available when the fish are.

PICKEREL

Pickerel are lean, sporty, evil-eyed bandits, and it's surprising that they aren't more acclaimed. They are virtually neglected by most non-winter fishermen, rarely specifically pursued by open-water anglers, and regularly downgraded by people who catch them unintentionally while seeking a species far higher on the popularity charts. Yet pickerel have fine sporting values. They are an aggressive, available fish, offering a good chance of angling success, and they are respectable battlers on appropriate tackle.

Not too many other gamesters will follow a lure right to the boat with such impugnity. It's commonplace for pickerel to strike viciously just as a lure is about to be lifted from the water, an action that is guaranteed to provide a thrill. Equally exciting is the observance of a fish making a V-wake in shallow water as he dashes from cover to head off a nearby lure. How many other fish will hit three, four, or five times in a row as they chase a lure? How many freshwater fish free-jump out of the water? Pickerel sometimes do, when they're speedily chasing a meal or when a lure comes by and startles them. They may attack your line in the water, too, without coming near the lure or even seeming to have been attacking it. And, in appearance if not disposition, pickerel are the proverbial villains. Long, slimy, toothy, camouflaged in chain-like markings and green-brown colors, and sporting cold-blooded eyes, the pickerel is a smaller but equally fearsome-looking version of his northern pike and muskellunge cousins.

Pickerel are most abundant in areas where pike and muskies are not found or are not very abundant. They range from Nova Scotia south to Florida and from Texas through most of the easterly states, though their primary abundance is in Florida and Georgia and from the mid-Atlantic states north.

They are referred to as chain-sides, snakes, jacks, jackfish, pike, and other names. They are not a jack but a member of the *Esox*, or pike, family. Pickerel are sometimes confused with walleyes, particularly in southern Canada where walleyes are called yellow pickerel, but the walleye is a member of the perch family and is unlike the true pickerel in nearly all respects.

Members of the pike clan have been referred to as water wolves, and this is a descriptive appellation. While a lot has been written about the variety of foods consumed by largemouth bass, they are out-gluttoned by pickerel.

Mostly pickerel consume other fish, such as small minnows and fry, but they are fond of mid-size fish like yellow perch and other pickerel in the 4- to 6-inch lengths. They'll even go for larger fish. It's not too uncommon, for example, to catch a large pickerel that still is trying to digest another pickerel half its own length. If you catch a lot of pickerel, you're sure to see some tooth-like scars on the back and sides where they've been grabbed by a hungry relative.

Pickerel may possibly consume, or attempt to consume (some have died with fish stuck in their throats), nearly everything that invades their domain. If pickerel are found often regularly eating other pickerel, it is usually because there is an overabundance of this species in that particular body of water. Their diet is principally made up of the most abundant and available forage in their habitat, and that is usually the prey-minnow species or the young of other predators.

The habitat of pickerel is somewhat similar to that of largemouth bass, particularly in regard to vegetation and abundant cover. Found in ponds, bogs, tidal and nontidal rivers, streams, lakes, and reservoirs, their prime habitat is lily pads and various types of weed beds, and sometimes they lay near such objects as stumps, docks, and fallen trees. Invariably, the waters with the best pickerel populations are those with abundant vegetation, much of which, incidentally, is found near the shore. Shallow ponds that are in medium to advanced stages of eutrophication are often prime pickerel territory. Large lakes and reservoirs devoid of weedy cover can also host pickerel (even very large ones), but seldom in significant numbers.

In typical pickerel water, the best fishing is had in the spring. Pickerel spawn in shallow bays and marshy areas shortly after ice-out in the North and in the mid- to late winter in the South. Water temperature and the development of cover are usually two indicators of progressing pickerel activity. Pickerel feed all year (they are a prime quarry of ice anglers) and can be caught in modest numbers in the cold water of early spring. When the water temperature passes 50, they become more active, and 55– to 70-degree water temperatures offer excellent conditions. At this time, weed growth is developing, providing more cover in which to lie motionless for the inevitable bait fish ambush. When vegetation becomes thick, which will be in the late spring or early summer, there is usually more forage available; these two conditions combine to generally lessen fishing productivity. From this time through mid-fall, it is important to be able to fish heavy cover effectively.

In the cold-water conditions of early spring and late fall, fish slowly for pickerel, as would also be done for bass. Shallow-running crankbaits and minnow-imitation plugs are best, though if you work a spinner so that the blade barely turns, this can also be productive and is probably the foremost pickerel-catcher through the rest of the season.

Pickerel are particularly attracted to movement and flash. Nearly any lure with a spinning blade or sparkle-like appearance will catch at least one pickerel in its lifetime, no matter how useless it may be otherwise. Standard spinners and small spoons are traditionally effective pickerel lures, but they are prone to hanging up in thick cover; spinnerbaits, weedless in-line spinners, and weedless spoons are a better option. Worms and jigs are also taken by pickerel, much to the annoyance of anglers using them for bass. Pickerel readily strike plastic worms, especially fire-tail versions; but, when they inhale the bait and the hook is set, the line rubs against their sharp teeth and gets cut off. Fly-fishing is also worthwhile for pickerel, streamer flies being especially

A spinnerbait, which fooled this nice pickerel, is one of the best early-season lures for these fish, which frequent shallow, weedy waters.

ravished. On a lake with plenty of pickerel, a fly-fisherman can be kept busy all day.

The time-honored lure for pickerel is a standard, red and white spoon, such as the Dardevle, or a silver- or gold-finished, weedless spoon such as the Johnson Silver Minnow, in 3/16- to 3/8-ounce sizes. Also effective, but not very popular, are spinners with bucktail or squirrel hair on the hook. Spoons and spinners have given way to spinnerbaits, however, which are as flashy or flashier and certainly more weed- and tangle-free. Tandem-bladed spinnerbaits with a white or chartreuse skirt are particularly effective, and it's often helpful to add a soft plastic, curl-tailed grub on the hook for spicing up the swimming action. Effective blade colors are silver, copper, chartreuse, white, and yellow. Where possible, spinnerbaits should be fished with a trailer hook; this will produce a lot of swiping, short-striking fish. With crankbaits and minnow-shaped plugs, a variety of colors work well. Silver or shad colors may be foremost, but gold, perch, and walleye representations are also effective.

Live bait may be the overall, top pickerel-catcher for most anglers, certainly in the winter. Minnows or shiners up to 6 inches long are the preferred baits. Pickerel often strike bait fish to stun or cripple them so they can re-attack and consume the prey, head first. This accounts for the common occurrence of missed strikes and repetitive attacks when using lures. Pickerel usually take bait, however, crosswise in their mouth and run off a bit with the bait, maneuver it around, then swallow it, head first. Because of this, you should give the fish time to swallow the bait before you set the hook. There's no question that fishing with live bait is effective, but a good lure angler can be more productive because he'll cover greater territory and make many presentations to fish-holding locales. For this reason and because pickerel caught with live bait are deeply impaled and difficult to unhook and release, we don't use live bait for pickerel, outside of ice fishing.

A moderate to fast rate of lure retrieve is preferred for pickerel, but it often pays to start a retrieval slowly and then quicken it. When a pickerel is following the lure to the boat, try speeding the bait up. This fish may think it's escaping and then pounce on the bait. Slowing the lure down works occasionally but is generally likely to alert the fish.

In pickerel angling, it really pays to be watching the water where your lure will exit. Pickerel are notorious followers. Many of them swirl after, but miss, a lure near the boat or simply trail it in and dart under the boat or down to the bottom nearby. If you don't watch, you may miss signs of activity that could lead to catching a fish. Many a time we've dropped a lure right back in the water or pitched it out a few feet and had a previously following pickerel nab it. Sometimes, upon spying a fish, we'll let a swimming plug come to rest on the surface just as a pickerel glides in and effortlessly clamps his toothy crushers around it.

Pickerel are usually caught in shallow water so you seldom have to do much searching for good hideaways. A half a foot of water to 7 feet deep is where you'll find most pickerel, and generally this is close to shore as well. In shallow lakes with a lot of cover throughout, you will find pickerel away from shore and slightly deeper. Anglers sometimes catch pickerel 15 to 20 feet deep in the open water of big lakes when trolling for trout, but this is not the norm, and such places do not provide good pickerel cover.

When fishing vegetation, it pays to concentrate on openings, pockets, points, channels, weed lines, and other irregular features. Casting parallel to the edges is often best for enticing fish that lie waiting just inside the weed line. Weedless surface lures and spoons are good for prospecting through the thick salad, and are probably more favored today than the traditional technique of "skittering," which entailed using a 12- to 14-foot bamboo pole to rake a spoon or pork chunk across the pads. The bigger pickerel, however, seem to pick the most desirable ambush points, near the edge of pads or weed beds, leaving smaller fish to stay further back in the cove.

Big pickerel are fairly hard to come by with regularity, perhaps because they are not as long-lived as other species, such as bass, or perhaps because so many of them fall to lures that few get to be old and large. In any event, big pickerel put up an excellent fight and, though they may fall to a medium-sized spinnerbait or plug, are more likely to take a larger offering, such as a 6-inch, minnow-imitation plug or tandem-blade spinnerbait.

Large and small pickerel alike will take a surface plug at times from late spring through early fall. In a small area, pickerel can get stirred into a feeding spree by the commotion of a surface lure and the activities of hooked or chasing fish. A wobbling or popping plug is sometimes useful for pickerel, but stick baits can be very effective. Pickerel are caught by many anglers while using the walking-the-dog stick bait retrieve for bass, and pickerel success can be had with the noisy, propellered models as well.

Big, treble-hooked plugs do pose a bit of a problem. When netting a fish with them, you'll have a real mess, yet they're hard to grab with all the teeth and hooks,

Big pickerel, like the nearly 6-pounder shown here, are hard to come by and usually take large lures. Various lures are suitable for catching pickerel, however.

and invariably there are several hooks in the fish as well. It's usually easy to unhook a fish caught on a fly or spinnerbait, but you may not mind putting up with this inconvenient aspect of using plugs when they're catching fish. Keep a pair of needle-nosed pliers or a surgeon's hemostat handy to reach down into a pickerel's mouth to unhook it without being cut, or, on small- and medium-sized pickerel, use some type of jaw spreader to keep the fish's mouth open while being unhooked. Use good judgment. No pickerel gives up once captured, and some reserve their best fight till they're in hand. With a prodigious array of teeth and a slimey protective mucous coating that makes them hard to handle, it can be easy to get cut up.

Any size pickerel can be handled effectively if grabbed by one hand just behind the top of the gill covers. Don't grab them by placing your fingers in the eye sockets unless they're destined for the skillet. It's worthwhile to keep a towel nearby for cleaning your hands.

Probably the principal reason that pickerel don't have better public relations is that they are often caught on tackle that is too heavy to allow them to make a good showing. The best gear for pickerel fishing is a spinning outfit with 4- or 6-pound-test line. Considering that the average pickerel weighs no more than a pound and a half, such thread seems to be an appropriate match. On light tackle or fly rods, they'll run, jump, and cavort in a pleasing manner. Only the large pickerel put up a really good fight on medium to heavy bass tackle. Where cover is really thick, and where largemouth bass are also being pursued, you'll have to temper this go-light advice with commonsense, but don't forget the sporting values of pickerel on the right equipment.